Neila Gore

Happy reading

Tony

Blessed
Assurance

Tony Earnshaw

ACKNOWLEDGEMENTS

Several years ago I wrote a short play about a disagreement between two friends, both vicars, and the impact on their friendship and their relationships. The late Trevor Danby suggested I write a novel about the four characters and their backstories, culminating in the crisis presented in the play. As I wrote, the novel took on a life of its own and the crisis proved to be a catalyst rather than a climax. As I developed the book, I had the advice, feedback and encouragement of Lynn Ruth Miller each step of the way. Without her suggestions, and nagging to produce more, I may never have finished. Both Trevor and Lynn Ruth are, or were, talented writers and performers, and I have benefitted from their insights and experience.

As I came to a final draft, I had the help of a panel of readers – besides Lynn Ruth they were Alex Birch, Tim Jenkins, Jane Stride and Jenny Monro. My thanks to all of them for their time and input. I was also fortunate to be asked, by Tim Jenkins, to appear as a guest reader by Phoenix Writing Group, and I'm grateful to Tim and the group for their encouragement and feedback.

Jenny Monro has been invaluable in keeping my website relevant and accessible, and for keeping me sane when technology let me down, and Neil Monro is the spreadsheet king. My thanks to them for that. Assistance and advice on how to take the final steps were available from the Alliance of Independent Authors and from SpiffingCovers, where the team were also responsible for cover design, typesetting, and much more.

I'd be in terrible trouble if I failed to mention Ruth Trattles for all her help and, last but not least, the focus on writing a novel gets in the way of other things. The main person to suffer from that is my wife, Estelle, and for that, for encouragement and support, and for so much more, I am eternally grateful.

Finally, one of the themes of this book is friendship and I have been conscious, while writing it, that I was privileged to have a friend from infancy with whom I could always talk things through. He is, sadly, no longer with us but the good things the book has to say about friendship are dedicated to Tony Spencer.

PART ONE

CHAPTER ONE

MOORS AND MEMORY

Tom's Story

I'd like to say the moors were my first memory, tuft grass and bracken stretching away into the mist, or the view across to Rawdon Billing from Dobrudden, but it would be untrue. And truth has become important to me as I grow older. My first memory is actually of scooping up handfuls of gravel from the drive and throwing them on to the lawn; to be accurate, the neighbour's lawn – an early lesson in boundaries. Or maybe it is of my mother holding me, my father coming home from work, or the search for my lost teddy bear. Memory is slippery, difficult to pin down, as is truth.

The fact is that the moors and hills of my home were a formative influence, but then maybe the gravel was as well. In my early years as a priest I would use something like that as sermon fodder. The gravel, I would point out, was like the seed in the Parable of the Sower, except for the depressing fact that none of it would bear fruit. But that, and the depression, came later. At the age of three, which is my estimate of age at the time of the gravel throwing incident, I was only aware of the texture of the stuff, of the fact that I could pick it up and throw it, that it was something over which I had some power, some control.

I don't know when I stopped simply throwing gravel and started to think about the meaning behind it, but I must have been very young. This 'stuff', as Liza calls it, has always been important to me. We'll come to Liza later, and at some length, but I want to chart my early years and mustn't rush my fences.

Why do I want to chart my early years? Because they feel important; because they might shed light on my later struggles, my path to enlightenment; because that mixture of Yorkshire common sense and wild beauty crept into my soul and still help me to experience transcendence while keeping my feet on the ground. If they are on the ground. There are those who doubt it.

If I am to convey a sense of my doubts and certainties, of the influences that have shaped my life, it has to start here, a West Riding town, on the edge of the moors, and on the edge of the sprawling conurbation which is Leeds and Bradford. West Riding has not been the official designation for many years, but I use the term advisedly. I remain, at heart, a West Riding man from a West Riding family – and a Noncomformist one at that. Here I am, at 60, all those years as an Anglican priest, many in the Home Counties, but I still see myself as a Yorkshire Baptist. And yet neither of those identities sit well with me in so many respects. Some of it does, of course; the places more than the religious identities, the people and the countryside more than the dogma and tradition.

So there I was, a post-war baby, one of many born into a world described by writers of the time as grey and austere.

That, I have to say, is not my memory of it. For me it was a magic world; playing cricket against a lamp post, or 'Cowboys and Indians' up and down the street, wandering with a great deal of freedom around the village, cycling across the moors; these were the activities that filled my days as I grew. And at home, there was security.

My own children had very different childhoods; more nomadic, less rooted. When I think of all the friends and parishioners I've pastored, I'm conscious of a feeling of difference. I can listen, help them think, get in touch with their emotions, but I'm a transient, in one place for a few years before moving on. Sometimes my own childhood feels more relevant, but the world has changed and in some respects that sense of place has gone and my childhood experiences can seem too different, too far removed to be of help.

Even now, on my rare visits to Yorkshire, I can see the child I was, walking up the 'bank' from Baildon Green, climbing the rocks on the Glen, cycling to Eldwick across Sheriff Lane. I walk the moors and feel that familiar spring of the turf beneath my feet, look out and see the old landmarks. Of course, much has changed. Housing estates have been built on fields and lanes I remember as rural. Pubs have closed; tea rooms have become pubs. Churches have changed too, services have modernised, some of the chapels have abandoned the organ altogether. Nonetheless, in essence, this is still the same place that formed me.

I suppose it was my uncles who sparked my independence of thought. We were Nonconformists of course, and expected to be independent, but in reality that simply meant conforming to a different norm. Most of my relations were also nominal Liberals in the way that many people are nominal Christians. They vaguely agreed with the Liberal Party but never voted for them because to do so might 'let the reds in', by which they meant the Labour Party. As I grew up, I struggled to see anything very 'red' about the Labour Party and scandalised the wider family by agreeing with Uncle John, the family's token 'red', on many issues while declaring myself a republican.

Besides Uncle John, the other strong avuncular influence was Uncle Newton, local politician and independent thinker, who was very happy to argue all day and defend his point of view. I may be seeing things through the rose prism of memory, but he never seemed to upset anybody in doing this – a skill I'm not sure I ever managed to acquire.

I never meant to upset anybody, but at school I irritated teachers by challenging opinions they were handing down as facts; at college the tutors wanted more orthodoxy; and in my career as a priest I have been variously held to be insufficiently enthusiastic about the 39 Articles, too liberal, too open, too friendly, and lacking in authority. In my personal life I have been accused of being too worldly, too other-worldly, too self-absorbed and too absorbed in other people. People other than Liza that is.

I wouldn't want to give the impression that I am just another curmudgeonly Yorkshireman, too busy calling a spade a spade to notice the impact on other people. Far from it. My ability to see both sides of an argument, my appreciation of nuance, has been one of the characteristics which have caused problems. The church is full of people who have no appetite for nuance, no taste for doubt or subtlety, 'Just give us the black-and-white truth' they seem to say, 'the Bible-based teaching. Don't ask us to think. Tell us how it is'.

Well, I'm sorry, I can't do that. People have to reach their own conclusions, by reading, thinking, arguing.

An argument was the focus of my first meeting with Pete. He was a skinny, serious kid with specs and a shock of blonde hair – he hasn't changed much really. He was playing football, never one of his strengths, and was brought down by an unnecessarily aggressive tackle. Being Pete, he apologised to the culprit, a wiry little kid called Mick who always went in hard and didn't care who got hurt. I arrived on my bike just in time to see the incident and couldn't believe this gangly kid with spectacles was apologising to Mick, who was clearly at fault. I weighed in, got told to butt out – not the terminology he would have used at the time – and found myself in the middle of a full-scale row. Boys took sides. There was a little pushing and shoving, then the game resumed. By this time I had been recruited to Pete's team, but when I looked round he was sitting on the sideline, chewing a blade of grass and taking no interest in the proceedings. I went over.

'Not playing?'

'They've got you now.'

'They were a man short. Still need you.'

'Okay. Sorry.'

'What for?'

'Don't know.'

'You don't need to be sorry. He chopped you down, you know.'

'I know. Thanks.'

And that was it. The game resumed and we were friends for life. The thing with Pete was he showed no sign of being scared of Mick; he just started from the assumption that it was his fault. I never met anyone so convinced of his own guilt or less likely to be the guilty party. If one of the gang fell off their bike, usually through taking a corner too fast, Pete would assume he had been in the way and apologise. When we were teenagers, he felt responsible for every relationship which broke up – a huge burden for a teenage boy. I used to have to repeat over and over 'It's not your fault. It's not your fault'. A bit like Robin Williams in that film, the one about the maths genius, only Pete was a little less tortured. As we grew older this changed to 'It's not your responsibility', but I'm not convinced he ever believed me. Believes me. It's still going on.

After the football incident, I found myself spending more and more time with Pete. He was interested in the same things as me; he actually liked to argue about something other than football and the latest fast car. We were an odd couple in many ways, but it worked. Still works, despite everything. We've fought over the years, competed. Pete married my first love; my first real love. I married her sister. She turned out to be my soulmate. It was the right decision, but it has been a little complicated at times.

But I'm getting ahead of myself again. Back in the days before Liza, before Anne, before girls even, Pete and I were a force to be reckoned with. We knew every bend in every road for miles around, every back way, every path across the moors. We knew how to get free pork pies for our Saturday lunch (wait for the local butcher to shut up shop, at about 1 o'clock, and clear out the week's leftovers), how to get in to see Bradford City for free (catch the bus after getting your free pork pie, wait until 20 minutes after kick-off and wander through the unmanned turnstiles) and the best vantage point to watch the game (the walkway above the Kop where the half-time results from other matches were posted). Of course, the police would often make us get down from our vantage point, but it didn't really matter – there was plenty of space at Valley Parade in those days so it wasn't difficult to get a good view.

In the summer, of course, there was cricket. The Yorkshire of Brian Close, Fred Trueman and a young batsman called Boycott. The test match on the wireless and endless days of playing makeshift games in which every wicket taken was hotly contested. Our day-to-day wicket was the metal panel at the bottom of the lamp post, not a big target to hit but the difficulty that implied was cancelled out by the tendency of small boys to hit the ball in the air and to run when there was no chance of getting in so most wickets were catches, run-outs or lbw. All this changed when I was given a cricket set – bat, wickets, bails and a convincingly hard ball. We then moved to the back garden and tested just how hard the ball was – harder than the kitchen window as it turned out.

The run-out and lbw controversies continued in the back garden. Numbers meant we only had one batsman at a time, so when he reached the opposite end after a single we needed a way of differentiating between taking the second run and simply getting back to take strike. The batsmen did this by shouting out 'walking' or 'ST' before setting off back to the home wicket. I never did find out what ST stood for, but it was widely embedded in local culture. Most of our childhood arguments seemed to revolve around whether the batsman had actually called 'walking' or 'ST', as he claimed, or whether he was just trying to prolong his innings by accusing the rest of us of deafness. Of course some batsmen would call 'ST' and then try and count the run which also gave rise to heated debate.

Pete maintains to this day that all this controversy was the perfect training for a career in the Church of England, that the male dominance and the reluctance to let our sisters bat (they were useful fielders) was a precursor of the women priest debates, and that a vicar should be allowed to get out of the church without being accosted by members of the congregation, if he was having a difficult day, simply by finishing the service with the 'grace', calling out 'ST' and making a run for it.

Anne's Story

Your average vicar. Black leather shoes, grey trousers (with cycle clips) and an old jacket over the clerical shirt and collar. Typical entry into the room too, armful of books, cycle helmet dangling from one finger, and an advance warning of his presence in the shape of a hummed hymn tune; if a hymn tune can be said to have a shape. Actually, this one was a bit misshapen. There was still a resemblance to the original, a tune called 'Assurance', but the resemblance was not obvious.

'Assurance'. Pete's favourite tune. There were those who felt that 'Diffidence' might be more appropriate, but no such tune existed, even in Anglican circles. To be fair, Pete was hardly diffident in preaching the gospel, just in his dealings with other people. For some vicars, the distance created by robes and pulpits is a key advantage of the job; one of the perks, if you like, a reminder that here is a man set apart, a man who can be forgiven a little social ill ease.

Not that they're all like that. Take Tom for instance, Pete's oldest friend, and another vicar. I know, it's London bus syndrome, nothing in sight and then you can't move for them;

story of my life. But Tom; Tom is something else. Confident, relaxed, attractive. Yes, I know, I'm married to Pete, so I clearly thought he was attractive once. Still do, to be fair. But Tom draws the eye; tall, well proportioned, with a twinkle in his eye, dark hair turning to grey – and presence. So it's charisma more than attractiveness I suppose. Charisma in a secular sense I mean, though he did flirt with the charismatic church for a while; part of his 'journey of faith' as he calls it. That's one thing he and Pete have in common, a love of cliché. A love of me too – once. As I said, like London buses.

So why did I choose the diffident one, the one who struggles with personal relationships, likes to hide behind the priestly robes? Not sure I could have had the easy-going, charismatic one in the end, not once Liza came on the scene, but I did choose Pete. I chose social awkwardness. I chose someone who thought he'd found the truth over someone who wanted to spend his life looking for it; a strange mixture of diffidence and certainty. But I suppose that really I just found Pete's foibles endearing – and endearing was more attractive than charming.

And he's still endearing, though he drives me round the bend too. Now, as he comes into his study, he looks a little surprised to see me – as if I'm some alien life form, an intruder in his inner sanctum. Well, I am really. This is male territory, clerical territory at least, and Pete hasn't quite come to terms with women priests yet, not that he has strong theological objections. He just finds tradition a comfort and change threatening.

But there I go again, defining myself by reference to the men in my life. Why do I do that? Force of habit I suppose. Can't be upbringing or Liza would do the same, and she shows no sign of that particular weakness. Oh, she has plenty of other weaknesses, my kid sister, but she has always been her own woman.

There are four of us with interwoven lives, interwoven relationships, interwoven struggles. Liza and me, plus Tom and Pete. Two sisters and two lifelong friends. Two vicars, God help us, and two vicars' wives. There I go again, defined by my husband's job. Except I'm not – not any longer. That, at least, is one lesson I've learned.

We've been close since we were 18 or 19, a long time ago. Liza and I have clearly been close much longer than that – all Liza's life and most of mine – and Tom and Pete met as small boys. What is it that has held us together? How have we survived the difficulties, the changes of viewpoint, the relationship issues, the controversies? How have we managed to stay so close? Are we as close as we think? And what about our faith? This is the big one for Tom. And yes, I'm aware that he is writing down all sorts of stuff about our backgrounds. That's what started me off really. Don't know if anyone will ever read this, but still.

Tom keeps coming back to core questions. What do we now believe? How has our core belief system changed? At heart, I think some of Tom's journey has been painful and he hopes to offer other people a shortcut. There is no such thing of course, but Tom is undisturbed by detail and we are caught up in the momentum of his enthusiasm – to the extent that I have started talking about his 'journey' for which some act of penance is surely necessary. I've yet to tell him I'm writing this.

Tom is one of the most open and honest men I know. I'm not sure I can be quite so self-revealing. What would the others make of it? Pete is Tom's rival in honesty but has a need for self-preservation which makes the concept of openness a little difficult. Liza will always tend to take a very partial view of everything so that would be interesting. I'm her sister of course, so I am hardly neutral. I love her dearly, but she has been driving me round the bend since we were tiny.

So, honesty about relationships first. I often feel like I'm the parent in the group. I'm older than Liza, obviously, so we have the whole big sister thing going there. The boys are different. Pete is a powerhouse when it comes to caring for others but a dead loss when it comes to caring for himself, so I've fallen into the trap of mothering him. I know; I'm making changes, but it's not easy. Tom, on the other hand, knows how to look after himself but is always full of enthusiasm for his latest idea, his latest interest. He always has a project. Other things get forgotten, unless someone reminds him. Pete isn't likely to notice, Liza isn't going to bother, so that leaves me.

Odd that we should have ended up as such a close foursome, and that Liza and I should be married to vicars. We were never very religious as children. Our parents sent us to Sunday School but didn't go to Church themselves. We went to the Church youth club, but only to meet boys, and the boys we met were only there to meet girls. Which brings me back to the point really – our background, my story.

We were brought up only yards from the sea in Goring, the Sussex one, disproving the popular myth that you have to be over 70 to live there. Looking back, I think there were quite a lot of older people, but when you are under 10 anyone over 25 has one foot in the grave anyway. In a bungalow too – another stereotype bites the dust – built in the 1930s with the outside half pebble-dashed and the inside all thin walls and round pin sockets. I loved it though, the bungalow and Goring as a place to grow up; riding my bike on Alinora Avenue and round to the seafront, roller-skating in the car park by the Sea Lane Café in the winter, and lazing on the beach in the summer in my teens. Worthing was a big attraction until we got older and wanted to go to Brighton to feel really cool. It's been a long time, but I'm still a south coast girl at heart.

We were a bit of a shock to the boys and their families, I think. Marrying girls from the south was not in the plan. Neither was a move away from the West Riding. Tom and Pete were deeply suspicious of anything southern, and the deep south started in Leicester as far as they were concerned. And here they both are, settled on the North Downs, only a hop and a skip from the south coast. And it's nice, having Liza close, so I can keep an eye on her, help out when needed, meet up for coffee. She has always been my closest friend. Well, always except when she isn't. You know how it is.

I still go down to Goring quite often. My mother's there still. My parents moved to Goring when they married and stayed put, grew into the place like a small child grows into clothes too big for it. After 50 years they were the right demographic. So I go down to see her in her bungalow. She's still independent; feisty, headstrong, and determined. Like Liza. I guess I'm more like my father. He was the maternal one.

Liza was born when I was just 18 months, so I really can't remember life without her. Nor would I want to. We were inseparable until the age of 13 when she discovered boys, make-up, and pop music, while I was focussed on ponies, tennis and drawing. I still tried to look after her but didn't really understand her world any longer. The hiatus lasted until we were 17 when our interests and obsessions came into line again. Oh, I still draw, still play tennis, but you know what I mean.

I could tell you lots about Liza as a girl; the name for a start. Her full name's Elisabeth, shortened to Lisa until she hit puberty when she decided that Liza was more her, more artistic, cooler. She had this annoying habit of reciting 'Liza with a zed, not Lisa with an ess' at us, and got annoyed when Dad said 'Zee, Lisa, if you're going to be American'. It seems a long time ago.

I could tell you how she tried to ride her trike (remember those?) to the Marine Gardens when she was five, and my father found her chatting to a bemused couple out walking their dog who, fortunately, were a little concerned about the apparent absence of a parent. How she tried to beg an ice cream from the Sea Lane Café in return for filling up the dog's water bowl. How she went out with a succession of unsuitable boys with whom she appeared to have nothing in common, except a desire to look cool and upset my parents. They achieved the second objective. Not sure about the first.

And me? Normal progress from dolls to ponies to boys. Average. Happy at school. Interested in lessons but not overambitious. Happy, I think.

Pete's Story

I sometimes think Tom believes sermons write themselves. Maybe his do. Mine are hard work; tedious sometimes. Not something that comes naturally, public speaking. Odd for a vicar I suppose, but if you're called to share the Word, as I am, then you have to do what it takes. The latest thing is to keep a journal. Where to start? Maybe I could just list my attributes.

1. Honest
2. Vicar
3. Married to Anne

Three points – that's all you're allowed in a sermon. You can cheat by using subpoints though.

1. Honest, partly due to:
    a. Personality
    b. Upbringing (Yorkshire where bluntness is valued)
    c. Faith
    d. Inability to be anything else

2. Vicar
    a. C of E; St Matthew's, Betcham
    b. Converted in teens; 'called' soon after
    c. Bible believing (not 'inerrant', which I take to be unrealistic, but true to the gospel, which is logical and sound)

3. Married to Anne
    a. Student romance come good. My second, no third, serious girlfriend
    b. Happy. Emotions are not my strong point, certainly not compared to Tom. I have a habit of comparing myself to Tom, not a good habit
    c. Anne went out with my best friend first but chose me; made me feel good if a little insecure.

The best friend in question is Tom, clearly

d.   No children (we couldn't – painful), but close to nephew and niece.

Should I finish there and let someone else take over? I'm not even sure I should be writing about me. It seems a bit self-indulgent, a bit removed from the 'death to self' that I preach from time to time.

Of course, Tom was the catalyst for this. As ever. He's recording and intending to share. I'm reserving judgement. And waiting to see what happens. Of course, his basic premise is interesting. Tom's ideas tend to be interesting. Dangerous sometimes, subversive, snares for the unwary, but interesting. This particular idea, though, is probably okay. Four friends, four journeys of faith – a phrase I like but Tom hates.

Where was I? Four journeys of faith; which Tom is to document. This is why I'm also trying to record things. Recollect things. In case my truth and his diverge too much. In case he gets it wrong. Not least because of the interlocking relationships. It has to be said that these have been supportive despite different life experiences and so on. Actually, and I suppose I must be honest here, there have been times when 'mutually supportive' has become a bit warped. The way of the world, temptations of the flesh. Anyway, for once I haven't told him what I'm doing – recording my own version of events, my 'truth'. Maybe he'll never know. Maybe this journal will simply end up in a drawer.

My personal inclination is away from the personal. When I came to faith there was a lot of razzamatazz all around me – music, people calling out, Billy Graham on the big screen – but I just sat there quietly and said yes, this is for me. It wasn't the emotional tone of Billy Graham's talk that got me but the logic, the attention to detail, the little cards with verses on them.

- Romans 3:23 'For all have sinned and fall short of the glory of God';
- Romans 6:23 'For the wages of sin is death, but the gift of God is eternal life in Christ Jesus our Lord';
- John 3:16… Well, everyone knows that one.

It just made so much sense. I wonder if Billy Graham ever took to PowerPoint? That feeling of everything slotting together was something I shared with Tom, although he was much more impressed with the emotion, the charisma, the feeling of sheer joy than I was; maybe because the rest of it was already familiar to him. He came from a family of lay preachers after all.

I've shared a lot with Tom over the years. We were boys together of course. He appeared in my life as a result of a game of football. I got involved in some fracas, entirely my own fault although the other kid was a bit of a bully. Well, Tom happened by, and he can't see any injustice without getting involved so he weighed in. The other kid was so busy switching his aggression to Tom that I was forgotten, so I went and sat on the sidelines while Tom took my place on the team. Being Tom, he wasn't comfortable with this and insisted that I play as well as him. I'd have been just as happy on the sidelines, but his intentions were good so I joined in again and somehow spent more time with Tom from then on in.

He could be exhausting to have as a friend. Challenging. Why? Well, we'd get on our bikes and head across the moors, but he would want to go off-road, not something people did in those days. Or we'd borrow a neighbour's dog and go for a walk, but Tom was never content with the normal paths. He wanted to explore. And then to Tom, a sign saying 'Keep Out' was an invitation; 'Trespassers will be prosecuted' was a challenge. I would try and talk him out of it, would sometimes refuse to go with him, but once he had the idea that it would be more interesting to trespass it was difficult to get him to stick to the tried and trusted. Still is.

When we got to Grammar school, Tom was in his element. There were so many after-school activities in those days. He joined:

- the English club,
- the debating society,
- the school orchestra (on flute) and
- the geography club – even though he had no aptitude for geography as far as I could see. I think he just liked the slide shows.

He started to take an interest in girls and got picked for the under 13 rugby XV. In the meantime, I just studied. Sounds boring I know, but I didn't fancy all this joining, didn't want to have to miss the free school bus every evening, and was completely intimidated by the girls in our form who seemed to come from a different world; a world in which studious boys of their own age were not welcome.

Given all this it's surprising that we stayed close, but differences and disagreements never seemed to matter. Not then and not now. We just spent time together when Tom was not doing all that stuff. And we competed for position in the form. I was usually in the top two or three for most things, much to his annoyance; hardly surprising given the differing degrees of focus. I could never beat him in English though – or in arguments. He always had an answer, even when I knew he was wrong.

It seemed odd to me that an only child should be so gregarious, so confident, so socially adjusted, but I guess he benefitted from his large extended family. He seemed to be related to half the village, while I just had my parents and sister, just parents really since Shirley was ten years older than me. She lost interest in me about the time I started to walk, and we've never been close; Christmas cards just about sums it up.

I was fifteen when Tom invited me to the Billy Graham crusade. 1966, the year we won the world cup. It was a time of general loosening of morals. Other teenagers were obsessing over short skirts and free love but Tom, who was still as socially popular as ever, took me to hear Billy Graham; not in person – he was speaking in London somewhere, Wembley probably or Earl's Court – but on some kind of video link in St George's Hall in Bradford. They had all the paraphernalia of the evangelists – counsellors, stewards, admin, handouts – it was just the main event that was on the screen. I was impressed. There was this huge organisation, with weeks or months of preparation (Tom had been to a weekly training session for 'counsellors' although he was too young to actually act as one), and it was all to save me. I had to confess to some trepidation – big emotional scenes, a manipulative speaker? Not for me. Tom just said 'Think of it as a new experience. Then you can take it or leave it'. I wasn't sure I wanted a new experience, but Tom was.

There was a huge build-up, as I remember. The band played, we sang hymns, the emotions were built to a crescendo and we were exhorted to expect the hero until he appeared on screen, approaching the microphone to rapturous applause. The talk itself was impassioned, beseeching, frank, emotional and shot through with a compelling logic. I was spellbound.

The message was simple:

1. God had created perfection,
2. We had spoiled it,
3. Someone had to pay.
4. God sent his 'only begotten' son to pay the price,
5. All we had to do was accept his son as our saviour and we were free.

Then we had to convince everybody else. I committed there and then to making it my life's work (although I prefer to use a three-point list). I didn't go forward, I was too embarrassed, but sat there in my seat and prayed the little prayer of commitment he taught us. Of course I later learned that many of the people who did go forward decided soon afterwards that it had just been an emotional high, and I can understand that, but for me it was a defining moment. I hope I give a more nuanced, less emotional message when I preach, but the underlying message is simple and straightforward. In my view, though not in Tom's.

Tom, in the meantime, was riding the wave of emotion, going forward, being counselled, returning home to tell his folks, full of the joys. I'm not sure his parents were as pleased as he expected. They were a little distrustful of Billy Graham, who was a bit expansive and manipulative in their view. A bit, well, American I suppose. It didn't sit well with serious Yorkshire Baptists. He calmed down after a while. He always does. We made a pact, to go to theological college together and really make a difference. I don't think we expected to end up in the Anglican Church. That came later. At the time, he would have regarded the Anglicans with suspicion, and I had no idea about churches at all.

At school, the consequence of our commitment to Christ was interesting. Some of our classmates were interested, some scornful. Tom, as always, made a drama of it and was the centre of attention yet again. I, on the other hand, found myself in quiet discussion or argument with some surprising people. I was getting a little more confident socially and, against my expectation, this seemed to help.

Of course, a zealous Christian commitment was a challenge for a sixties schoolboy, maybe for any teenager, with all the prohibitions about experiences we were keen to have. I found that it gave a moral underpinning to my natural shyness, while Tom's solution was to argue at length about precisely what behaviour was acceptable or unacceptable. It turned out that most of the unacceptable behaviours were the province of governments – war, the bomb, wealth at the expense of others – and most of the things he wanted to do were fine. This obviously included drinking and sex.

Liza's Story

I don't know that I should be doing this. It's dangerous. Oh, I know what the others would think. I'm the dangerous one, the loose cannon. Maybe they're right, but I don't want to hurt anybody, never have, and there are a few issues which are a bit sensitive, I think. I mean, think about it. You've got four people who have been close forever. Friends, lovers, married, sisters, you know. Stuff happens. Secrets are kept, blind eyes are turned. And now Tom wants it all out in the open. 'For the greater good' he would say. For his benefit, I think. Still, it's Tom and he's set on writing things down, so I'm going to do the same. Not for publication, but just so I'm clear myself. Just so I can argue if necessary. He may need some edits. I love him dearly, but his version of events may not be mine.

Of course I can't just sit and write, it'll never happen, so here I am, playing with voice recognition, hoping I can make it work. Then all I need to do is talk, play to my strengths. Scary. The end result will probably be a bit boring, a bit like those canal holidays, long periods of floating along with nothing happening and then a burst of activity and high stress as you try and berth up, or go through a lock or something. Maybe I'll focus mainly on the locks.

Some of it's embarrassing too, mind you. I haven't always behaved as well as I could. Maybe none of us have. I could certainly tell you a thing or two about my sister – and Tom. Maybe Pete's the innocent in all this. The thing is the three of them are my family, my life. I love them. I hope they know.

I grew up in Worthing, well Goring really, a very boring place, full of old people. Well, that's what I thought at the time anyway. Lots for small children I suppose – we had greens and beaches and stuff to play on – but nothing much for teenagers except places to hang out. And our parents didn't like me just hanging out. 'Where are you going?' they'd ask and the answer they wanted was somewhere definite. Somebody's house maybe? Right – with their boring parents instead of mine. Or a coffee bar. Don't know where I'd have found one of those. Anyway 'Out' was not regarded as a good answer, so I had a problem. I said to my children when they moaned about Molebridge, 'You should try Goring!' Anne was happy of course, bless her, she could be happy anywhere. She had her tennis and her horses and her other interests; and me to mother – a mixed blessing for me. Oh I loved her to bits, don't get me wrong, but she did have a tendency to smother.

I was always the creative one. Not academic, but give me some paper and crayons, or paint, or anything really, and I was away. I was a dab hand with plasticine too. Do they still have that? Of course they have Play-Doh now, don't they, but then it was all plasticine. And I was the papier mâché queen as well; spent hours designing stuff.

I was a bit disengaged from the more academic stuff, a bit dyslexic. I didn't know that then, just thought I wasn't that way inclined. Always felt a bit inferior. Now, well, did you know that Roald Dahl was dyslexic? And W B Yeats? A lot of creative people obviously, but they were wordsmen. I wish I'd known earlier, might not have overcompensated so much. I don't know, maybe it wouldn't have made much difference but my teen years; I must have given my parents nightmares. I was very art student for one thing – hippy trippy and on another planet; sometimes without the aid of drugs, darling, sometimes with. And boys… long-haired boys with army greatcoats and loons, boys with guitars permanently attached to their shoulders, boys with pockets full of Rizla papers, and boys who called my father 'Man'. Called my mother 'Man' too sometimes.

So what happened was there was this boy, Robert, an arty boy, like the rest, but a bit more serious, you know? And he said to me one day that he thought I was talented, that I should take my art a bit more seriously. Well I told him to lighten up, obviously, get off my case, but he insisted and we had a big row. And, you know, it was his parting comment that got me. He just said 'Fine, waste your talent. Be a hairdresser all your life'. Not that there's anything wrong with being a hairdresser obviously, but me? I didn't think so. And then I thought, well what else would I do? And I didn't fancy anything really, just art, or something to do with art. So I did buckle down and take it more seriously. What? Oh, I dumped Robert, too heavy, but I got on to a foundation year, at Kingston. Which my parents hated, by the way, worried sick about what I might get up to – with good reason.

Kingston was wonderful, a year with sparky, arty, creative kids all with the same focus – well, similar anyway – and a great social life too. It was all over too soon really, but it got me into Lothbury which suited my parents a lot better. Well, Anne was there, and she could keep an eye on me. Poor Anne! And that's where I met Tom, and Pete.

CHAPTER TWO

TEENS

Tom

Pete becoming a Christian complicated life rather. I think I expected it to be a purely positive thing, but life is always more complicated than that. To start with, the Christian thing had always been my province, my differentiator and it was something I wore lightly. It was simply part of who I was. Then Pete came along and colonised the area. With all the zeal of the converted, he started to make a nuisance of himself around the school and his increasing unpopularity rubbed off on me.

To make matters worse, I was busy trying to be cool and popular, despite being a Christian, while he saw it as legitimising who he was, his lack of coolness and popularity included. He revelled in being the odd one out, and now he had a rationale for it. And every time I said or did something which he felt fell short of Christian perfection, he was there to remind me of the example I should be setting. Worse still, whenever I did something which I thought fell short, a much lower hurdle, he was there at my shoulder, a nagging externalisation of my own conscience.

So all this took some adjustment. And our shared interest in politics and current affairs didn't help. Pete adopted a fundamental, legalistic approach to faith which made him judgemental in relation to matters of individual morality and tolerant of the decisions of government and authority. Whenever I challenged him on the latter, he would talk about 'rendering unto Caesar' and those placed in authority over us until I wanted to hit him. On the other hand, on matters of sexual conduct he was as strait-laced and judgemental as it was possible to be. My own conduct in that arena as a late teenager was more experimental than scripture based and that led to a few rows. I felt then, and still feel, that the church takes an excessive interest in what people get up to in the bedroom and not enough interest in the sins committed on our behalf by government and others in positions of authority.

This all went on for some time. Cricket was a shared passion. We were both from long-established Yorkshire families after all. This caused another rift between us when the D'Oliveira affair reached its climax with the Stop the Seventy Tour campaign. The D'Oliveira affair erupted in 1968, less than two years after Pete's conversion. Basil D'Oliveira had left his native South Africa some years earlier because, as a 'coloured' man, he couldn't achieve his potential. He was barred from first-class cricket at home. Achieving your God-given potential has always seemed to me one of the prime responsibilities we have as Christians but that's by the by. 'Dolly' became English and in due course was selected for England. All well and good until England were due to tour South Africa and the South African authorities made it clear that he would not be welcome.

Then all hell broke loose. The England selectors caved in, there was a campaign in the press, one of the tour party was unfit, and Dolly was selected after all. High drama. And in the end the tour was cancelled.

I was incensed at the whole thing; at the idea that politics could be more important than cricket in putting a team together, at the idea that the MCC might cave in to pressure, and at the idea that Dolly might not go. He was one of our best and most popular cricketers. An all-rounder – and boys love an all-rounder. Pete, on the other hand, took the view that the politicians and MCC committee knew best. They were in authority and we should let them make the judgements. It drove me round the bend. We argued about it all summer. Yes, he said, he agreed the apartheid system was a moral cesspit (my words, not his), he agreed that it ruined lives and needed to be defeated, yes he agreed that Dolly should be in the team. 'So?' I said. So? So, it was down to the authorities to make the decisions, he said. We came closer to not speaking than at any time in our lives, which was quite something given what came later.

Pete's resolve to stand with the authorities clashed with my more individualistic tendencies again two years later when South Africa were due to tour England and the 'Stop the Seventy Tour' campaign was launched. It was a heady time for me, a chance to make a difference, but for Pete it was another example of a failure to 'render unto Caesar'.

All this boiled over one heady day in Manchester. The Springboks were playing at Old Trafford and the activists were out in force. With many others, I headed west to get there and hear Peter Hain haranguing the demonstrators. The idea was simple – hit the apartheid regime where it hurt, in their sporting pride, refuse to allow teams selected on racial rather than sporting grounds play, show that the people of the UK were not as weak and ineffectual as their government and sporting authorities. The aim was for peaceful demonstration but tempers got frayed, and I narrowly escaped arrest after a scuffle with the police. I went home feeling pleased with myself and exhilarated. We were making our point strongly and the signs were that the cricket tour planned for the summer was likely to be cancelled, as indeed it was. Pete saw it differently, gave me a hard time, suggesting I was irresponsible.

It was our first major argument.

The interplay between faith and politics is still a closed book to Pete. He always wants to keep things separate; compartmentalised. And yet this is the guy who stands up to preach, Sunday after Sunday, and tells the congregation they shouldn't be 'Sunday Christians'. It's a seven day a week thing, he says, it should be there in every little aspect of your lives – at work, at home, in the kitchen, in the bedroom – but not, apparently, in your politics. Personally, I think that's crap. And anyway, apartheid wasn't really about politics, it was about basic human dignity. In fact, all the stuff I got involved in back then seemed to me, still seems to me, to be about much more than politics – the bomb threatened to annihilate us all, the war in Vietnam was about killing innocent people. And yes, I marched through Grosvenor Square chanting Ho, Ho, Ho Chi Minh. I sang 'We shall not be moved'. I wrote to the press. And Pete? He just wanted to concentrate on spreading the gospel of salvation. Couldn't see he was getting trapped in a prison of his own making.

Anne

We've been through a few ups and downs, Liza and me. Sisters do, I suppose. Sometimes I think she was put on this earth specifically to wind me up. Again, not untypical I guess. I'd still put my life on the line for her though, still be there if ever she needed me. Actually she often does need me, though sometimes in circumstances which strain the relationship a little.

I suppose it started at school. There's only 18 months between us, she's a September baby, I'm March, but the result was she was just the one year below me. And the girls in the year below were always after the boys in my year. Rows over boys were a frequent occurrence. I'd find myself a dishy boyfriend, take him home and my outrageous, arty sister would come on strong, flirt like mad and I'd be left struggling to compete. Of course they didn't all fall for it, but it was just enough to hurt.

I think my problem was, is, that she is way more confident than I am. I have lots of interests, I'm fairly outgoing, and happy in my skin. But Liza… That girl is something else; outrageous, dippy, clever, creative, gorgeous, and a little volatile.

We had a huge bust-up when I was about 16, probably our first. Oh, we had plenty of squabbles before that, sister stuff, but this was something else. I went into the kitchen looking for a snack, a distraction from homework, and there she was, on the phone. We kept the phone in our kitchen at home. No mobiles in those days of course, and no cordless either so you made your calls where the phone was. Most of our friends had their phones in the hall, a bit draughty but at least your calls could be reasonably private and it didn't interrupt what everybody else was doing. For some reason, ours was in the kitchen. Anyway, there Liza was; phone in one hand, the cord twisted round the other in her normal way – it used to drive my father barmy the way she messed up the cord. She had her back to me so she didn't notice I was there at first. You could tell from her tone that she was talking to a boy. She always sounded different, had her special voice on.

'It's your choice,' she was saying. 'I won't tell her if you don't.'

'Tell who what?' I said as I went for the biscuit tin.

She swung round, guilt and anger fighting for control.

'Go away. I'm on the phone.'

'Who to?'

'None of your business.'

'So why are you so sensitive?'

'Sorry, it's my sister.' This was said to the phone. 'It's okay. I'll deal with it.'

'Who are you talking to?'

No answer.

'Liza!'

'None of your business.'

'Who are you talking to?'

'Go away!'

I'm really annoyed now. I know she's hiding something. Her defensiveness is a dead giveaway. I grab the phone. She resists. I hear a voice say 'I'll call you later' and the dialling tone. I know that voice. Andy Milner – my boyfriend of a week. She's pinching my new boyfriend.

'You cow!'

'Give me that phone.'

'That was Andy.'

'So?'

'Get your own boyfriend.'

'He is my own boyfriend.'

'No he isn't.'

Just as the argument started to get more physical, Mum came in. I had a hank of Liza's hair in my hand, while she was trying to scratch my face with the hand not holding the phone.

'What on earth is going on?'

'She's trying to steal my boyfriend.'

'No, I'm not.'

'You can't steal a person, Anne, they're not property.'

'Well she's trying hard.'

'He just thinks I'm more fun than you.'

'I bet he does!'

'What's that supposed to mean?'

'You know what I mean.'

'Girls! Stop it now! Anne. Lounge. Now. I'll be there in a minute. Liza, you stay here.'

After separate talks, and a 'talking-to' each, things calmed down a little. It wasn't the last argument over a boy, but she was never quite so underhand again. And I was never so naive. So strangely, our bust-up helped us to deal with later events in a calmer way. And there were later events, later quarrels, some of them about boys. As for Andy, he dropped us both, and started going out with Andrea Smith.

'Snake,' said Liza when we saw them together.

'Lucky escape,' I said.

We made a pact that day. No boy, or man, would come between us again. We were too important to each other. Of course we broke the pact, several times, but the understanding was there, the pledge of loyalty – severely strained as will become clear, but there nonetheless.

Pete

Here's a list of reasons Tom and I started arguing in our teens:

1. I became a Christian. I thought he'd be pleased, but he seemed to feel I was on his turf.
2. I took Christianity seriously. He didn't.
3. He felt I was a prig.
4. I thought he treated Christianity as a trap, while for me it was liberation.
5. He was popular with the girls. I wasn't.
6. He felt that sex was okay for a Christian. I thought it wasn't.
7. He felt strongly about politics. I thought politics was irrelevant.
8. He felt. I thought.

The whole cricket and rugby thing was a case in point. He was all excited about the South African tours. He was quite into cricket and rugby anyway, which I wasn't – very boring – and there was this whole political element which got him all excited. He felt so strongly about it in so many ways, while I thought the sport was boring and actually so was the politics. I realise that sounds very self-centred. I think at some level I knew he had a point and was ashamed that I didn't care more which made me even more negative about what he was doing. At the time, it just didn't resonate with me.

While Tom was busy with his protests and his sport, and seeing how many of the girls in our year he could go out with, I was trying to learn more about Christianity. I went to Bible study and prayer meetings, and started reading the Bible daily. I used the 'Daily Bread' study notes and made lots of notes of my own. I got involved with one of the local Anglican Churches, not the one in the village but in neighbouring Shipley. Tom didn't approve. In his mind the C of E was the Tory party at prayer and it was way too hierarchical and rule-bound, all of which added to the appeal for me. But the main reason for going there was Jim Barr. Jim was the curate; young, dynamic, and interested in what teenagers thought.

Jim ran the youth club, a teenage study and discussion group, and various other activities, all of which gave me a chance to meet with other studious and devout teenagers. I first met him when I saw a flyer for a 'squash' on a Sunday evening. I had no idea what a squash was but something about the leaflet interested me so I went along. The squash was held in the church hall and turned out to be a sort of youth club with choruses. I stood at the side for a while, feeling a bit out of place, when a tall guy in his mid twenties approached me. He was wearing a leather jacket and a dog collar, a combination I hadn't seen before, and his hair was down to his shoulders.

'Hi. Welcome. Don't think I know you.'

'No.'

My monosyllabic response only seemed to encourage him. He beamed at me.

'I'm Jim. Pleased you could come.'

'Thank you.'

I was beginning to regret it. If I could have turned and run I would have.

'And you are?'

'Oh, Pete. Pete Ogden.'

'Well you're very welcome. What brings you here?'

'I, er, saw a leaflet.'

'Ah, our wonderful flyers team,' he beamed at me. 'And are you just curious Pete, or do you know the Lord?'

That felt a bit direct.

'I, well, yes, I'm quite new to this. I, er, made a commitment at the Billy Graham meeting.'

'Hallelujah, a new brother. Well, come and meet some people.'

And he dragged me across the hall to where a group of other kids were drinking Coke and chatting.

'Guys, a new friend for you. This is Pete. He's a new Christian. Pete, meet Phil, Guy, Kathy, Sue, and Jane.'

I was worried that I might be butting in, but they seemed friendly, made space for me to sit with them and were happy to explain what was going on and answer my questions.

'Is Jim the vicar?'

'No, he's the curate. He's cool.'

'I've never seen a vicar with long hair before.'

'Or a leather jacket, I bet. You should see his motorbike.'

The boys were clearly very impressed with this, the girls less so.

'He's a biker?'

'Yes, he's got a Bonny.'

'A Bonny?'

'A Triumph Bonneville.'

'Oh, sorry, I don't know much about motorbikes.'

Less than I knew about the church actually.

'Well a Bonny's about as cool as it gets.'

'Unusual for a vicar.'

'A curate, but yes. How many vicars do you know who want you to call them Jim?'

'I don't know any vicars, but the Baptist minister's Mr Jones.'

'Well, there you go. He's cool.'

During this exchange with Phil and Guy, the girls had been looking a bit bored. One of them now jumped in.

'So where do you go to school, Pete? I haven't seen you around.'

'Oh, Salts. You?'

'Bingley. We all are apart from Guy, he's at Beckfoot. Do you live in Shipley?'

'No, Baildon.'

'Not far then.'

The other girls giggled and nudged each other.

'Ignore them. They're just jealous.'

'Jealous?'

'That you're talking to me.'

'Oh, I'm sorry.'

'Don't be sorry. I'm not.'

I think I may have blushed. Jane became my first girlfriend, overcoming my shyness by just assuming we were going out so I didn't need to ask her. She was ideal for me at the time. Outgoing enough to overcome my shyness, attractive enough to make my heart race and Tom to make positive comments, her dark hair cascading over her shoulders, she was a little shorter than me and slightly built. She was serious but fun. And we shared a faith.

I became a regular at the church, a stalwart of the youth club, and soon found myself leading a weekly Bible study.

This was a group of young people like myself who were not regarded as 'cool' and were a little out of step with the times. Tom was a little embarrassed. He recognised the shared faith but they were precisely the kind of Christians he wanted to keep at a distance; too serious, too earnest, too 'holier than thou' – in his eyes anyway. Maybe he was right. Jane he made an exception for. There were two reasons for that I think, one being to please me, the second being that she was an attractive girl and he was very susceptible.

I loved the Bible study, preparing it, working out the questions, having some answers ready in case there was silence. I found I had free rein to write lists – five lessons in this passage, seven questions raised, that sort of thing. The fact that the word 'wealth' appears 15 times in the New Testament and 'wisdom' 52 times, and the inferences that could be drawn from comparing this with the figures for the Old Testament (71 and 164 respectively). The difference between the versions fascinated me as well. I liked to use the Revised Standard but a lot of the group preferred 'Good News for Modern Man' which was the latest NT translation at the time. The full Good News Bible came out a few years later. It was popular because the language was more contemporary, too much so for my taste. I'd have been happy to stick with the King James but that would have been an uphill struggle.

Jane took the mickey a bit, I have to admit. She found my fascination with lists and numbers eccentric and, fortunately, a little endearing. We grew steadily closer, and did a lot of our growing up together; my first serious girlfriend, not that there were many. We lasted until leaving home split us up. I think we both found when we went off to our new lives as students that we didn't actually miss each other. We had become a habit. We split by mutual consent during the Christmas holidays at the end of my first term at Lothbury. In the couple of years leading up to student life though, we were very much a couple at the core of a thriving group of friends.

We struggled, of course. There were a number of tricky issues. Sex was one of them – how far to go, how far was right. Nature and dogma had always been at odds on this I suppose, but we felt we were fighting our peer group expectations as well. We were odd ones out and the feeling that we might be missing out was too much at times, or almost too much. Frustration can lead to arguments, and we had a few of those.

Tom wasn't much help. He was, I think, genuinely fond of Jane but had little time for her reservations, or mine.

'You've been going out forever,' he said to me one time. 'It's not normal.'

'What's not normal?'

'Abstinence. Not expressing your love physically.'

'We do express our love physically.'

'I thought you didn't. I thought that was the point.'

'We express it physically up to a point. That's the point.'

'And what point is that?'

'Well, you know.'

'No, I don't. Tell me.'

This was getting awkward.

'Well, we stop before. We… Look, I don't want to talk about this, okay?'

Tom was not ready to give up.

'Okay. Just trying to help. Do you want me to talk to Jane?'

'No, I don't. Don't even mention that I've mentioned it.'

'Why not?'

'Because it's personal. Because she'd be embarrassed.'

'Not as embarrassed as you, I bet.'

'Maybe not, but she'd not like the idea of me talking to you about it.'

Tom was almost affronted.

'But I'm your friend. Who else would you talk to?'

'Nobody.'

'So?'

'So, just don't, okay. Just don't.'

'Okay, okay.'

'Promise?'

'I promise.'

'Change the subject, yeah?'

'Okay. Whose round is it?'

'If it wasn't mine, you wouldn't be asking. Same again?'

And so my life ran along a fairly comfortable routine, my time split between Jane, Tom, church stuff and A levels. And underneath it all, the questions we were all facing; what to do at university, which course to apply for, what grades would be needed.

My thinking was this – one, I wanted to go into the Church; two, I would benefit from doing a secular degree and then studying theology; three, it didn't really matter what the degree was but I stood the best chance in maths; four, moving away from the home area was an important part of the student experience; five, it would be good to be fairly near Jane; and six, it would be good to be near Tom.

Tom also wanted to do a secular degree and test his commitment to theological training. I think he also saw himself as a latter-day St Augustine – he wanted to be good and celibate, but not yet. Jane was keen to do teacher training and our attempts to apply for courses near each other became more and more complicated as we narrowed down the options, not least because she wanted to live at home and I didn't. She was a little put out that I seemed more bothered about being near Tom than being near her. Understandable I suppose. She didn't quite understand how much I relied on him. We had some difficult conversations. She would suddenly start:

'Why can't you find a uni near here?'

'Because I'd have to live at home.'

'What's wrong with that?'

'Living away is part of the point. Independence, student life, you know.'

'We could be together if you went to Leeds. Or Bradford. Or York even.'

'We could be together if you came down south.'

'I don't like it down south.'

'You've never been.'

'Well I don't like the sound of it. I don't like the way they think of the north.'

'Think of it as breaking down barriers.'

'I don't think so.'

'You're scared.'

'Okay. Yes, I'm scared. Everything's changing. I'm happy with my life. Now everybody's going away, I'm leaving school, the youth group's breaking up, and you're deserting me.'

'I'm not deserting you. Look, there are 52 weeks in the year and with three ten-week terms I'll be home for 22 of them. Add in a reading week each term and that's 25. If I come home three weekends every term that's the equivalent of another three weeks, so I'll be here 28 weeks and away 24. You'll hardly notice I'm gone.'

'You think there's a maths answer for everything, don't you?'

'It's fact.'

'No it isn't. You'll get involved. You won't want to come home. There'll be a Christian Union, study, commitments, other girls. You'll forget me.'

'No, I won't – ever.'

We were both right of course. There was a Christian Union, study, lots of things to take up my time, so I only ever went home for the holidays. But there were no other girls, not for me, not so long as I was still going out with Jane. So I was right too. I didn't forget her – ever.

Liza

So, here we are again. This is great, I can just talk. It's like having a shrink. Or one of those things that great men of letters had. You know, like Boswell and Dr Johnson. An a menu thingy… Amanuensis; yes that's the thing. Anyway, here I am; coffee in hand, laptop at the ready, sunny morning, talking about me. God, does that sound self-obsessed?

So, where had I got to? My late teens and foundation year – God, what a time. This is one of the embarrassing bits; my sultry period. I thought it was sexy to pout a lot. Yes, all the S's – sultry, sex and substances.

How much detail to go into? I was a wild child. But do I want to say just how wild? Don't know. Perhaps I'll just go for it. Edit out any bits I think are too much afterwards.

I think the sixth form was my favourite bit of school. More freedom, you know? Wear what you like, well not quite in my case but near enough I guess. There was more of an equal relationship with teachers; too much so in some cases. I remember snogging David Jones, the French teacher, in the cloakroom at a Christmas party and enjoying the notoriety. He'd be fired today of course, but nobody seemed to bother then and he was gorgeous. One or two people said to watch him, he had a different sixth-former every year, but I just said 'I snogged him, I'm not jumping into bed with him; unfortunately'. He was after me all the time after that. Never told Anne, she'd have gone mental. I kept him at arm's length, but I have to admit I was a terrible tease. He was used to getting his own way, and I kept him thinking he might. It was a dangerous game I suppose, but I thought I was in complete control. And I didn't want to jump into bed with a teacher, even one as drop-dead gorgeous as David. I was getting what I wanted in that department from Billy Harrison.

So, I can see the reactions now. Shock horror, Vicar's wife had sex? Get used to it. And this was sex before vicar, you know. Like sex before marriage only not. Well it was that too I guess. We were at the beginning of a sexual revolution, and I wanted to be at the forefront. It ticked all my buttons. In so many ways darling! No, really. The way I saw myself, I was a rebel, a bohemian, an artist. It was my duty to disregard convention, to do what I'd been brought up not to do, to shock the bourgeoisie. And I liked it. Sex I mean. It was great. Still do. I bet Tom won't put this in what he's writing, but he's a great fuck. More shock, horror… Vicar's wife swears! This is great.

So, darlings, you might think Worthing wasn't much of a happening place for a hippy chick. Well, you'd be right. I couldn't wait to get out, get to London. Be part of the scene. Here's the thing though. I never made it. Got as close as Kingston, then Lothbury, suburbs. It was closer than Worthing but not the real thing.

I used to moan about Worthing. 'This is so boring' I'd say. 'Dragsville'. Yes, really. People did say things like that then, trying to be trendy. 'Nothing happens here' I'd say. Then one day Dad just snapped. Got fed up I guess. 'Well stop moaning and make something happen' he said. So I did – parties, protests, happenings and sit-ins. I had a little group of friends, and if we liked something we had a party, if we didn't we had a protest – simple.

Tell you what, though, they were pretty much the same, the parties and protests. See, for a party, we got all dressed up, drank wine and passed joints round, got off with boys we fancied, played loud music and sang along. For a protest, we got all dressed up, drank wine and passed joints round, got off with boys we fancied, chanted slogans and sang along to some guy with a guitar. Not much difference really.

I was really into my art, you know. It made me quite focussed in a way. And over the moon when I got into Kingston – the only one from my little group to get in. Ironic that I should go there – Anne had been intending to be there doing teacher training before she changed her mind.

I loved Kingston; and student life. I had all these other artists round me, spent my time immersed in it, and the foundation building was right next to the Union Bar. How good was that? Of course, it wasn't London but it was close, we could get in for exhibitions and stuff. And we had the river. Shows my seaside roots maybe. I need water. Spent hours by the Thames on the path there, watching the wildlife, the odd rower, sketching.

Kingston was a bit different back then. If you go now it's all changed. I remember the bit behind the market square, the other side to the river. That was a warren of little streets, and there was a brewery I think, and pubs that aren't there now. They pulled half of it down, moved the roads. It's odd because so much of it looks like it's never changed, but it was a real mess of demolition when I was there. Not the riverside. They've developed that since, but it was untouched then.

Anyway, darlings, Kingston was just a staging thing really. Staging point? Staging post? You know, an interlude, a stepping stone from school to my degree course. A year goes pretty quickly, even at 18, and I was soon heading for an art degree at Lothbury – another London suburb, a bit leafier, a bit more settled, for me at least. And, to the delight of my parents, somewhere that Anne could keep an eye on me.

CHAPTER THREE

LOTHBURY

Tom

When it came to choosing where to go after school I was not very fussy. I wanted to go somewhere far enough away from Baildon to have a complete change, and I didn't want the grades required to be too demanding – I really didn't see the point of increasing the stress levels, not least since it was already in my mind that I'd go on to study for the ministry.

As a result I spent a lot of time on the train over the months of my upper sixth heading north to Edinburgh, south to London and the southern universities and polys, west to Manchester and east to Hull. I loved the interview process. It was a day out, a chance to see somewhere new, an hour or so talking about what I wanted to do and why, and then a train journey back with a can or two of beer and a book.

Of course, sometimes there were bumps in the road, like the interview I went to wearing an ex-RAF greatcoat and nearly got arrested by the military police. It was all quite innocent on my part. Ex-RAF greatcoats were very trendy at the time, and I wore mine everywhere. I had embellished it by sewing on military badges and insignia

I'd picked up on the market and felt I was the bee's knees. There was no mistaking me for a military man of course, not with my shoulder-length hair and student slouch, so when I interviewed at Enfield Poly, right next to an RAF establishment, there was trouble. I spotted this big saloon slowing down ahead of me and waiting as I walked up the road, so I crossed over to avoid any trouble. The car promptly did a U-turn and stopped next to me. Two officers got out and approached.

'Where did you get that coat?'

'On the market. Why?'

'You've no right to wear an RAF coat.'

'It's an ex-RAF coat.'

'What are those badges?'

'Ones I bought.'

'Have you earned them?'

'No. I bought them.'

'Where?'

'On the market.'

'What market?'

'Shipley.'

'Where's that?'

'Yorkshire.'

'You're a long way from home.'

'I'm here for an interview.'

'An interview?'

'At the poly.'

'You're going back home today?'

'Yes.'

'Well, don't let me see you wearing that again.'

'It's not likely you will.'

And they got back in the car and drove away, leaving me feeling I'd had the better of the conversation but still vaguely unsettled, and less enthusiastic about Enfield than I had been. It was a good story for the lads, but I was happy when I was on the train out of there.

On another occasion, at another poly – Lanchester I think – the interviewees were all given a guided tour finishing at lunchtime, so we all decamped to the bar while we waited our turn. The beer consumed before the one-to-one interviews no doubt helped some and hindered others. At the time, I felt it was one of my best interviews, and I got an offer from them so it can't have been bad. Alcohol also played a part when I found myself on the train back from an interview with a squaddie on leave – very friendly but with a far greater capacity for alcohol than I had, as I soon discovered.

In the end, although I had a number of offers, it was all a bit of a waste of time since I didn't get the grades I needed and had to go through clearing, ending up at Lothbury Poly in south London. A good result as it turned out.

I took to student life like I was born to it; a never-ending round of parties, beer, gigs, and Chinese takeaways with a wealth of student societies to join and an interesting but undemanding course. Only twelve hours of contact time and plenty of other time to read around the subject, argue the toss and generally put the world to rights.

Southern beer was a challenge. After the Yorkshire beer I'd been used to it tasted sour and thin, so I spent the first six months at Lothbury disguising it with brown ale or drinking bottles of Sam Smith's. The palate adjusts over time though and by Easter of my first year I was relishing the well-kept Young's in our favourite hang-out, the George. Every evening at around nine, we'd convene, Marj, Jim, Anna, Scouse Bob, Dave and me; maybe a few others. Sometimes Pete would come along, when he could be prised away from his books. Pete was there the night Anne walked in. It was May 1971, a warm evening, the pub busy with thirsty students, many spilling outside on to the pavement. We were in our usual alcove arguing about whose round it was when I saw this girl go by, long, dark hair, bewitching smile, and a great figure. I had to act.

'My round then.'

'What?'

'You just claimed you bought the last one.'

But I was already heading for the bar and catching the barman's eye.

'Same again Bert please. Oh, sorry, were you first?'

'You seem to be able to catch the barman's eye.'

'I'm sure you could catch his eye if you wanted.'

'Oh I don't know. I'm too reserved.'

'Well you certainly caught mine. Can I get you a drink?'

'Oh, I don't think so.'

'To apologise for butting in, it's only fair. And for your friend; I assume you have a friend somewhere around?'

'I'm supposed to be meeting someone.'

'Don't tell me you've been stood up.'

'A girl.'

'Well, come and join us while you wait. What can I get you?'

'Okay, you win. White wine please.'

'Add a white wine to that could you Bert? Thanks mate.'

By the time we got to the table her friend had turned up, so I persuaded Pete to buy her a drink while I introduced my new friend to the others. To be honest, I had two reasons for doing this. First, I could see that Scouse Bob and Pete both fancied her and I wanted to avoid unwelcome competition. Secondly, I could feel that knot of excitement in my stomach which told me this had the potential to be a significant relationship. It did, of course, though not in quite the way I envisaged.

'Guys, this is Anne. Anne, meet Marj, Jim, Anna, Scouse Bob, Dave and that's Pete at the bar.'

'He looks sweet.'

'Ignore him. He's bookish, intense. Not your type.'

'And what is my type?'

'I am.'

'You've a high opinion of yourself.'

'No. Don't get me wrong. There's nothing wrong with Pete, or any of these guys – well, most of them anyway.'

'Steady!' This from Scouse Bob.

'There's nothing wrong with Pete, but when I look at you I can't envisage you and Pete wandering hand in hand into the sunset. Can you?'

'Don't know. I haven't spoken to him yet.'

'Exactly. Whereas you and I… Doesn't your stomach flip when you look into my eyes?'

'You're making me heave, that's for sure.'

'Shut up Bob. Come out with me Anne. Tomorrow. Do you like curry?'

'Love it.'

'Well then. Come and have a curry with me tomorrow night . At the Ashok. Do you know the Ashok?'

'Why should I come out with you?'

'Two, no three, reasons; because I'm asking; because you like curry; and because you want to. You know you do. Go on, we can get to know each other over a madras and a glass of wine. You won't regret it.'

'All right then. I'll take the risk.'

'Yes!'

Meanwhile Pete, having bought a drink for Kath, Anne's friend, was deep in conversation with her and appeared to have forgotten the rest of us. Not normally great shakes in the chat-up department, he seemed to be getting on just fine. My stratagem for keeping him away from Anne seemed to have worked better than even I expected. He'd been a bit down in the mouth since splitting with Jane over Christmas and a new love interest was exactly what he needed.

The girls were soon off to meet more friends in the Union Bar, and Pete and I were left feeling smug.

'Did you see that? The most beautiful girl in the pub, and I have a date! The old magic still works.'

'She only said yes because she couldn't believe what she was hearing.'

'She said yes because she is not only beautiful but also intelligent and discerning; unlike her friend who had to settle for Pete.'

'There are three reasons why Kath is going out with me...'

'So you've got a date as well?'

'Naturally. The Ashok, tomorrow.'

'You can't.'

'Why not?'

'Because you'll cramp my style that's why not, that's where I'm taking Anne.'

'Well, be that as it may, there are three reasons why Kath said yes. 1. She was relieved not to be chatted up by you. 2.

She can recognise a gentleman when she sees one and 3. I asked nicely. Oh and 4. I'm irresistible.'

'You're both jammy buggers.' Scouse Bob again.

'Indeed we are. But we can't both go to the Ashok.'

'I can't do anything else. That's where we're meeting and I didn't get her number.'

'Sounds like she's got yours.'

'She'll be there.'

'What time are you meeting?'

'7.30. You?'

'Same. But we're meeting in the Fishes for a drink and then going on.'

'Well, that should give us some space. We'll be past the poppadom stage by then.'

'Is that a euphemism Pete?'

'No it isn't.'

'Ignore him. He's jealous. The girls will have compared notes by now. We'll just have to play it by ear. And well done, mate.'

'Well done?'

'On getting a date and starting to put Jane behind you.'

'Yes, I calculated that the right length of time had passed and was just looking for someone who met my criteria.'

'Which were?'

'1. Attractive. 2. Intelligent. 3. Available and 4. Interested in me.'

'Better than Tom's criteria, right lads?'

'Go on Bob, enlighten us.'

'Just two criteria for him.'

'And what are they?'

'1. Female. 2. Breathing.'

'Very funny. Just jealous.'

'I agree, Tom. Anne met my first three criteria as well.'

'Well, she's not available now.'

'Quite.'

The following evening wasn't quite what I'd planned but was still a great success. The girls had, of course, exchanged details and decided that since Pete and I had both plumped for the Ashok, we should make it a foursome. It meant that there was a little less time for gazing into each other's eyes, and I was a bit concerned that Pete's tendency to take life seriously might put a dampener on proceedings, but I needn't have worried. We all got on like a house on fire.

It seems odd to be talking about Anne like this, after all these years, but away from the crowded pub what shone through was her unique mixture of caring sensitivity and common sense. She was so grounded. Still is. Look at the four of us now – take the curry house four and substitute Liza for Kath – and what have you got? Pete, very precise, list oriented, emotionally constrained. Liza, very 'out there', extrovert, arty, big hearted, temperamental. Me, governed by ideas and feelings. And Anne, rock steady, looking after us all, the cornerstone. Of course, she's not perfect, as we will no doubt see, and when she strays the ripples spread, but she is still the cement in our lives. It doesn't sound very glamorous, but she was very beautiful. Still is, in my opinion. They're a beautiful family.

Anyway, that evening I was entranced. Kath was a pretty girl, full of fun; Pete was in good form and seemed to be coming out of his post-Jane depression; and Anne sparkled. The wine flowed, the food was good, and I felt on top of the world. Pete managed to make a list of ten reasons for eating curry, nine reasons for drinking wine and eight reasons for going for the madras instead of the vindaloo before we moved from the getting to know you stuff to philosophical arguments.

Both girls were a little surprised that Pete and I had ambitions to be ordained, that we had callings, vocations, whatever. The life of faith was outside their experience. A life without faith was outside mine. It was left to Pete, who had experienced both, to mediate. With all the enthusiasm of the convert, and all the particular character traits that make him Pete, he was soon drawing diagrams and flow charts to explain the Trinity, the Fall and redemption, and the history of Israel. Fortunately, it was a curry house with linen napkins so he was restricted to the paper in his pocket or we might have had to resort to force-feeding him vindaloo to keep him quiet.

What did come out in that discussion, somewhat to my surprise, was the difference in motivation between Pete and me. The girls were pressing us on why we were so set on the Church as a career. My answer was to do with ideas, truths, the search for meaning; all the things which fascinate me. Pete's answer was to do with saving people. I'd never thought about the difference before. He feels responsible – for everybody. Always has. If they don't get to heaven, it's his fault for not hunting them down and preaching at them, or for not preaching well enough or some other failing. Me, I'm not convinced it's any of my business. I'm interested in connecting with God, the Divine, whatever you want to call it, and I'm interested in sharing that connection with anyone else who wants to know. The whole evangelistic bit feels a bit controlling to me and doomed to failure, not to mention riddled with holes.

Now, in case you're wondering, we did talk about lots of other stuff. Uni gossip, bands, home towns, and so on. The Beatles or the Stones? (Beatles won 3:1.) Hendrix or Clapton? Ginger Baker or Buddy Rich? We all, as I remember, had a ball.

Walking Anne home that night I had an amazing feeling of well-being. It was a clear and starry night, I had my arm round a beautiful and engaging girl, Pete seemed happy for the first time in weeks, and I had eaten well.

Over the next few weeks this feeling of contentment increased. I spent an increasing amount of time with Anne. We walked by the river, went to the pictures, studied together, and spent lazy mornings squashed together in her narrow bed, my bedsit not meeting her high standards. Pete and Kath seemed happy too, though Pete's conscience ruled out the mornings in bed.

I'm conscious that Pete has probably painted me as some kind of teenage Lothario, and it's true that I played the field a fair bit in my schooldays. Not in cynical or cruel way, but just a natural result of being very susceptible to female beauty and not yet being sure how to manage the feelings that brought to the surface. I'd started life at Lothbury in much the same way with a succession of short-lived relationships, most of which seemed to end of their own accord with no hard feelings or major emotional effect. All that changed with Anne. I was smitten. Lothbury was surrounded by old style Victorian pubs with snugs and alcoves, and we sat in most of them at some point in the following weeks, fingers intertwined, eyes locked, unaware of the noise around us. There were other students playing bar billiards, people coming along to pinch the stools from round our table, laughter, arguments, and bursts of song. We hardly noticed. And then the summer holidays came. We delayed going home as long as we could but, in the end, we had to return to our families, and to some temporary employment, and face the separation.

I remember my mother on the phone, reminding me that Pete had already been home for a week or more, my father telling me of various summer job opportunities. Pete had gone back as soon as term was over, partly because that was the logical thing to do and partly because his relationship with Kath seemed to have lost its sparkle. Anne and I agreed to phone and write regularly and tore ourselves away, but not before we'd agreed that I would go and stay with her in Goring in August.

Once home, I was happy enough. The moors were enough to lift my spirits and it was good to catch up with the old crowd from school – and my parents of course. I did the rounds of uncles and aunts, had tea with my grandparents, and was generally treated like a prodigal son. At Church that first Sunday, Gerald Sutcliffe, the church secretary, welcomed my return from 'the mission fields of the South East'. This was a joke, but only just. Gerald was wary of anywhere outside Yorkshire and regarded anywhere south with deep suspicion. To make matters worse, I had told him that there was no Baptist chapel near Lothbury and I had taken to attending the local C of E. He was worried, I could see, but his response was straightforward – 'Aye, well happen you'll educate them lad'. What could I say? 'Happen I will' was my reply.

I got a job for the summer which restricted my moorland wanderings a little but which also kept me in beer and petrol. I enjoyed the job too, working in the post room of the Provident Loan Group. I just googled them. They're still going, offering loans at 400% APR. I had no real idea of their business then, or interest, it was just a friendly place to work. I spent most of the day sorting letters into piles for the different departments, arguing about football, swapping jokes and playing tricks on the other workers. There were two other students with summer jobs besides me, and I'd been at school with both of them. In fact we landed the jobs because Ian, one of the other guys, had an uncle working for the Provident. The uncle would appear from time to time to make sure 'the lads' were all right, and generally I felt part of the Provident family from day one.

I've never quite got my head round this. Here was a firm lending money to people who had very little and charging them obscene levels of interest, yet everyone seemed benevolent, friendly, and caring. I worked plenty of places where the student temps got abuse but not here. And yet this is the one temporary job which would raise eyebrows if I put it on my CV.

In the evenings I'd meet old school friends in the Malt or The Fleece, or drive out into the Dales with Pete. Returning home, I'd sit down with my father and continue the argument I'd just been having with Pete. I usually found I could disagree with both of them, even when they were taking completely different positions. I loved it.

I wrote to Anne two or three times a week, and seemed to get a letter back every day, much to my parents' amusement.

'I didn't know you could write letters' was my father's comment. 'We never seem to get one.'

'I wrote last term.'

'Aye, I know. I framed it.'

The truth was I was missing Anne rather less than I had expected, less than she appeared to be missing me. I wondered what it would be like when we were reunited. Don't get me wrong, there was a stack of things I wanted to share with her, and I was missing her. I was just more easily distracted than I had expected. And, to be fair, it was a busy summer. I was out of the house by eight to get to work, was back about six, would wash and change, then eat, and off to meet the crowd in the Malt around eight. I'd then dash a letter off to post the next morning. Fortunately at the bottom of the street was a postbox – a rather unusual one on a metal stand which one of the lads round the corner had tried to melt down for scrap without success.

Anne's letters to me were longer, more detailed, less hurried and probably more loving, so at the weekend I'd try to do better. But at the weekend there were the moors to wander, a dog to walk, and other activities which appealed more than letter writing. I suppose my equivalent today would take photos of where he was and send them, but I felt a certain pressure to describe the moors and other activities. Sunset over the gorse is a sight to see, the hills and dales over to Rawdon Billing, or to Keighley Gate have an amazing combination of rugged charm and soft beauty, but I never felt capable of doing justice in writing to what I could see and feel. Anne, on the other hand, could wax lyrical about the sea, the waves, the sun on the water, and about our relationship. It all felt a bit unbalanced.

The time came, of course, when we were to meet again, at her parents' place in Goring, and I boarded the train with a mixture of eagerness and trepidation. I'm still not sure how I feel about all this, about Anne reading it all, even after all these years, but the truth is I was longing to see her and I was dreading seeing her. I really didn't know how it would be.

When I got there it was great. She was looking great in tight jeans and one of those smock things all the girls used to wear. And boots. And a smile to drown in.

We walked along the front, threw pebbles in the sea, and snogged as if it was going out of fashion; it was probably the longest anybody has ever taken to get from Worthing Station to Goring. I was elated, relieved, in love again. Then we got to her house and met her parents – who were charming – and her sister. And my heart stopped. I couldn't breathe. To me, Anne was beautiful, lovable, fanciable, bright, warm; I could go on. But Liza… Liza looked at me and all I wanted to do was hold her. She was a bombshell, a revelation, the sexiest woman I'd ever seen. I couldn't believe it. All my certainties evaporated.

Even after all this time, I can't understand how two perfectly ordinary people like their parents could produce two such extraordinary women, or how I could fall in love so deeply with both of them, or how I've come through it not unscathed but in one piece. At the time, I just tried not to be too moonstruck over Liza, to be attentive to Anne, and to enjoy my stay. Liza was a bit reserved – I later learnt that there had been words between her and Anne on the subject – and that helped a little but, deep down, I knew I was in trouble.

Pete

Five reasons why the first year at Lothbury was difficult:

1. I lost Jane, my first significant relationship.
2. Tom was always obsessing over some girl or other.
3. The Christian Union was full of people I didn't like, and I felt I should.

4. I was homesick.
5. I was always broke.

Five reasons it improved:

1. I met Kath (a good thing but not without stresses).
2. Tom settled with Anne (a good thing, but I wished I'd seen her first).
3. I met Anne (a very good thing).
4. Tom and I got on better and spent more time together.
5. I got used to the place, the people and the lack of money.

Actually, that first year was very significant for me in many more ways than that. First, I found I could survive away from home, though I always had Tom there, which could be regarded as cheating. I still don't know how I would cope if Tom was not just round the corner somewhere – I've never had to. Secondly, I found that I could manage on relatively little money, which is a good thing as a vicar. The Church of England still seems to assume that vicars will have a private income and don't really need paying properly. Thirdly, I had a lot of practice at sticking to my beliefs, not least with Kath who really didn't understand my objections to sex before marriage. Most of her friends were busy trying to hold boys off, and she felt it richly ironic and not a little frustrating that she wanted sex and I was holding out on her. Tom didn't help.

'Look at Tom,' Kath would say. 'He's not saving himself.'

'It's a bit late for that,' I'd say.

'Yes, but he's a Christian too; intending to go into the Church, right? And I don't hear Anne complaining she's not getting any.'

'Tom's views are different. I know what I think is right.'

'Don't you want to? Is it me? Don't you find me sexy? Is that it?'

'No, that isn't it. It's a matter of principle.'

'You might sound a bit more convincing.'

'Sorry. Yes, of course I fancy you. Of course it isn't you.'

'Mm, that's still not very convincing.'

And then I'd have to demonstrate how much I meant it, but without crossing the line. It was a bit stressful. And of course I was a bit jealous of Tom. I would have loved to feel I could justify ignoring the Church's teaching and jump into bed with Kath, but I couldn't. I just couldn't.

Tom wasn't much help either. In his view, I needed to either sleep with Kath or dump her and find a girl who would share my beliefs. He suggested trying the Christian Union. There were two problems with this. 1. I liked Kath and 2. I didn't like most of the girls in the CU.

Then there was Anne, Kath's friend and Tom's girlfriend; sparkling, beautiful, and adorable. We quickly became friends. I found I could talk to her and she rapidly became my closest friend other than Tom. I don't think I was aware of how much I fancied her in those early months, but looking back I think I was always a bit smitten. But she was with Tom and I was with Kath, so the idea of going out with Anne never seriously entered my head, not until much later.

I should have realised she was special if only because she made such a big impression when I first met her. I was in the pub with Tom and some of the others when she came in.

She looked gorgeous, and Tom was by her side in an instant, like a rat up a drainpipe. I could only watch and wonder. But then Kath appeared and somehow we got talking. I hadn't had much success with girls since breaking up with Jane, or even been very interested, but I was very taken with Kath and soon forgot about anything else. I was a bit nervous, to be honest, when I asked her out and a bit relieved when I found we'd be on a double date with Tom and Anne. Tom thought it was an unfortunate coincidence, but I'm pretty sure the girls rigged it, safety in numbers and all that.

I talked about the sex thing with Anne. Tom was a bit taken aback. He would never talk about sex with anybody as far as I could see, other than me; the one person who was most likely to find it awkward. 'Best friends' he'd say. 'Why wouldn't we talk about it?' Otherwise, he was all for it but thought it was private. I think he was embarrassed that I was so frank, and worried that Anne would be frank back. A bit rich, given the grilling he'd given me about Jane, back home. As it happened, Anne did not return my frankness in kind, which was a good thing as it turned out. I remember the first time I asked her advice. It was a sunny morning, and Anne and I went out for coffee between lectures. She was sipping her coffee when I asked her how she'd feel if Tom didn't want to have sex with her and she nearly choked.

'Can you not do that when I've got a mouthful of coffee?'

'What?'

'Ask me something like that – out of the blue.'

'Sorry.'

'Look, I know you like to just deal with the facts Pete, but couldn't you wave a flag or something, tell me you're about to raise a personal issue?'

I may have coloured, just a little. 'Sorry. Is it inappropriate?'

'Yes. No. I don't know. Why do you ask?'

'Because if it's inappropriate…'

Anne would soon realise that I can be a bit literal. Patiently, she clarified. 'No, why do you ask about the sex thing?'

'Oh, well, I wondered.'

Anne stirred her coffee again, a habit of hers.

'This isn't about Tom and me is it?'

'No. Of course not. I didn't mean to pry.'

'It's you and Kath.'

That was helpful, we were getting somewhere. 'Yes. I can't sleep with her. It's wrong.'

'You think it's wrong.'

'It is wrong. The Bible…'

She was firm on this point.

'No Pete. You think it's wrong. Other people disagree.'

'Well, that's not really the point.'

'I guess not. The point is that you don't want to sleep with Kath and she's upset.'

'Yes.'

'And you thought she'd be pleased.'

'Yes. I thought a boy who didn't pressure her would be a welcome change from all the sex maniacs out there.'

'They're not sex maniacs Pete, most of them anyway. And you and Kath seem quite serious.'

'I'm always quite serious.'

Anne smiled at this.

'True. But that's not what I meant.'

'So what should I do?'

'There's no point in asking me that. You know what you want to do and what you think you should do, right? What do you want to do?'

I think I needed a swig of coffee before answering this one, but the answer was clear enough.

'Want? I want to go to bed with her, but I'm being strong. And she hates me for it.'

'No. She doesn't hate you. She's very fond of you Pete. Believe me, she's my friend. I'd know if she hated you. She just doesn't feel attractive, desirable. She thinks there must be something wrong with her.'

'There's nothing wrong with her. I've told her. It's my beliefs.'

'I know you've told her. And she believes you. But she can't help thinking that if she was a bit more attractive, you wouldn't hesitate.'

'She's wrong. Really she is.'

Anne took a deep breath.

'Well, she sees Tom, with the same beliefs…'

'Yes, I thought Tom would come into it. We don't have the same beliefs.'

'Clearly not, but it's very confusing. You both want to be Anglican priests.'

'Yes, but the Church of England can accommodate a lot of different ideas. We have the same core beliefs.'

'Well it's confusing from the outside.'

'I suppose.'

'So, clarify it for me.'

'Clarify?'

'Yes. Explain. Help me to understand.'

'You really want to?'

Anne looked at me as if I was daft, took a breath, and responded.

'It's important to Tom and it's important to you, so I think I need a better handle on it; Kath too.'

'Okay. Well, it's quite logical really. Think of it as a progression, a journey. Step one is creation by God, step two is betrayal by us, step three is redemption by Jesus, step four is acceptance by us of that redemption and step five is us living that redeemed life.'

'So where does sex before marriage come in?'

'Oh, well the Bible is like a manual for life, and if you accept Christ you try to live by the rules. The sex thing is just one of them.'

'So why doesn't Tom see it like that?'

'He interprets some of the passages rather differently. You see, we agree, more or less, on steps 1 to 5 but differ on what constitutes living the redeemed life.'

'So it's open to interpretation?'

'Tom seems to think so. It seems pretty clear to me.'

'Neat and tidy?'

'I suppose.'

'Which is how you like things.'

'Doesn't everybody?'

'No. Not Tom for a start.'

'How about you?'

'Oh, I don't know. I'm not sure I trust neat and tidy. But I can probably reassure Kath a bit now.'

'Can you? How?'

'The way I see it, Pete, is that you like rules, need them maybe, and you've found your set of rules to live by, right? And if you break the rules it feels wrong, unsettles you. So you might want to sleep with Kath but there's too much risk involved. It might unbalance you.'

'Oh dear. I sound a bit unstable.'

'You just need the right woman, that's all.'

'And that's not Kath?'

'Don't know. Time will tell.'

Of course, at that time, I had no idea who the right woman would turn out to be but it was a helpful conversation nonetheless and marked the start of a new understanding between us.

With Kath it was a different story. We carried on for a while and she claimed to understand me a bit better after my talk with Anne, but I think she was a bit put out that Anne could understand me better than she could. As the summer term drew to a close we had a talk. Well, Kath talked mainly. The gist of it was that she was very fond of me, we'd had a good time, but she didn't see a future in the relationship so it was best to finish now and start the next academic year as just friends. That was it; done. All I had to do was agree. So I did.

The summer started off a little awkwardly. I went back to St Peter's, met the old crowd and Jane was there, looking stunning – tight jeans with big flares, and a cheesecloth blouse. We had a slightly stilted conversation.

'Hi Jane. How are you?'

'Fine.'

'Good. College okay?'

'It's fine.'

'Good. Er. Back for the summer then?'

'Yes.'

'Well...'

I didn't know what to say. I looked at the stained glass window (the martyrdom of St Stephen) and ventured an inanity.

'Er. Lothbury's good.'

'Good.'

'Yes, good. Nice to see you though.'

'Yes.'

'Well. Catch you later.'

She hesitated. Bit her lip. Spoke.

'Pete.'

'Yes?'

'Are you happy?'

'Happy?'

'Yes, happy.'

'Yes, I think so.'

'Happier than when you were with me?'

'Happier? No. I liked being with you. It just...'

'Didn't work out. I know.'

There was something else on her mind.

'Pete, when we were together...'

'Yes.'

'Why didn't you make love to me?'

'Why didn't I...? You know why. We discussed it at length. We both thought it was wrong.'

'I wish you had.'

'I don't believe I'm hearing this.'

But she had slipped away and was deep in conversation with someone else, making me wonder whether I'd misheard. It left me wondering though. The ground beneath me had somehow slipped. Certainties no longer held. I confided in Tom, naturally. He was curious.

'So you think you missed out?'

'How do you mean?'

'Well, she said she didn't want to but maybe she did.'

'I don't think she was lying to me.'

'So she's revised her opinions in retrospect?'

'Maybe.'

His conclusion was typical.

'So she's sleeping with someone now.'

'You think so?'

'Why else would she be talking about it? She's feeling guilty and trying to make it your fault.'

'I don't understand why she isn't sticking to her principles.'

'She's human.'

'And I'm not?'

'You've not succumbed yet, that's all.'

'Well it seems quite simple to me. You believe something is wrong, you don't do it.'

'Sounds simple but isn't – not to most people.'

'Kath didn't understand either.'

'Oh well, they're both history. Let's see how you feel next time.'

'It's not about how I feel. It's about what I know.'

'We'll see. Another pint?'

It was typical of Tom to think of it in terms of feelings rather than of logic. And to finish the discussion with a casual 'We'll see'. I knew what I knew. The Church said it was wrong, so it was wrong. St Paul said we would be tempted and tested. I was being tempted and tested. I needed to resist, so I would resist. Simple really. Not easy, maybe, but simple. For now, of course, it was both easy and simple, as I had no girlfriend to tempt me. It felt quite a relief to be able to quietly get on with my studies and prepare for the new term. What with that and my summer job, there was little time to do anything apart from go for the odd pint with Tom, or try not to beat my father at chess, so I hid away and had a quiet and happy summer doing just that.

I confess to feeling a little abandoned when Tom went off to Goring, and a little jealous. Here was fickle Tom managing to continue with a relationship while I had failed. And there they were, probably my two best friends now, taking romantic walks by the sea and gazing into each other's eyes, while I was left at home with my books. I had known I'd miss Tom. I was a little surprised at how much I also missed Anne. I was also a little surprised to feel so enthusiastic about returning to Lothbury and my studies.

Anne

When it came to choosing a university my criteria were clear. I wanted somewhere away from Goring but close enough to get back easily and cheaply. I got a place at Gipsy Hill, a teacher training college near Kingston, aiming to be a PE teacher, but first I took a year out, coaching tennis and working out whether that was something I wanted to focus on. It wasn't. I enjoyed myself but couldn't see it as a long-term career.

So, what to do? London and its outskirts were still an obvious choice and I decided to switch to Social cience – nicely non-specific and covering lots of stuff I was interested in. I ended up at Lothbury. That's where my life changed, where the pattern was set for everything that followed.

I loved Lothbury. I'd found a bedsit near my site – Lothbury was a multisite institution with Arts and Humanities on one site, Art and Architecture on another and the engineers hidden away somewhere else so they couldn't see how much time the rest of us spent in the bar and canteen. The bedsit was my own little world, private, quiet, with my bits and bats around me. After a day of study, debate, and socialising I could retreat into this safe place and rest; wonderful.

And in the day I was with friends, equals, people I could relate to. Some of the lectures were a bit tedious of course, but the seminars were interesting and the other people on my course were great. I made loads of friends. At home, Liza was the gregarious one, but here I came into my own. I joined societies – tennis soc., lit soc., geogsoc., dramsoc., socsoc., you name it. I drank coffee by the gallon at Annie's, just across the road – a bit upmarket for students but irresistible. I walked down to the river, watched the boats glide by, and the well-toned boys propelling them through the water. I enjoyed watching the ripples made by the cross-currents, the glint of the sun on the surface, the feeling of peace among the bustle of the town. And, for this first year at least, I was free from responsibilities. No little sister to watch out for. I missed Liza, of course, but it was good to have a break, to be able to blossom a little.

I was lucky with my accommodation; I found a bedsit in a house of bedsits. There were three other girls in the house and a communal kitchen which soon became the hub for gossip, confidences and study. We all got along pretty well. There were a few arguments about milk and stuff to start with, but I got a kitty system going so nobody could be accused of stealing the basics. I spent hours in that kitchen, with its red Formica surfaces and bentwood chairs, drinking coffee and talking, delaying the return to study. A fair few bottles of Oddbins' plonk got consumed there too. The three other girls were all first years too. There was Kath (geography, from Luton), Wendy (law, from Devizes) and another Anne (another social scientist, from Nottingham). The other Anne was Anne 2, to Kath and me at least. She argued that she was Anne 1 and would sometimes get support from Wendy. As I said, we all got on, but Kath and I rapidly became close friends.

We'd sit in my room, or hers, for hours putting the world to rights, arguing about our courses, about the books we were reading and the films we saw. Our rooms were carbon copies of each other. A bed, an armchair, a desk and chair, a reading lamp, a chest of drawers; those were the basics. To this we'd both added a scattering of cushions, a throw on the bed, arty posters on the wall (Aristide Bruant dans son cabaret, Jimi Hendrix, Che) a tranny and piles of books. Tranny, in those days, meant transistor radio.

One thing which strengthened our friendship even more, before more or less wrecking it, was the night we met Tom and Pete. We'd arranged to meet in the pub and I got there first. The pub was heaving, mainly students, with a lot of familiar faces. One face stood out from the crowd for me. Tom. It was as if he'd been waiting for me. I headed for the bar and there he was, in front of me, with that crooked smile of his, and I was lost. There was a bit of chat, some badinage, but I knew he was more than just another guy as soon as I saw him. I think you have to understand, if you're going to persevere with my story, our story, just how strong that chemistry was. For both of us, I think. How strong it still is, despite everything. Yes, despite the choices we've made, despite our love for Pete and Liza, despite feeling these were good choices, there's still a charge in the air when I see Tom. But I'm getting ahead of myself. I was meeting Kath that evening, and it soon became clear that she and Pete were attracted to each other. Pete had been sitting quietly with the group, but when Kath came in he came alive. Very convenient for me, and for Tom, and the evening was a turning point in my life, though I would have struggled to predict how things would actually turn out.

Tom and I arranged to meet the next night. Kath was keen to make it a foursome so I agreed, a little reluctantly, to curry for four. I needn't have worried. It was a dream evening. We all got on like a house on fire. It's a strange expression, sounds like a bad thing. Anyway, the conversation rattled along, the wine flowed, we shared and laughed, and left the curry house as established couples. The odd thing was that I fell in love that night with a man who was to become a lifelong friend and made a good friend of the man I was later to love and marry. It sounds complicated and sometimes it has been.

As for Kath, she was more than a little taken with Pete. His shyness, his slight air of otherness, his gentleness all appealed. It's difficult now to look back and say with any accuracy what she felt, although we talked long and hard about it then and later, but she was a bit smitten.

Over the months that followed we spent a lot of time together. It seemed natural; two couples, two sets of friends, shared interests. Of course there were strains. Sex for one thing. Not for me, or Tom. I'm a little uncomfortable talking about this now, but Tom and I spent many nights in my single bed. I refused to stay at his place, it was a mess. We enjoyed each other in all senses of the word. I'd get up, a little flushed, to go and make tea and bump into Kath. Worse, Tom would go for tea with something inadequate wrapped round him and he would bump into Kath. Kath was feeling frustrated and unattractive because Pete wouldn't sleep with her, so our obvious enjoyment of each other was like rubbing salt in the wound.

Why wouldn't Pete sleep with her? Because he thought it was wrong. Why did she have to pick the one boy in the college who objected to sex? She couldn't say. I'm sure he wasn't the only one, but it felt like that to Kath. She was ready to commit, to explore, to enjoy a full relationship and he just wouldn't. It was very frustrating for her. Not only that, but she couldn't shake the belief that somehow it was all her fault – and all his assurances that this was a matter of conscience couldn't quite put her mind at rest.

It was a problem for both of them, not helped by the fact that Tom shared a faith with Pete but took a very different view of sex. What neither of us knew was that Tom and Pete had always shared a basic faith but had never agreed on any of the detail; sex, politics, biblical truth, the interpretation of key verses, the role of the Church, individualism, corporate responsibility, you name it, they had completely different views and interpretations. Knowing what I know now, I'd say Pete found faith and fell in love with religion The clarity, the rules, the certainties. Tom, on the other hand, had a deep and intuitive grasp of faith but distrusted and resented the religion which had been built around it. One man's secure place is another man's prison. I keep saying 'had', but nothing has changed, after all these years. Every discussion is still an argument. And yet, they love and support each other, whatever else is going on in their lives. It's quite something – drives me mad sometimes.

What drove me mad at that time was the way both Kath and Pete seemed to think I had the answer to their problem, that I could wave a magic wand and make it all go away. Kath would share her worries and insecurities with me, late into the night, and then Pete would want to meet for coffee and share his. That was when I first got close to him really and saw what a dear, sweet man he was; how anxious he was to please Kath, how desperately worried he was about doing the wrong thing, how hopelessly rule-bound – then and now – but lovely, and impossible to argue with. He always had an answer to any point you could make, usually a list of answers. In the end I realised that all I could do was listen. So I did. I listened to her, made sympathetic noises, and reassured her as much as I could. I listened to him, made understanding noises, reassured him as much as I could. And I tried not to feel smug. It was no surprise when the relationship tailed off towards the end of the first year.

My main concern, as the year drew to a close, was how to handle the holidays. I wasn't really looking forward to going back to Goring, to be honest. I had a job in a shoe shop (Stead and Simpson's, remember them?) so I'd have money, but I wasn't expecting to enjoy it. I'd be without Tom and without the freedoms of university life. On the plus side, I'd arranged for Tom to come and spend some time with me towards the end of the holidays and was looking forward to seeing him, and to showing him off. I counted the weeks and played a lot of tennis.

I think my parents were counting the weeks too, to be honest. I was restless and difficult, usually Liza's province, and they were clearly interested to meet this boy I talked about so much. Liza was very interested too. We had a serious talk about it. Her year at Kingston had clearly agreed with her. Never short of self-confidence, never a shrinking violet, she had blossomed. Somewhat to my surprise, I found I'd missed her, and we spent much of the summer going out together, sharing our experiences of the last year. We became close again, closer than we'd been since we became teenagers. It's never been an easy relationship, but we have always had that underlying closeness, despite everything.

Of course I'd told her all about Tom, and Pete and Kath too for that matter, and she was keen to meet him. I gave her the 'hands off' talk.

'Be nice to him,' I said, 'but not too nice. He's mine, okay?'

'Okay. I learnt my lesson.'

And she did as she promised – overdid the reserve even. He was fascinated. Oh, he tried to hide it. He tried to ignore her. He paid lots of attention to me. We had a good time. But I knew, deep down, I was in trouble.

Liza

So, where was I? Oh God, yes, that summer. Put the cat among the pigeons that did. See, there I was, happy as Larry, great year at Kingston, if a bit full on. You know, parties, notches on the bedpost, grass, Oddbins' finest. And I was looking forward to Lothbury, and ready for a bit of downtime, ready to chill. And there was Anne, love's young dream, looking great, fulfilled, and happy – chilled even. So we had an amazing time together. It was the best sister time we'd ever had. We shared, gossiped, empathised, drank too much wine and giggled a lot. You get the picture.

I told Anne about Kingston, she told me about Lothbury. I told her about the foundation course. She told me about

Social Sciences. I told her about Greg and Barry and Mick and Dave. She told me about Tom Raistrick. I told her about Roddy and Nigel and Tim and Phil. She told me about Tom Raistrick. Okay, she mentioned Pete a few times too, she was clearly close to him, but that summer it was all Tom. It was fun, but frankly, by the time he was due to arrive, I was already bored of him. She even warned me off him, which I thought was a bit of a nerve, and quite unnecessary. I'd already decided he was too good to be true, but hey, good little sister time. So I was very reserved when he finally made it to Goring, almost formal. Course, I could see he was very attractive, but I wasn't letting on. I was determined to support Anne, not undermine her, and they were very close.

Nonetheless, to be honest, I felt a frisson, a charge of electricity between us. I was being reserved and would have been quite happy not to be. He was being cool, and I just knew he'd sooner be hot. Well, you know, don't you? And I was thinking, what if they stick together? Am I going to spend my life wanting to jump into bed with my brother-in-law? Ironic, given the way things worked out.

And there was the vicar thing too. Couldn't get my head round that. It was outside my experience. Why? That's what I couldn't work out. Not sure I've got it sussed even now. And how Anne managed to acquire two of them, one as lover and one as a sort of best friend, well, it was beyond me.

Tom's visit went fine, I think. I kept out of the way as much as I could. Oh, we went out for a drink, the three of us, a couple of times and it was fine. We even went to the beach once, and I have to confess I wore my skimpiest bikini, but I don't think Anne noticed. Tom did though, and when the conversation turned to skinny-dipping I could see his mind racing. Apart

— 79 —

from those two slips, I was very well behaved, went out with my friends, kept him at arm's length and almost called him Mr Raistrick. That might have been a tad over the top though.

The thing that was troubling me wasn't so much those few days as the next couple of years. Actually, the rest of my life, but I was going to have to survive a couple of years at Lothbury first, with Anne and Tom drooling over each other. Anne tried to suggest I hook up with Tom's friend Pete, but even she could see I wasn't going to commit to a relationship without sex, however sweet he was. And I should say, for the record, Pete is the sweetest man on earth – was then and is now. I love him to bits, but we never had that frisson. He really is like a brother to me. Bless him. He was a bit out of his depth at Lothbury, I think, with everybody else playing to different rules, until Anne rescued him, but we're getting ahead of ourselves a bit.

As it turned out I got a bedsit, not far from Anne but far enough, if you know what I mean. The art students didn't mix much with the others, different site and so on, so we weren't thrown into each other's company, and I just caught up with Anne every few days while spending the rest of my time with other artists. Catching up with Anne sometimes meant Tom too, and sometimes Pete. Actually, I bumped into Pete in the supermarket a couple of weeks after the start of term, and we went for a drink, which was interesting. He was just so... so nice. I can't think of another word for it. He was interested in what I was doing, he was funny – and meant to be, I think, though some of it could have been naivety – and the time passed very quickly. We talked about Anne and Tom, of course, and it was obvious that there was an issue there so after a while I called him on it.

'Come on Pete, what aren't you saying?'

'How do you mean?'

'Tom and Anne are these wonderful friends for you, but – there is a 'but', right?'

'Yes, there's a but.'

'And?'

'Well, I can talk to Anne, about anything. I have done, at length.'

'You seem to be able to talk to me.'

'True. You're very alike.'

'Really? Anne and me?'

Pete thought about this, took a pull at his pint in the straight glass he and Tom always insisted on drinking from. A 'schooner' he used to call it, even though he got some odd looks and one barman asked if he wanted beer or sherry. He shrugged it off. Southerners, it seemed, were a weird lot.

'Well, in a way. You're easy to be with, to talk to. I don't always find it easy with girls, especially attractive ones.'

'No problem there, then.'

'No problem at all.'

'Thanks.'

'You don't need to fish for compliments, Liza. You're one of the most attractive girls I've ever met.'

'Just tell me that whenever I'm down.'

'The thing is, I can talk to you, or Anne, about the most personal stuff, no problem. And with you, that's no problem, but with Anne there is a problem. Two actually.'

'Two?'

'Yes. One: I think I'm in love with her. I keep telling her all the ways I make a useless boyfriend and all the time I'm just wanting to kiss her.'

'And two?'

'Two?'

'What's the second problem?'

'Oh, Tom of course. My best friend. I feel disloyal even talking about it.'

'And what does Anne feel?'

'You tell me, you're her sister.'

'Well, she's besotted with Tom, obviously.'

'Obviously.'

'But she's very fond of you.'

'If I had a pound for every time I'd heard that.'

'What?'

For a moment he looked quite sorry for himself.

' "I'm very fond of you Pete, but not in that way". I've heard it a dozen times.'

'Not from Anne though.'

'No, but only because I haven't given her the chance.'

'You should.'

'You think?'

'I'm probably the wrong person to ask.'

'Why's that?'

'I have an agenda. I've got the hots for Tom.'

'Another one. But not me?'

'I'm very fond of you Pete, but not in that way.'

'Well, that's okay, because I'm very fond of you, but not in that way.'

'Pete, I think we need each other.'

'Friends?'

'The best of friends. Give me a hug.'

We hugged, parted, kissed. A more or less platonic kiss – not a lovers' one anyway. We've been close friends and allies ever since. In the short term, we agreed to keep our secrets, and we went out a few times as a sort of foursome with Tom and Anne and got along famously. In fact, I saw quite a lot of Pete that year. Looking back, I think neither of us wanted to commit to anyone other than Tom or Anne, so our best friend and default partner set-up worked well. Oh, I had a couple of flings, Pete dated a little bit, but no real relationships, nothing heavy. And for any significant moments, any real support, we had each other. It was a bit like having a brother. Not entirely. I mean, I probably wanted him around more than I would have wanted an actual brother – don't know, never had one. And although it was a best friend sort of thing, we did yield to a bit of snogging from time to time, you know. Nothing more, of course, he was very puritanical.

I remember one night, I was pretty pissed – too long in the union bar and not enough food – he walked me home, looking after me, see? Anyway, he got me into my room and fussed around me and I was, well, not much help. So he gets my shoes off and laid me on the bed, tries to put a blanket over me, and says 'Sleep it off' or something like that. But I'm not having any.

'Can't go to bed with my clothes on.'

'I think you should.'

'No. 'Snot right.'

And I started to get undressed, but the buttons were getting tangled.

'Help me, Pete.'

'I can't.'

''Sall right. I don't mind. You're my bestest, bestest friend. In the world. Ever.'

'Well all right. Just your jeans.'

'Thas right. Whoops! Knickers came too!'

'Liza.'

''Sall right, can manage now. Look!'

I jumped, unsteadily to my feet and pulled my T-shirt over my head. I was braless so stood before him completely naked. He stepped away, as I recall, and looked embarrassed.

'Liza, please.'

'You don't fancy me.'

'You're lovely Liza, but I'm the wrong man.'

And he let himself out. When I woke up the next day I felt awful. Well, I had the mother and father of a hangover but also a burning sense of embarrassment, and a terrible feeling that I'd messed everything up. I agonised over it all day, hardly noticing the stick I was getting from my course mates who always took great delight in anyone else getting drunk – and even more from the next day's suffering. I didn't see Pete; he wasn't in any of his normal haunts. I did bump into Tom though.

'Hi Tom. Seen Pete?'

'He was just here… Don't know where he's gone.'

'He was with you?'

'Just now.'

'Okay. He's avoiding me.'

'Avoiding you? Pete? Why?'

'Oh nothing.'

'Pete avoiding you? That's not nothing Liza. He thinks the world of you.'

'I know. It's just. Well, I got drunk last night and crossed a line.'

'Right. So he's embarrassed?'

'Very, I should think. So am I. But I want to get things back to normal. I need to talk to him.'

'I'll tell him.'

'Thanks. Don't tell him that you know though.'

'I don't know anything, not really. He's a lucky man though.'

'How do you mean?'

'Well, sounds like you threw yourself at him a bit, right?'

'You could say that.'

'Well most guys would see that as an answer to prayer.'

I could see we were getting close to dangerous ground. Tom continued.

'Never the right one though, right?'

'Oh, Pete's not the right one. We're best friends, not lovers. I'm frightened I've messed that up.'

'He'll come round. I'll talk to him.'

And he did. Pete was round that night, with flowers. Flowers! How sweet.

'I should be the one giving you flowers.'

'That would be weird.'

'Weirder than a naked, drunken friend?'

'I wasn't going to remind you of that.'

'Well, it has to be faced. I was out of order. I'm sorry.'

'Don't worry.'

'And I'm scared.'

'Scared?'

'Scared I've ruined our friendship.'

'No chance.'

'Really?'

'Really. You are very special to me, and I'm sorry I'm not the right man. It would make life a lot simpler. But we both know I'm not, quite apart from my beliefs about sex.'

'Quite apart from that, yes. Sorry, that makes it worse.'

'It's fine. Girls aren't in the habit of throwing themselves at me, even if they are thinking of Tom really. No, it's okay.'

'Okay.'

'Just one thing, Liza.'

'What?'

'Don't do it again… I'm only human you know.'

'You're superman.'

'Seriously. It would have been very easy to get into bed with you, and then what? Our beautiful friendship changed forever.'

'Maybe for the better.'

'You know we'd both be settling for…'

'For second best?'

'You know what I mean. And what we have is special, isn't it?'

'Yes. Best friends, right?'

'Best friends.'

And we settled back into routine. But something had changed, you know? Mainly for the better, strangely enough. I now knew what I'd only suspected before which was that Pete was completely trustable, he was never going to take advantage. I was also touched when Tom took the time to check I was okay, and that neither of them told Anne.

Tom found me in the cafeteria the next day, sat down opposite, smiled that wrinkly smile of his and made my heart jump.

'Just wanted to check you're okay.'

'Hi Tom. Yes, fine thanks. Pete came round last night. All sorted.'

'You were right. He was embarrassed.'

'Did he say why?'

'No, just that you were a little drunk.'

'A little. I was way over the top. Very unsubtle.'

'Sounds like fun.'

'Tom!'

'Seriously, we all mess up sometimes. No big deal. Glad it wasn't me though.'

'Oh, thanks.'

'I'm not as strong willed as he is.'

'I'll try not to get drunk and naked then.'

'Naked?'

'Oh yes.'

'Good test for him then.'

'Which he passed with flying colours. Don't suppose I was looking my best though.'

'I'm sure you were.'

'Tom?'

'Sorry. Inappropriate. Girlfriend's sister.'

'Are you and Anne okay?'

'Yes. No. I'm not sure. Sorry, me spending time alone with you is probably not going to help.'

'Oh. The old sister jealousy thing.'

'Partly. And partly because… Oh it doesn't matter. Better be off.'

'What doesn't matter?'

Just then Anne appeared, carrying a tray with coffee and some kind of sticky bun.

'Interrupting something?'

'Hi Anne. No, just chatting.'

Tom got up.

'Take my seat, darling. I've got Plato with Mike Gordon now.'

'Okay, see you later.'

They kissed.

'See you later. Bye Liza.'

Anne settled down. She looked at me suspiciously.

'So?'

'What do you mean, "So?" '

'That wasn't a casual coffee chat. What's going on?'

'Hasn't he told you?'

'Told me what?'

'About my embarrassment. Obviously not. He's been a sweetheart.'

'He does that. Too much.'

'No, listen Anne. I made a prat of myself with Pete, okay? I wasn't going to tell you, but I can see the way your mind is working. I got drunk, threw myself at him.'

'You could do worse.'

'I know. But not that way. And we're friends, Anne. Not lovers. That would spoil things. Fortunately, he was strong and kind and firm.'

She raised an eyebrow. Something like that anyway.

'Firm?'

'Don't. But yes, I rather think so.'

'Result.'

I think there was a bit of sisterly giggling at this point. Which helped.

'Thank you, that's the first laugh I've had about it. I was so embarrassed, couldn't find Pete the next day. I think he was avoiding me, but Tom saw something was up and I think he talked to Pete. Anyway, he was just checking everything was okay now.'

'And is it?'

'Yes, very much so I think. Pete came round – with

flowers. We talked. I apologised. He was great. He managed to make rejection sound like a gift. Which it was actually. So we're best friends again.'

'All platonic?'

'Yes. Look, I know everyone thinks it's weird, but we are just very good friends. I love his company. It could have got all sexual, nearly did, and probably would've with a different guy, but I think that would spoil it. I don't think we'd last as a proper couple, but I can see us being best of friends forever this way.'

'Assuming your future partners understand.'

'Well, we'll cross that bridge when we get to it. How about you? You seem a bit on edge.'

'Oh, just the sister jealousy thing. Sorry.'

'Really? No more than that?'

'I don't know Liza, something's changed. Difficult to put your finger on.'

'Tom you mean?'

'I think he's losing interest. Sometimes it's as if his mind's elsewhere. I don't know what to do.'

'Anne, I'm sorry.'

'Well. My mind's wandering a bit as well, to be honest.'

'Really?'

'Not sure I picked the right one.'

'You should have picked Pete?'

'You said yourself, he's strong, kind and firm.'

I may have blushed at that point. Yes, even me.

'Doesn't believe in sex, remember.'

'Before marriage.'

'That sounds like getting ahead of yourself.'

'Does a bit, doesn't it? Ignore me.'

'It's what I do best.'

CHAPTER FOUR

ALL CHANGE

Tom

Going back to Lothbury for the second year felt very different. I knew the place by then of course, felt at home, and I was going back to friends, established routines, and Anne. And Liza. I knew I was going to have to be very careful not to mess up. Every time I saw her my heart sank. Maybe that sounds a bit contrary, but I had this internal voice saying to me 'You're with the wrong one. You're with the wrong one' and I couldn't work out what to do about it.

I tried a few things, a few stratagems. I tried avoiding her, but it was impractical. I practically threw Pete at her. That helped a bit. Oh, they never got romantically involved, but they did become pretty well inseparable. I think Liza and Pete connect at some deep but platonic level as if they were destined to be best friends – even now – but no more than that. There was the incident when Liza got drunk and ended up standing naked in front of him, but Pete was the perfect gentleman, didn't let it embarrass him, refused to discuss it, and carried on as if nothing had happened. Liza was mortified. She's not one to embarrass easily but that did it. More than that, she was scared she'd lost him. I had to pour oil on troubled waters.

The funny thing was I really enjoyed that year, despite everything. I spent most of my time with Anne, Pete and Liza and, despite the undercurrents, they were the three people in all the world that I was happiest spending time with. And there were undercurrents. Some of the magic had gone out of my relationship with Anne, Liza and I were trying to pretend some kind of friendly indifference, Pete and I were at loggerheads over the validity of the charismatic experience (I know, but it mattered to us) and Liza and Anne were, well they were Liza and Anne. Some things never change. Talk about sibling rivalry. They would go through fire for each other but fight over the matches.

I think the thing with Anne and me was unacknowledged dissatisfaction. Everything had been going fine until I met Liza, and even though I tried to ignore my feelings, I couldn't. Meanwhile Anne was tiring of me. She could tell you why better than I can, but the Liza thing clearly didn't help. We both tried to continue as the dream couple we'd invented in our heads, but it clearly wasn't working.

It was towards the end of the college year when it all went pear-shaped. Maybe I should rephrase that as the outcome was my marriage, but at the time it was pretty painful. It all started out with student politics. It doesn't seem to happen now, but in those days we were forever staging a sit-in over something and this time it was a decision to cut the welfare staff. This involved redundancy for two long-serving women in particular – women who were dedicated, diligent, and (perhaps most significantly) mother figures to a couple of thousand students. The students' union held a special meeting, emotions ran high, the politicos jumped on the bandwagon and before we knew it we were marching into the offices of the principal and deputy principal and occupying them.

I suppose it was predictable that both Liza and I would be there and equally predictable that Anne would be lukewarm about the whole thing, while Pete would see it as totally reprehensible. What also looks inevitable with the benefit of hindsight was that Liza and I would go off together when we got bored and hungry. At the time, I saw nothing amiss. We were close friends after all, and we had to eat. We lasted till about eight in the evening, before slipping out. There was a sort of shift system going and no shortage of other activists waiting to take our places. I looked across at Liza and mouthed 'Hungry?'. She nodded, and we headed out. Liza was the first to break the silence.

'God, that was boring.'

'I know. It sounds glamorous but no, not really. Where do you want to eat?'

'Let's have a drink first.'

'Okay. The Queens?'

One drink became three before we headed off for a pizza, and a bottle of Chianti. We saw no-one we knew and were soon completely wrapped up in each other. We talked about college, politics, Lothbury, home, friends, you name it. After all the months of tiptoeing round each other it was like a dam had burst. At the end of the meal Liza slipped her arm in mine, and we wandered through the streets happy and content.

Without consciously intending to do so, I realised I'd walked her home when she stopped and said, 'Well, this is me. Thanks Tom.'

'Thanks?'

'For a great evening.'

'Oh, no. It was you. You make things great. I…'

'No arguing. Night.'

'Night.'

And without thinking, I kissed her. Not a friendly peck on the cheek, not a hug, but a full-on, no mistake about how attractive you are, can't get enough of you sort of kiss. She wasn't slow to respond. Another dam had burst.

'You'd better come and have a coffee.'

'Coffee. Right.'

In fact it was some time before I got my coffee – several hours in fact. I woke up in a strange bed to see a naked Liza padding towards me with two mugs. She took my breath away.

'Hey you.'

'Morning gorgeous.'

'Coffee.'

'Thanks. That took a while.'

'What?'

'Coffee. I'm sure I was offered coffee several hours ago.'

'Is that a complaint?'

'No. No complaints.'

'Well, we've really done it now.'

'The cat is among the pigeons.'

'And out of the bag.'

'Only if you want it to be.'

'Tom, I've tried to hold you at arm's length but I can't do it any more.'

'Me neither.'

'Anne's going to hate us.'

The doorbell rang.

'Right on cue.'

'What do you mean?'

'That'll be Anne. Nobody else calls at this time in the morning.'

'Shit. Ignore her.'

The bell rang again.

'Why? What's the point? We've got to face her sometime.'

'I'm not dressed.'

'She's seen you naked before.'

'Not with you.'

'Put something on then. I'm going for the door.'

'Liza!'

But she'd gone, pulling her dressing gown round her and leaving me to hop about finding my clothes which were scattered around the floor. I was just pulling my T-shirt on when the door opened and in they came, Anne first. She stopped talking mid sentence, stopped moving, almost stopped breathing. She just stood there.

'Anne, say something.'

'How could you?'

'It just happened.'

'How could you? You bastard.'

'Anne, it's not like that. He...'

'And you! Up to your old tricks.'

'I'm sorry, Anne. I never meant to hurt you.'

'Really?'

'Yes, really. Neither of us did.'

'You've a funny way of showing it.'

She turned to go.

'Well I'm out of here. And I don't want to see either of you, ever again.'

'That's going to be a little difficult.'

'I don't care.'

Liza blocked her way.

'Okay. Go if you must, but hear me out first. This. This was bound to happen. I adore Tom. I have done since I first set eyes on him, but I knew he was out of bounds. I kept him at arm's length, avoided being on my own with him. I tried so hard Anne, for you. And then last night we, we were thrown together and it was like I'd come home. I'm sorry, really I am, but…'

'But you found an opportunity and snatched it.'

'Anne, no, it was both of us. You're very special but Liza, she's my soulmate.'

'Second bloody prize.'

And Anne collapsed in tears on Liza's beaten up old armchair.

'Anne.'

'Fuck off.'

'No, listen. I love you, we've had great times together, but you got bored with me a while back. I know you did. And…'

'And so you thought you could jump into bed with my sister.'

'Oh God, it wasn't like that.'

'God. Yes. How does that square with your morality?'

'Anne.'

'Leave me alone. Keep away from me. Just. Just…'

And she stormed out.

'That went well.'

'Yes. We had our say.'

'I was being sarcastic.'

'I know. But I know my sister. She's in a state right now, but she'll be quoting it all back to us in a few months' time.'

'You think?'

'Yes. Her pride's hurt, but you're right, she's been looking for a way out of your relationship for months. We just gave her it.'

'Did you mean what you said?'

'Of course. I know her.'

'No. Not that. About me.'

'Are you completely stupid? Of course I meant it. I've been in love with you since that first night in Goring. Pete knows. Ask him.'

'God, Pete. Is he going to give me a hard time!'

'You'll survive, you and Pete. Anyway, he should be pleased with you.'

'How do you make that out?'

'The field's clear. He can ask Anne out now.'

'Anne? Pete?'

'You are stupid.'

'Thanks.'

'But lovely. Pete has fancied Anne forever. He couldn't do anything about it because there you were. In the way. Now, the coast is clear. Unless you tire of me and go running back, of course.'

'I'll never tire of you.'

'No?'

'No. I've fought my feelings for you for so long. I've watched you and felt more and more sure. I love you. I'm stuck with it. I...'

'Tom.'

'What?'

'Shut up.'

And she started to take off the clothes I'd so hurriedly found and put on.

Anne

I don't want to talk too much about that second year at Lothbury. It's too painful, even now. The thing is I love Tom, he's a dear, dear friend and part of the family, but back then I hated him. Well, not to start with. For months we were a sort of cosy foursome; Liza and Pete, not a couple but thick as thieves – which they still are by the way – and Tom and me, an old couple starting to get bored with each other.

So really, when it all fell apart, at the end of the year, it was no bad thing. I was ready for a break from Tom; more than ready. What I wasn't ready for was finding him in bed with my sister, and after our teenage rows over boys as well. But I think they needed each other – still do. They meet a need in each other for difference. Liza and her artistic, slightly countercultural streak. Tom being so grounded. Anyway, I was hurt and disappointed, bitter and angry. I spent months hardly speaking to them and passed a summer in Goring with our parents wondering what was going on until Liza spilled the beans. Then she got it in the ear from Mum for her trouble. The strange thing was that when Mum attacked her I found myself defending her, saying things like 'I was bored with him anyway' and 'Liza and Tom are soulmates, anyone can see that', quoting the clever bitch. Sorry. I love her too, but you know how it is – sisters.

So what happened with me after the big scene? Pete did, I suppose. Who else was I going to talk to? I had three close confidants and two of them had just run off with each other. Pete was a tower of strength, a gentleman. He can listen can Pete – too much sometimes, to too many people, but it's good when he listens to me. And he was always there. We ate in the refectory together, went out for walks and drinks; became a couple in many ways. The other girls talked about him as my boyfriend and I'd say 'We're just good friends', not convincing any of them, but we were, for quite a while.

Then one evening, walking by the river, he suddenly said, 'I don't think I can do this any more.'

'What? Walk on the riverbank?'

'Be good friends.'

'But you are a good friend, Pete. The best.'

'It's not enough. Not for me.'

'I'm sorry.'

'Don't be. Look, Anne. One, you're the best friend I've ever had, Tom notwithstanding; two, you're absolutely beautiful; and three, you're intelligent and sensitive.'

'Sounds okay so far. I can't see the problem.'

'The problem is I'm in love with you.'

'Oh.'

'Oh? Is that it?'

'No, I was thinking that only you could turn a declaration of love into a three-point list.'

'Sorry, but the thing is, it's getting to me. This being good friends, it's a sort of torture.'

'So what do you want to do?'

'I don't know. Stop seeing you so much, I guess.'

'Is that going to make you feel better?'

'It's worth a try.'

'Is it the only option?'

'I can't think of any others, can you?'

'Well, you could always ask me out.'

'What? On a date?'

'It's what people do Pete.'

'I know, but...'

'But what?'

'But you don't feel the same.'

'How do you know?'

'Do you?'

'Why don't you ask me out. I might say yes. Then we could find out how we really feel about each other.'

'Well, one, I...'

'Pete.'

'What?'

'No three-point lists. Just ask me out.'

'Sorry. Anne, will you come out with me, on a date, not as good friends?'

'Of course I will.'

'You will?'

'It's about time we moved this relationship on, don't you think?'

'Yes. I do. So, what now?'

'You could try kissing me.'

And he did, without another three-point list, thankfully. After that the relationship did in fact move on; quite a bit. And quite quickly. After all, we had been going through the 'getting to know you' stage for some time.

There were two issues we had to address as it turned out. Well, three actually – Tom, Liza and sex. Since I was barely speaking to Tom and Liza, relations between Pete and them were also a little strained, but Tom was his oldest and closest friend and Liza, well apart from being my little sister, she was also one of Pete's closest friends. So, somehow, we had to call a truce, make up, and put it all behind us. We talked about this a fair bit without reaching a conclusion, so in the end I just turned up at Liza's door, like in the old days.

'Anne!' was her greeting.

'Can I come in?'

'Oh, of course.'

'Not in bed with anybody are you?'

'Maybe you shouldn't come in.'

'Sorry. Cheap shot. We need to talk.'

'Okay. I probably asked for it. Come on up.'

'Liza, I…'

'Cup of tea?'

'Thanks. Yes. I. I've… Look, this has gone on long enough. I'm still angry, but I can't go on punishing you.'

'I never meant to hurt you, Anne. I tried hard to keep away from Tom, really I did.'

'Yes, well, he was right, you know.'

'Who was?'

'Tom. I was bored with him. I don't know why. I think we'd run out of steam somehow and neither of us could quite admit it. It's just, well, jumping into bed with my sister is hardly the gentlest way of ending with me.'

'No.'

'I mean, he could have talked to me. Ended it.'

'Anne, it just happened. We didn't plan it. It was, oh I don't know, like a train coming towards me and I couldn't get out of the way. I'm sorry. No, really.'

'Right. God, Liza, this milk's off.'

'Sorry, it'll have to be black then.'

'I'll have a coffee in that case.'

'Okay, sorted. Why are you here Anne? Why now? Don't get me wrong, I'm pleased you are but… why?'

'Well. Where do I start? I'm in a better place, a more forgiving one. I miss you. And I've moved on. From Tom. Which is complicated.'

'Complicated? Sounds like life is getting simpler.'

'I'm going out with Pete.'

'Pete? Okay, that is complicated.'

'You might be happy for me.'

'Oh, I am, but Pete's hardly spoken to me since Tom and I...'

'He's not been on the best of terms with Tom either.'

'No, but that's normal. They've been falling out every couple of weeks since they were five.'

'Anyway, Pete and you is part of the issue. And Pete and Tom. I've missed my little sister, Pete's missed his two best friends, I've been mad at you both but it's killing me, I can't keep it up, and I think Pete's good for me. I feel happy, Liza. The only thing that's not right is you and me. If we can fix that the rest will fall into place.'

'Even you and Tom?'

'It'll be a bit awkward for a bit, but yes, even me and Tom.'

'So kiss and make up then?'

'Kiss and make up.'

We hugged – a breathtaking, world-encompassing hug. A hug that took me back to home and childhood, to my difficult and annoying sister who I loved so much. I think we cried too – I know we did – and talked, all morning, about Tom and Pete, about the two of us, about Liza throwing herself at Pete, about Tom helping her overcome the embarrassment, about the future. I don't think we quite realised the complications we would face in the future, but we did get a glimpse of the strength of the bond between the four of us, which I suppose is what this whole exercise is about.

Liza

Such larks! End of year two and I find myself in bed with Tom! That put the cat among the pigeons. Anne didn't speak to me for weeks; nor did Pete really, no more than he had to. And he and Tom had a blazing row – another one. I played it down to Anne when we started speaking again, but it wasn't their normal row over some point of principle, this was full-blooded and bitter. I hadn't realised Pete could be so... What's the word? Bitter? Vitriolic? Maybe just angry. Righteous anger, you think? Tinged with jealousy, of a sort. Tom had the girl he, Pete, wanted and was messing her about; adding insult to injury. Anyway, big bust-up, and then they were terribly polite to each other for weeks. It wasn't pleasant.

The thing is, I didn't plan it, Tom didn't plan it, it just happened. Irresistible forces and all that. I suppose, in the back of my mind, I knew Anne was tiring of Tom, well she'd more or less said so. Also, in my defence Your Honour, I knew there was a frisson between her and Pete, but essentially I'd spent a lovely evening with the man I fancied more than anyone I'd ever met, I was pleasantly drunk and he kissed me. One thing led to another, and I wasn't about to call halt. It was very bad of me – and him; let's not forget his behaviour – reprehensible. Thank God! Anyway, it worked out in the end – mostly.

After that it was cloud nine time, Tom and me time, sex in the afternoon time. There were only two clouds in my coffee; a sister-shaped cloud, dark and silent, and a Pete-shaped cloud, dark and polite. Pete was polite and reserved, no three-point lists, not the natural order of things. Anne, annoyed with me, was more normal, although I had resolved not to give her cause. Well, sod 'em, I thought.

Both were a bit of an issue though, and I had no idea how to get over the rift in either case. Fortunately, Anne sorted it for me by falling for Pete and deciding enough was enough, so no need to go crawling. Just a sisterly morning of hugs and tears and we were good to go again, more or less anyway. There was a bit of embarrassment, the odd moment of recrimination, but essentially we'd all managed to end up with the right partner; a relief all round.

I suppose Anne knew her prospective brother-in-law (we were very quickly talking in those terms) a little more intimately than most and vice versa, and my new, prospective brother-in-law knew me fairly intimately too (Anne and Pete were not much slower in talking in those terms either), but we were soon on a fairly even keel and set for the great adventure into post-student life – together – my sister with my closest friend, and me with the love of my life, the man most capable of driving me to distraction, in so many ways. Still.

Pete

This is just a list of things I gained from Lothbury:

1. My wife. Still can't believe I found Anne, or that she fell for me
2. My oldest friend as a brother-in-law

3. Technically that might be brother-in-law by marriage as he married my sister-in-law
4. My other closest friend as a sister-in-law
5. A degree which enabled me to go on to train as a priest
6. Somewhere to put my emotions. Not my strong point, but with these three I feel safe.

All that late teen and post-teen angst about sex seems a long time ago now. I felt so out of tune with the times, but Anne was much more understanding than my previous girlfriends. We didn't wait long to marry though – neither of us wanted to. It was a church wedding – had to be, for me – in Goring, the local Anglican church in Anne's parish with the vicar in his robes, Liza looking stunning as chief bridesmaid, and Tom pretending he'd lost the ring. He was best man, of course, and made a great speech that had everyone in stitches. I returned the favour when he and Liza got married, though I think my speech was dryer. I toyed with the idea of telling the story of Liza drunk and naked but thought better of it. It would have been inappropriate, and maybe best not to let on that I still had that mental image.

We arrived at Lothbury almost as two units of two, just ready to meet up. Not as simple as that, obviously, but we were a foursome of sorts most of the time we were there. Even the period when we were a little estranged was defined by that estrangement. And we've been a solid group pretty much ever since, despite later ups and downs. More of that later, I suppose.

PART TWO

CHAPTER ONE

JONNY NOWER

There was a hint of September rain in the air as Jonny Nower stepped out of Mercer's and headed east along Threadneedle Street. A rather patrician figure in pinstripe and brogues, Jonny was a little preoccupied, and it was only as the first drops made themselves felt that he paused, swore, and headed back inside. Re-emerging, he took shelter under the brolly he had forgotten and headed off again.

Back to Bishopsgate, or was it still Gracechurch Street at that point? Jonny was never sure. Anyway, north up Bishopsgate was where he was heading, past the market, past the building sites which dominated the junction with Camomile Street and eventually into his office on the third floor of one of the office blocks which bordered Broadgate. The rain was getting heavy by the time he reached Liverpool Street, and he was relieved to reach the covered walkway and shake the wet from his umbrella.

When he was a younger man, City workers had carried their umbrellas tightly furled, not an art he had ever mastered. Umbrellas had been black back then too. Now, like most of his friends, he carried a golf umbrella emblazoned with the logo of a service provider. He had a selection to choose from.

Today's choice was a purple affair with the eagle emblem of the Taylor Trust Company, which acted as a custodian bank for Nower Asset Management, the company he once owned.

As he reached the foyer it occurred to Jonny that things he once owned were a dominant theme in his life; the business, the estate, even the church. Technically, of course, the estate and the church had never belonged to him but to his family, his forebears, but it still felt like these had once been his. Indeed, he had been accused of acting as if they still were from time to time. A fair criticism, he supposed, but a habit hard to break.

Jonny was one of a dying breed, or so he liked to think. Born into privilege, he had joined the stockbroking firm of Handley Prior straight out of university. Tom Handley had been at school with his father, so Jonny had been spared the endless round of dreary interviews young people seemed to have to endure nowadays. He found he had a knack for the business and, in particular, for investing client money, so when Big Bang came and Handley Prior disappeared into the clutches of one of the banks, Jonny jumped ship and set up his own investment firm. There his ability to work happily alongside the sons of dukes and barrow boys, in complete social ease, enabled him to build a strong and successful team. Assets under management grew, his reputation grew, and his wealth grew. The only cloud on the horizon was the way in which his family money was reducing, eaten away by death taxes and frittered away by his elder sister and younger brother.

Jonny took action, engineered a sale of the estate to a local businessman, retaining some land and buildings on the periphery to be the new family home, and set up trusts to protect the remainder. He also set about converting his paper worth into hard cash by selling Nower Asset Management to an American boutique of boutiques. Now here he was, former owner of the firm, reduced to a grand but meaningless title and the care and responsibility for a handful of long-term clients. He had become the face of the business, where once he had been the heart of it.

'Jonny!'

Riding the escalator up from the foyer to the first floor of the building, he passed Dave Pullman heading in the opposite direction. Dave was tall, thickset, and difficult to miss. Difficult not to hear too, as he was blessed with a resonant bass which carried across the hubbub.

'Jonny! Need to talk to you.'

'Come back up. I'll wait.'

It was a long wait, or felt like it, it was a long and slow escalator, but Dave was that rare commodity, a colleague he actually trusted. As he waited, he remembered their first meeting, just before the turn of the century. It was at a point where business appeared to be booming, the bigger players were looking to add assets under management, and Jonny was being courted from all sides. Among the suitors was Blue Island Trust, a Midwestern trust bank with an East Coast asset management business looking to expand.

Blue Island made their initial approach through Dave, a savvy investor from Queens, who was direct and friendly. He and Jonny had met at industry conferences, round tables and the like and knew each other well enough for straight speaking, so when Dave invited himself to the Nower offices for a chat, he got straight to the point.

'How long're you going to run your own little empire Jonny?'

'Do you want the client answer?'

'Yes. But also the honest one.'

'Well, the client answer is forever, I've no interest in retiring, I'm still a relatively young man. Don't worry.'

'And the honest one?'

'Not so different. Just change the 'forever' to 'not for the foreseeable future'.'

'Be nice to share the burden a bit though, I guess.'

'I've got colleagues, you know. Partners. Senior staff.'

Dave grinned and sipped his coffee.

'So why do you still own 90%?'

'Oh, I think it's a bit less than that.'

'Not a lot less. 86.5.'

'You've been doing some homework.'

'You could say that. And that kind of ownership can look bad. Look Jonny, this is off the record, right? Between us.'

'Okay.'

'Blue Island wants to grow a little faster than the sales figures, know what I mean?'

'You have a war chest?'

'A little put by for suitable acquisitions.'

Suitable acquisitions – Jonny grimaced.

'And you think we'd fit? You think I'd fit?'

'Well, here's how I see it. We send the men in suits in to agree a sensible price, and you, Jonny, become a very wealthy man...'

'I already am.'

'On paper, yes. I mean really. Hard cash, or our paper, which is effectively the same thing.'

'It would certainly improve my liquidity position.'

'It would realise the value of what you've built up.'

'I can't abandon my colleagues.'

'No need. They're good, right? Otherwise they wouldn't be here and you wouldn't be so successful.'

'We have a certain culture.'

Dave took a piece of A4 from the file he had placed on the desk and turned it so Jonny could see.

'Look, this is just my very rough assessment. Key people; retention terms – ballpark you understand. Next layer down – assurances, benefit improvements. Decision-making structures – guarantees and continuity. Just to show we mean business – and that we'd play fair.'

'I don't see my name on the list.'

'What do you want? It's yours.'

'Within reason, I assume.'

'Always within reason. The way I see it, both sides would need you to stick around, for a while at least. But you could shed some of the executive and admin rubbish. Focus on key clients. Enjoy it a bit more.'

Jonny grinned.

'What makes you think I don't enjoy it now?'

'My guess is you enjoy the investing, you enjoy talking with clients and helping them manage their wealth. You even enjoy the in-house investment committees and so on. But the housekeeping? The compliance? All the stuff about appraisals and recruitment, capital expenditure, budgets. Not you, Jonny. Must drive you mad.'

'So, what you're saying is I get to do the bits I like and you pay me a shedload of money to stop doing the bits I don't like?'

'Got it in one.'

'And you'd protect my partners, the staff?'

'Absolutely. A minimum of disruption.'

'Meaning?'

'Meaning we're acquiring assets under management here, this isn't a cost-cutting exercise – so we need most of your people.'

'And the others?'

'At the margin, there might be some duplication, but we'd find other roles where we could, agree good terms where we can't.'

Jonny leaned back in his antique leather swivel chair and surveyed the expanse of mahogany between them.

'And no imposition of corporate style in office furniture and so on?'

'Can't promise, Jonny old boy, but can't see a problem. Blue Island won't want to destroy your culture.'

'So, if we assume there might be interest?'

'Then we get our people to talk to your people and see what happens. We get the lawyers to draw up confidentiality agreements and take it from there. What do you say?'

'Well, I certainly think there's no harm in exploring the idea.'

'And any issues, any concerns, call me. I'm your go-to man. I won't be involved in the nitty–gritty, but I'll make sure you're heard. Fair enough?'

'Fair enough.'

They shook hands.

What followed was a round of talks, negotiations, explanations, the setting up of a data room and a lot of time spent reassuring people. First came the partners with succession aspirations, disappointed to have the carrot stolen from under their noses. For them the reassurances about culture and the obvious need to keep the clients happy helped, as did the financial incentives offered by Blue Island. As Jonny pointed out, on more than one occasion, they all had good track records to fall back on if it all went sour, and the financial handcuffs would be bought out by any serious suitor. It was a comment he had cause to remember on several occasions in the years that followed.

Next came the senior professionals hoping to make it to the top level. Similar arguments applied to them, with the added bonus of possible openings in the wider Blue Island empire.

The support staff were perhaps the most concerned, and concerning. Here there were bound to be some casualties, and the fact that the numbers were likely to be low was of little comfort to people who thought they might count among them.

The whole process was exhausting, and Jonny had little time, or energy, to consider his own position, why he was going down this path. Part of him wanted to call a halt, but he was getting more and more committed as the days went by. Deep down, he knew this was a good move. He had built and run this business, made it his main focus, been breadwinner, mentor and father confessor to eager young men and women, neglecting his home life. It was time to explore other options. Jancy certainly thought so, and had been nagging him to spend more time at home, with her, or at least to ease up on the corporate stress. Maybe this would give him a chance to do so.

If dealing with colleagues and employees was tough, dealing with those outside the company was worse still. The choreography alone was a major challenge. Trying to get the message out to clients simultaneously, manage the press, and reassure the intermediaries while still maintaining focus on what the business was all about was draining, if also exhilarating. Daily meetings of a war cabinet were set up, specifics addressed, plans made and adjusted.

In all this, Dave Pullman and Jonny acted as co-heads, the old and the new acting in concert. They made an odd pair, the smooth New Yorker with his trademark beam and the slightly patrician, silver-haired and rather serious-looking Nower. Pullman was well over six foot while Jonny was barely five seven. They understood each other though and a good working relationship was forged, which had survived despite the gradual erosion of many of the reassurances and safeguards over the years.

The problem with Blue Island, as Jonny was to discover, was that it was a many-headed hydra and the revolving senior management had different views on how subsidiaries should be run. The board member responsible for the boutique of boutiques structure when Jonny and Dave first spoke was Clayton Jones, a man with a vision of a range of boutiques all operating independently and feeding the centre with the resulting profits. Under this model there was little interference and the maintenance of the existing culture within each boutique was a positive. When Clayton was rotated to a new role, his place was taken by Bob Junker, a smooth Californian of Dutch extraction who took the view that the centre should, above all, be in control. This meant shared accounting, shared platforms, centralised support functions, rebranding. The fact that written assurances had been given meant little. Agreements could be rewritten with a little cajoling, bullying, rational argument and, if necessary, some financial incentives.

Jonny found himself sidelined, powerless to defend colleagues who felt let down and betrayed. Accused of feathering his own nest by people he had nurtured and supported was hurtful, even though he would probably have taken the same view had the positions been reversed. Losing all control when he had hugged control, and ownership, to himself for so long was difficult. Being accused of recalcitrance by Junker at the same time led him to say a few things which might have been better left unsaid. The American did not take kindly to Jonny's suggestion that Blue Island was untrustworthy, apparently believing in the corporate values of integrity and plain dealing, even while ignoring written agreements. Jonny found himself even more sidelined and with time on his hands.

Some of his senior colleagues wanted him to jump ship and set up a new business, to start again. It was tempting, and the golden handcuffs were growing looser as time went by, but he was unsure of his appetite for building another business.

Throughout all this, he and Dave remained firm friends. Dave was a fixer, a man who could get things done, who could extract assurances and broker agreements. He had charm and, Jonny still felt, integrity. Management changes above his head were not his fault. Less close to Junker than he had been to Jones, Dave could nonetheless smooth the difficult relationships now involved and protect the firm from some, at least, of the central diktats.

Right now, Dave was nearing the top of the escalator. Jonny moved forward to intercept him and they drew away a little to one side.

'Don't want to worry you, Jonny, but we have a problem.'

'A problem?"

'An opportunity to excel.'

'Oh, one of those. What's gone wrong?'

'Scafell. Just a few jitters.'

Blue Island management were highly sensitive to any potential breaches of client confidentiality, even to the point of naming some of the family offices and UHNW (ultra-high net worth) clients for whom they worked. Code words abounded within the organisation. It was one of Jonny's little jokes that, as every time one of these clients was mentioned there seemed to be a mountain to climb, the code words would themselves be mountains. This particular deal was with a very large UK client; the largest Jonny had dealt with, so the project was named after the largest mountain in England.

'You want to talk about it now? You were on your way out.'

'I was only going to grab a latte. I could be back and in your office in five.'

'Okay. Anything I should be thinking about?'

'Yeah, Jonny. Your role. Who fronts it. Keeping New York happy.'

'That should fill the idle minutes.'

'What?'

'Get your coffee. I'll be waiting.'

Jonny headed through the largely open-plan office to one of the few private offices to survive the recent changes. Investment managers nowadays were required to behave as a team, with an emphasis on transparency and shared ideas in an open environment. The friendly competition of Jonny's youth had been a casualty of the move from a focus on the individual to a focus on the 'house' and the consequent need to control the dispersion of returns with the result that all the hands-on portfolio managers were based in one big room, personal space only identified by photos, and personal memorabilia scattered on their desks beneath the twin screens of their computers.

Reaching his office, he sank into his chair, checked his voicemail and glanced at his inbox. One of the messages was from Jim Ferguson at Scafell asking him to call back. Better wait, he thought. One of the others was from one of the key client managers at Blue Island in New York, wanting to talk with him urgently about Scafell. Better wait, he thought. It was a little strange to feel so sidelined and yet to be so much in demand.

It was also interesting that Jim Ferguson was calling him. Scafell was his family business but he normally left his in-house chief investment officer to deal with Blue Island and, while Jonny and Jim went back a long way, the recently appointed CIO was also an old sparring partner. Dan Murphy was an ex-trader from the East End who had worked for Nower early in his career and had maintained friendly contact with Jonny since leaving. It wasn't difficult for him to pick up the phone. Jonny wondered if there was some agenda which was a bit sensitive for the ex-trader's no-nonsense approach. He was still musing on this when Dave appeared, clutching a cardboard mug of coffee.

'A few voicemails waiting for me, Dave.'

'Scafell?'

'Jim Ferguson and Biff Johnson.'

'You haven't responded?'

'Before getting the low-down? No chance.' Jonny poured himself some sparkling water from the bottle in his cooler. 'Want to tell me about it?'

'Storm in a teacup probably, but everyone's getting aerated. Dan Murphy's making demands. Junker won't budge. Biff's in the middle.'

'Let me guess, Junker expects Biff to keep the client happy but won't do anything to help make that possible.'

'That's about the size of it. And your old pal Dan...'

'...is being a pain?'

'He's making silly demands. Not sure why. They've got a good deal.'

'So where do I come into this?'

'Jonny! As if you need to ask. You're going to pour oil on troubled waters. Tell them all to play nicely.'

'Blessed are the peacemakers.'

'Exactly.'

'Okay Dave, give me the detail.'

'Well, you're going to love this. Dan has a shopping list. He wants more access to senior staff...'

'More? How could he have more?'

'Maybe he wants to sleep with Junker.'

'Nobody wants to sleep with Junker.'

'Probably true. He wants a few bips shaved off the fee. No wait, there's more. He wants first dibs on new investment opportunities, and he wants representation on the board.'

'What board?"

'We're running the Scafell business as a separate company, for tax reasons.'

Jonny considered this.

'So why can't Scafell be represented?'

'Because it's an internal solution, to help us run things efficiently.'

'Okay, let's work through this logically. First off, the senior contact thing is purely cosmetic. They're already as close as they can be, so we just need to make them think they've got more.'

'Without scaring Junker.'

'Without scaring Junker. Then the fees, well I guess that's tricky. Can we shave anything off?'

'What do you think Jonny? It's cut to the bone already.'

'So we say no.'

'And risk losing it?'

'It's a straight choice, Dave. Do we want to keep the business or not? How profitable does it need to be?'

'We might have a little room for manoeuvre.'

'Good. So we explore what little room we have. What's next? First dibs on new opportunities. You're going to tell me that falls foul of the regulators.'

Jonny smiled.

'You know I am. TCF.'

'Treating customers fairly – the opposite of what Dan wants – but at least we have something to hide behind. Is that it?'

'That's it.'

'And Biff wants rescuing. Wonder what Jim wants. I should probably talk to Biff first.'

'I'll leave you to it.'

Dave threw his coffee cup into the bin and left. Jonny grimaced, picked up the phone, and got through to Biff's voicemail, which was par for the course. He left a message and sat back. The phone rang.

'Nower.'

'Jonny. Biff.'

'That didn't take you long.'

'I just had to finish a call. Has Dave filled you in?'

'He just left.'

'I think your powers of diplomacy may be called for. I'm getting nowhere.'

'Junker in one ear and Dan in the other?'

'Junker's telling me not to give way but to keep Dan happy. It can't be done.'

'And Dan?'

'Well, he's got a shopping list.'

'So I understand.'

'And he doesn't want to budge.'

'So what do you want from me?'

'Help. You're the only one who can fix this.'

'There'll need to be a bit of give on both sides, whatever Junker says.'

'Look Jonny, I don't care. If you authorise the concessions I'm in the clear. And you can stand up to Junker. I can't.'

'I'm a lost cause already in Junker's eyes, it's true.'

'That's not what I meant.'

'It's okay. It's true. I'm an embarrassing legacy; something he inherited with the business. And I have the advantage that I don't actually care what he thinks. You don't have that luxury.'

'So you think you can resolve it?'

'Square the circle? Probably. I'll make a couple of calls. Get back to you later.'

'Thanks Jonny. You're a lifesaver.'

'It's what I'm here for.'

Jonny's next call was to Jim Ferguson. It went straight to voicemail, so he left a message and got on with his afternoon, knowing that Jim would respond when he could. Sure enough, his mobile went as he travelled home that evening. He ignored it. Not a conversation he could have on the 6.20 from London Bridge. It would have to wait.

*

That evening was taken up with church matters. The Parochial Church Council met monthly and that evening's meeting would be the first with the new 'priest in charge'. As a small, former estate church close to Molebridge, St Aidan's had become the responsibility of the team ministry at St Peter's. The designated 'priest in charge' for St Aidan's had recently changed and was the new vicar of St Peter's, Tom Raistrick. Jonny had yet to spend much time with him, but so far he liked what he saw. Gregarious, easy-going and personable, Tom was just what St Aidan's needed. His predecessor had been devout, spiritual and thoroughly focussed on his faith but totally incapable of relating to his parishioners, a key element in a village church. He had moved on to academia, a sensible move in Jonny's view. He was all for faith and spirituality but some interpersonal skills were also needed in his opinion.

The previous incumbent had also been very poor at chairing meetings. In fact, Jonny could remember no clergyman who wasn't very poor at chairing meetings, so his hopes of improvement with the new guy were not high.

The church was poorly heated and had no rooms large enough for the PCC other than the body of the church, so it had become a tradition for PCC meetings to be held in Jonny's sizeable lounge. Members started to arrive as he was grabbing a quick sandwich and cup of tea. Not for the first time, Jonny felt a tinge of irritation with people who insisted on turning up early when he was always rushing from one thing to another.

The PCC were a motley bunch. Jan Rycroft, the secretary, and first to arrive, was a northerner who had migrated to Surrey with her husband as he followed job opportunities. Jan was a teacher and equally in demand wherever she lived. She had blonde hair tinged with grey, loved horses and had become quite the country woman since settling in Micklebury. Her 'playground' voice carried well across the fields and stables but could be a little overpowering in the confines of a PCC meeting. Still, Jonny liked Jan, she was the salt of the earth and spoke her mind.

Next to arrive were Nick Jennings and Terry Derbyshire who were friends and neighbours and in the habit of sharing lifts. Jonny still found it amusing that these two friends carried the names of close friends from the Jennings books of his youth, but they never seemed to see the joke – or indeed any joke – they were a dour pair.

As 8 o'clock approached, there were more arrivals – Anne Johnson, large but quiet; Fiona Wilson, the youngest, and a little unsure of herself; Sally Roberts, attractive, outgoing, always full of energy; and Steve Ede, reliable, practical, and a father of six. It was just turned eight when Tom Raistrick arrived. Jonny felt an immediate change in the room. A well-set man in his fifties, Tom had presence. And, of course, he was still new enough to pique interest. This was his first PCC at St Aidan's.

'Sorry everybody. I'm a bit late. Never seems to be enough time. How are you all?'

Mutters of forgiveness and responsive enquiries about his health, his wife, his day followed and everyone settled. Tom started the meeting with prayer then looked at his agenda.

'Right, forgive me; new boy, long agenda. I'd like to suggest we take a few minutes to agree how long we want to spend on each item and aim to finish by ten.'

'That'll be a first.'

'I know. PCCs can be interminable, but not when I'm in the chair. My experience is that we tend to get bogged down in minutiae and leave no time for important stuff, so we all get home late feeling frustrated. Sound familiar?'

'You've been a fly on the wall.'

'It's the same everywhere. Trust me.'

There was a rustling of papers. Nick Jennings was looking doubtful. Jonny thought he should step in.

'Is something troubling you Nick?'

'It's all very well saying we'll have short meetings but all these things need discussing.'

'Not for hours and hours.' This from Sally. 'We spent forever arguing about the washbasin in the ladies last time. A complete waste of time.'

'You wouldn't have said that if we'd not sorted it.'

'It meant we didn't talk about any of the big issues until we were all dead on our feet.'

Tom had been listening carefully to this exchange.

'What I'm hearing is that we need to give appropriate airtime to all the issues which face us and to do so when we're fresh enough to give them proper consideration. Right?'

There was a general murmur of assent.

'Well, what I propose is that we establish a number of subcommittees or working groups if you prefer. They can do the detailed work on their areas of responsibility and simply report back to the PCC.'

'The PCC is responsible. We have to make the decisions.'

'You're exactly right Terry, and that's why we have to be careful to set out what the subcommittees can decide and what they need to refer back to the PCC.'

'That would be everything.'

'Really? Let's use the washbasin as an example. It was old, cracked and leaking as I understand it.'

'A bit like some of us.' This was a rare interjection from Anne Johnson.

'You speak for yourself.' This from Nick, but with a smile on his lips.

'So the PCC knew it needed replacing. That's a two-minute discussion. Why did it take so long?'

'Because we had to agree how many quotes to get, who from, what sort of style to go for, whether we should decorate as well. You name it.'

'Exactly. Well, what I propose is a maintenance subgroup. They would have authority to sort all that stuff out within agreed budget limits and just report back... But if, for example, they found the structure was unsafe and needed major work then they would present a proposal to the PCC for discussion.'

Sally perked up. 'So no more of my life wasted on 18 models of tap?'

'Not unless you're on that group.'

'Please, no.'

'So, the first thing is to agree what the groups will be, who will be on them, and what we don't want to delegate.'

At 9.30, as they finished an agenda item relating to Advent services, Tom checked his watch and made an unusual proposal.

'It's now half past nine. We have another half hour for this meeting so let's just spend a moment allocating time to what's left on the agenda shall we?'

There was a murmur round the room.

'Is there a problem?'

It was Jan Rycroft who spoke up.

'We normally just go on until we finish.'

'Not now we don't. I need my beauty sleep.'

'But what if we don't get through it all?'

Tom smiled reassuringly. 'There are two issues here. How many things to discuss and how much time they need. My suggestion is that the world will not end if we have to defer some items. Not only that but we have several items we can either discuss briefly or simply delegate to our new committees. Humour me. See if it works.'

Ten o'clock came round. Tom closed his notebook and suggested ending with a prayer.

As they all left, Jonny muttered to Tom, 'Do you really need your beauty sleep or can you stop for a coffee?'

'A cup of tea would be good.'

Settled in Jonny's study, the two men sipped tea.

'You didn't tell me I'd have to drink from a Fulham mug!'

'You've got to support the local team.'

'Fulham can't be the closest team. Wimbledon I would have thought.'

'Ah well, there are limits.'

Tom laughed. 'A pragmatist.'

'Yes, and I was impressed by your pragmatism this evening.'

'The first PCC is always a bit nerve-racking. I hope I haven't shocked them too much.'

Jonny laughed.

'Terry Derbyshire's face was a picture. They'll get used to it. And some of them caught on to the benefits right away.'

'And you approve?'

'I certainly do. I think you're the first clergyman I've ever met who can chair a meeting.'

'It's not traditionally been seen as a top priority.'

'No, but it can drive you round the bend - interminable discussions about trivia. Not sure I've ever understood the appeal of minutiae.'

'It keeps people in their comfort zone. It's stuff they can relate to, understand, control.'

'You've given this some thought.'

'When I was a curate I used to watch the vicar struggle with these meetings; get bogged down, frustrated. Used to hear other people moaning about the time taken up. Listened to what they were saying. I had a good friend in the congregation who ran a sizeable business, so I asked him how he would do it. Simple really. Once I got him to talk about his business, rather than the church, he just gave me a template for management.'

'I bet he didn't talk about comfort zones though.'

'No, he was focussed on using expertise – getting Terry to run the buildings and fabric group, given his experience as a surveyor, is an obvious one. What I found was that people became very comfortable, in a good way, in the groups because they could use their experience and knowledge from their day-to-day lives. What becomes more of a challenge is what's left for the main PCC, the responsibility for the spiritual and pastoral welfare of the congregation and the parish.'

This was an issue close to Jonny's heart.

'We never seem to talk about that.'

'What?'

'Spiritual questions. Pastoral oversight. Your predecessor was strong on spirituality but weak on communication. And pastoral care? That meant relating to real people. He ran a mile. Sorry, hobby horse of mine.'

'We all have different strengths. I'm not sure day-to-day pastoral care is one of mine, but I'm sure we have people who are really good at it. Anne or Sally maybe. Or Nick.'

Jonny considered this.

'I'm not sure about Nick. Practical stuff is his forte, not a listening ear.'

'Well we can explore that. You were saying spirituality was overlooked?'

'Was I? I suppose so. It seems to me the church is in danger of being little more than a community hub.'

'A valuable thing to be.'

'But not its main purpose Tom, surely.'

'What is the main purpose, do you think?'

'I'd struggle to give you a quick answer, but it's something to do with our relationship with God.'

Tom grinned. 'When I was a kid at Sunday school, the answer was always Jesus.'

'And it isn't now?'

'I can see we're going to have some interesting conversations Jonny. No, I think Jesus is sometimes the answer, or maybe always he's part of the answer, but there's much more to it than that – and much less.'

'You intrigue me.'

At this point there was the sound of a car pulling up outside. Jonny smiled.

'That'll be Jancy back from bridge.'

'I should go.'

'No, stay and say hello.'

They listened to the car door slam, the crunch of footsteps on the shingle drive and the key in the lock.

'In here, darling,' called Jonny and Jancy's petite frame and fine bone structure appeared at the door. Her face lit up.

'All finished? That's a record.'

'Tom is a diligent chairman. This is the new normal.'

'The two of you yacking over tea, you mean?'

'That too, probably.'

Tom had risen to his feet to greet Jancy, and now made as if to go.

'Don't feel you have to rush off Tom, it's nice to see you. And I want to know how you're settling in.'

'I should go now, while you've the chance Tom.'

'It's very nice to be made so welcome.'

Tom sat down. Jonny turned to his wife.

'You missed a treat, darling. You should have seen Nick's face when Tom curtailed the discussion on the gents' loo.'

'You didn't!'

'I'm afraid so.'

'I don't think we've ever had a PCC without at least half an hour on the plumbing. I think Nick thinks that's the main purpose of the meeting.'

'Well, he should be happy now.'

'Why's that?' queried Jancy.

'Because Tom's given him a whole subcommittee to chair.'

'Not on plumbing?'

'On the fabric. It includes plumbing. Also the paths, the light bulbs, the stonework and so on.'

'That should keep him quiet.'

'Quiet and happy – and useful.'

'Tom is busy harnessing our skills, darling.'

'So, Tom, have you found Jonny's skills yet?'

'There are so many to choose from Jancy, I'm not sure which to harness.'

'Oh! A diplomat as well.'

'Seriously, what I'd like to do is focus the main PCC discussions on the direction of the Church, the vision, the pastoral side and leave the mechanics to the special interest groups. That probably means there's a small number of PCC members who will be crucial for the future. Jonny's obviously one of them, but he can also help identify the others. Sally, I would have thought – or maybe Fiona, or Steve?'

'There's a danger it will be mainly the women. Not sure that matters, but our male PCC members seem to be focussed on nuts and bolts.'

'Well, let's see how it develops. For now, I think we've made a good start. It's a nice group – and a nice break from St Peter's.'

'Not a nice group down there then?'

'Not what I said. No, just a bigger group – more formal. And I've yet to find people I can sit and chat to like you guys. Speaking of which, I should be off. Get out of your hair.'

*

Another wet morning. The 6.30 train. The Waterloo and City Line. A walk up from Bank and Jonny was behind his desk by 8 a.m. It was a good time to call Jim Ferguson he thought. And so it proved. Jim picked up straight away and was eager to talk.

'Thanks for calling, Jonny. I'm sure you've heard from your people by now.'

'Sounds like we have a bit of an impasse.'

'Which I'm hoping you can help resolve. Dan doesn't think we've got a very good deal. He's getting a bit frustrated. And you know what he's like.'

'Not tackling the issue very subtly?'

'Quite. Look, Jonny, I don't want to be thought of as the client from hell. I'm not sure Dan cares, but he's only trying to get the best for the business, you know that.'

Jonny pulled his scrawled notes from the previous day towards him – a shopping list.

'Perhaps we should talk through the demands?'

'Demands? Is that how they're seen?'

'Pretty much.'

'Okay. Shoot.'

'First thing is more access to senior staff. That's a difficult one, Jim. Not sure how we'd do that.'

'How's that?'

'Well, you already have dedicated senior RMs, regular discussions with the heads of business and a hotline to Junker. What else does he want?'

'He feels we get the runaround.'

'To be honest with you Jim, I'd say that was a result of too much access, not too little. Junker prevaricates because he's not close enough to the action and doesn't want to say so. I'd get lynched for saying this but Dan and Junker aren't a good mix. Junker's probably terrified.'

'I won't tell. So what's the solution?'

'Something that saves face but gives Dan a bit more of a feeling that he's being listened to. Is he happy with Biff?'

'Yes. No problems there as far as I know. Maybe you could be more involved. Dan trusts you.'

'I'm hardly senior staff these days, Jim.'

'You're president or whatever it is the Americans call you.'

'A courtesy title. I'm sidelined, just there to troubleshoot.'

'Which is what you're doing now, right? And you're in a position to stand up to Junker, which I imagine is difficult for Biff.'

'Well, you're right there.'

'So my suggestion would be that you put yourself forward as our local ambassador, a high-level client executive, or whatever you want to call it. You talk with Dan whenever and have a regular catch-up with him and the client team in the States. Up to you, Jonny, but I'd be happy with that, and I'm sure we could sell it to Dan.'

'Okay, I'll see what I can get through internally. Next thing. Fees – obviously.'

'Obviously?'

'I've never seen a client shopping list which didn't include lower fees. I gather that the internal view is that we're very close to paying you rather than the other way round.'

'Is that true?'

'I'm sure we can find some give somewhere, but it won't be much.'

'Well, let's not get hung up on that. See what there is. His next thing was early access.'

'Yes, first dibs on new investment ideas. No can do, I'm afraid. It falls foul of the TCF requirements.'

'Not if we instruct you first.'

'Well, not if it's your idea, but as I understand it, Dan wants to benefit from our ideas before anyone else.'

'Maybe if he's talking with you on a regular basis that would keep him happy?'

'Not sure why it would. I'm not the young, thrusting ideas man any longer.'

Jim laughed. 'Maybe not, but you can add people to the call.'

'I'd have to control what they said.'

'Even so.'

'Okay, Jim, we can try it. What about this board thing?'

'You've set up a board to run our affairs and we're not represented.'

'It's supposed to be independent.'

'It's not very independent of Blue Island. Your guys just want control.'

'So what do you want?'

'I want Dan on it. This is my demand, not his. And if your guys want you there as well, to act as a buffer, that's fine by me.'

'And Dan?'

'Dan hates boards. He knows he has to do it, but I think he'd feel it had more chance of being useful if you were there as well.'

'Okay Jim, leave it with me. I'll have a few internal conversations.'

'Thanks Jonny. I appreciate it. How's things with you anyway? Jancy okay?'

And the conversation turned to other things. As Jonny came off the phone a few minutes later, Dave stuck his head round the door. Jonny waved him in.

'The very man.'

'Sounds ominous.'

'Just come off the phone with Jim Ferguson.'

'Is he the good cop or the bad cop?'

'Bit of a mix. I think it's soluble.'

Dave grinned at this.

'What?'

'I had a bet with myself that you'd sort it within the day.'

Jonny spread his hands in a gesture of supplication.

'Let's not get carried away. All I've done is work out what we need to do. Want me to tell you now?'

Dave settled in the chair, crossing his legs.

'Good a time as any.'

'Okay, so this is what they want. They want me involved. Sorry, I know that won't go down well with Junker but they know and trust me…'

'And, by implication…'

'Well, we can put it diplomatically but no, they don't have the same level of trust in Junker. Anyway, they want me as a senior client executive or something like that. Then they want something shaved off the fees; a token. We could push back on this if we give them everything else – maybe.'

'We're more or less paying them as it is.'

'Yes, I told him that.'

'You're a brave man.'

'He's an old friend. So, the first dibs on new ideas thing. They understand the issues. It's more about communication really. Regular discussions between Dan and me with bright, young investors pulled in from time to time. And Jim wants Dan on the board. Wants me on it too, I think. Said it was up to us, but reading between the lines he thinks it would be wise.'

'It's supposed to be an independent board.'

'I told him that Dave – he said it's not very independent of Blue Island.'

'Touché.'

'It's their money. We're just looking after it.'

Dave grinned.

'Try telling Junker.'

'Oh, I have. That's why he doesn't like me.'

'He doesn't understand you, Jonny. Everything he does is Blue Island. It's his religion. And you're not a company man. Complete culture clash.'

Jonny played with the Post-it pad on his desk before answering.

'You know how I got successful, Dave?'

'Yes. You focussed on clients. I know.'

'That's what we're here for. And if we look after them, by and large they'll look after us. Simple.'

'And it's what you're still doing.'

'When I'm allowed, Dave, when I'm allowed.'

'I'll talk to Junker – probably this evening. Can you keep Biff in the picture?'

'I'll give him a call. Let me know how you get on in the morning.'

'Will do.'

Dave threw his coffee cup in the bin and sauntered out. Jonny reached for a pack of tissues and wiped the coffee marks from the desk before settling down in front of his screen. Nice guy, Dave, he thought, don't know why he can't use a cup and saucer. However, right now he had other jobs to do. One of his roles was to chair a range of committees aimed at controlling risk, the main one of these being the operational risk committee or ORC, an acronym much favoured by the younger staff. Today's meeting was about to start.

ORC was an international committee and this morning the London members were foregathering in the main meeting room to conference with their colleagues in the US, Europe and Japan. The meeting room was old style, mahogany furniture dating from days of independence, but overlaid with white boards, conference facilities and video screens. When Jonny arrived, Joe, one of the team, was fiddling with the drinks, setting out papers and adjusting seating. Jonny was followed in by Kathy, shivering.

'Is it me or is the air con a bit fierce today?'

Joe was more interested in where everyone else was, and irritated that they had sent someone out for coffee.

'I ordered coffee already.'

'We wanted decent stuff. It's really cold in here.'

'We'll still get charged for what I ordered.'

'So don't order it.'

'Then I wouldn't get any coffee.'

'Have you turned the air conditioning up?'

'No. Not much. Just enough to keep sharp.'

'So that's no as in yes? Anyone on the line?'

'I haven't dialled in yet.'

Jonny listened to this exchange with amusement. He was with Joe on the coffee and couldn't see the attraction of the milky concoctions sold by the American chains unless you were actually in the States where, he agreed, almost anything was better than what passed for ordinary coffee. He did feel the air con was a bit fierce though, so strolled over to the controls and adjusted it.

'Let's dial in. By the time we've done that everyone will be here.'

Joe dialled in. Listened to the greeting – 'Welcome to Meeting Place. Please enter your six-digit PIN followed by the pound sign' – entered the number, and followed the next instruction – 'The moderator has not yet entered the meeting, enter your access code now.' He entered the code. 'You are now entering the meeting. You are the moderator.' Nobody else was on the line.

Jonny looked down at his papers. They were expecting Chuck and Biff from New York, Hiro from Tokyo and Hans from Frankfurt. The meeting had been set at an unsociable hour for Tokyo, but Hiro seemed not to care. He gave the impression of working 24-hour days. There was a ping and the disembodied voice announced that someone had entered the meeting; Chuck. It seemed Biff had gone out for coffee. ('I hope he's getting you one,' muttered Joe.)

Within five minutes, they had been joined by Hans, Hiro and Biff on line, and Bill arrived with a tray of coffee and a youngster who was introduced as Scott.

'I should explain to you all,' said Bill, 'that Scott is with us for a couple of weeks to see how things work. His father is Jim Ferguson of Scafell, so he has quite a bit of insight already, and knows Jonny I believe.'

'We're old friends,' confirmed Jonny. 'I agreed with Jim that it would be helpful for Scott to see how things work from our side of the fence. And I'm encouraging Scott to stop us and ask any questions he needs to ask. So welcome Scott. And let's start. So, new committee, first meeting, which means our first job is to define and identify different risk streams, therefore agenda item 1 is a brain dump. Who wants to start?'

Kathy started. 'Key operational risk, executives freeze to death because Joe is in charge of the air con.'

There was laughter. 'Thank you Kathy. I've adjusted it. You should feel warmer in a few minutes. I suggest we look at what risks we have and how we mitigate them.'

Joe jumped in. 'Investment risk.'

'Well yes, but we need that if we're to make any money.'

'Volatility?'

'Again, necessary, but measurable and controllable. Note that one Joe can you?'

'Peer group risk.'

'By which you mean the risk of underperforming them?'

'Mitigation: do better?'

'Market risk.'

Jonny looked across at Scott. Confusion was written across his face.

'Keeping up, Scott?'

Scott looked a little embarrassed. 'Not really. I'm struggling to understand what you're talking about.'

Jonny could remember feeling at sea himself with no-one to rescue him. He felt the youngsters had to work some of it out as they went along, but he liked to ease the pain a little.

'Don't worry. Specifically what?'

'Anything really. Investment risk, volatility, peer group risk. Anything. Sorry, I don't want to be a nuisance.'

'Not a problem. Probably won't hurt us to go back to basics. Bill, perhaps you can explain.'

Bill looked at his notes and started.

'Well let's start with investment risk. That's the risk that the investment might be a bad one.'

'You mean it might be a con?'

'No, that would be risk of fraud. It's more that we might buy something expecting it to go up in price, but actually it goes down.'

'So it's the risk of getting it wrong?'

'If you like.'

'Because you're not very good or because you're unlucky?'

Jonny smiled at this. It was a question worthy of Jim Ferguson. They agreed that while everybody got things wrong, they could not afford to be wrong too often – say 30 or 40% of the time, and exceeding this number could mean they weren't as good as they thought they were, or that they had been unlucky. They moved on to market risk – not dissimilar, Scott concluded, except on a bigger scale. Jonny was enjoying this. Volatility was next.

'That's an easy one,' claimed Bill. 'It's simply the risk of things going up and down a lot.'

'I thought that's what things did.'

'Well yes, but if they go up and down too much and we need to sell when they're down we'd lose money.'

Kathy butted in. 'Strictly speaking our clients would.'

'Indeed. So we need to understand the risk of losing our clients' money – and, potentially, our clients. What else?'

'Peer group risk,' offered Joe.

'Okay. That's the risk of doing worse than the competition.'

Scott needed clarification. 'You mean the risk that you don't do well but everybody else does?'

'Could be, but it doesn't matter really how well we're doing. I mean, if we do badly but everybody else does worse that's obviously better than if we do well but everybody else does better.'

'Is it?'

'Well, obviously, the clients wouldn't be better off elsewhere so we keep the business.'

'So is it your risk or the clients'?'

'Good question,' said Jonny. 'Both. Our interests are aligned. Look at your father's business, Scafell. He wants us to produce good returns without risking too much loss. If we don't, he could move his money somewhere else so we're also motivated to produce good returns without too much loss, so we're aligned. But if we make spectacular returns for him, having taken too much risk, we could use those figures to tempt other people to hire us. They might be blinded by the success and overlook the risks. Your father wouldn't. So we need to make sure we can measure and control the risks so that an ambitious individual doesn't get carried away and that's what this committee is about. But it's also about asking questions and challenging, so this is a good discussion, very worthwhile. Goes to show that having someone here who doesn't feel he should already know the answers is a bonus. I'd like to look at it from a different angle now though. The challenge we face is to give this process teeth, avoid reducing it to box ticking once Scott is no longer with us. How do we do that?'

The truth, as Jonny was very well aware, was not as straightforward as had been suggested. In his view, there was a major risk which was insufficiently acknowledged and this was the risk of the business itself being overambitious and putting undue pressure on individuals to perform. In his day, he had maintained client relationships by constant communication, realistic expectation setting and trust. Now he felt there was a danger of this being undermined by a hungry corporate entity. The danger of antagonism between Junker and his peers on the one hand and the Scafell team on the other was only too real as Blue Island tried to squeeze more out of their clients and Dan Murphy tried to protect Jim Ferguson's interests by taking more control and squeezing costs. If fees were squeezed, the pressure to grow more assets would become more intense, and there was an issue here for Jonny in that his loyalties were conflicted. He had built this firm, looked after Jim as a valued client, and been a trusted adviser and friend. He had been honest when he said he and Scott were old friends. He was a family friend of the Fergusons. He was paid to look after business for Blue Island but was that his first loyalty? He had not felt this conflict when the business was his. Indeed, he had known that the better he looked after Ferguson, the longer they would work together; the two loyalties were mutually supportive. He was no longer sure that this was the case, and he was getting increasingly uncomfortable.

He had not expected the presence of Scott Ferguson to throw matters into such sharp relief but felt this was a constructive development as he sought to find his own way forward. Maybe it was outside Blue Island – maybe outside the business. This threw up its own issues, of course. If he left then who could protect Jim's interests as well as he could? Here again, Scott provided some answers. The young man's ability to ask questions and put his elders on the spot reminded Jonny of Jim in earlier days. He could see the father in the son and knew that both were very capable of looking after their own interests. Plus they had Dan Murphy onside of course. No, he had no need to be overanxious about the Fergusons, although Jim would be one of the first to know if he did decide to leave. In fact, he might well discuss the options with him before making his decision.

CHAPTER TWO

MOORS AND HEATHS

Don Raistrick was taking his time selecting a club when his companion spoke.

'Use the seven iron.'

'Why?'

'Because you always do.'

Fred Ogden was joshing, but also getting a little impatient. The ritual observed by Don on nearly every hole was to go through all his options and then decide that a seven iron met his needs. There were exceptions, of course, but Fred knew that Don used the seven for two thirds of his shots and just wished he would get on with making that decision. At the same time, he knew that rushing Don achieved nothing, so he tended to hold back until he could hold back no longer or made a joke of it.

They had been playing golf together since their boys had been teenagers. It had started as a foursome, lads and dads, but neither Tom nor Pete had stuck with it. Tom had discovered girls and lost interest. Pete had found God and became obsessed with theology. The two men had continued, found a common interest and became firm friends.

Now here they were, the two of them, battling the wind on a moorland golf course, competing for space with sheep, horse riders and dog walkers, and arguing about which club to use. This was the last hole; the nineteenth was already beckoning with the obligatory ham sandwiches and that traditional Yorkshire pub dish of pie and peas. First though, they had to make it to the green and sink their putts. They were playing the back nine, a full round being a bit much for Fred these days. The eighteenth could be clearly seen from the clubhouse window and Don tended to get unnerved by the audience, not that most of them were paying any attention. Fred, on the other hand, felt no embarrassment about his golf. He was as good, or bad, as he was and people could just accept that.

Don took his shot. It was a little short and went into the bunker. At least that made the choice of the next club easy. Don was an experienced hand with a sand wedge. He had been in many bunkers and had lots of practice. Fred was already on the green so waited while Don extricated himself from the sand before putting. A two putt. A good end to the round.

'That's a pint you owe me.'

'Another one. Next time I'll get you.'

The two men shook hands, scraped mud off their shoes, stacked their bags against the clubhouse wall and headed for the bar.

'How's your lad finding his new parish?' asked Fred as he held the door for Don.

'Challenging, I think. Good to be near Pete and Anne though.'

'I always feel happier when they're able to support each other. It's nice for the girls too. What'll you have?'

'Bitter I think – the Tetley's. You eating?'

'Oh yes, not missing the pie and peas.'

Pork pie served hot with mushy peas and mint sauce was a particular favourite of both men, and they were soon tucking in. Fred broke the silence.

'Good pies these. Wonder whose they are.'

'Used to get them from Curtis's in John Street.'

'Gone now. Maybe the butcher's in the village.'

'Aye, 'appen that would be it.'

Don took a pull at his beer and returned to the subject of the lads.

'Seems like Tom's found someone he can talk to in his new job, a churchwarden at the smaller church.'

'What church is that then?'

'Old estate church in one of the villages. St Aidan's I think. Seems this chap is from the old family. You know, minted, posh, but seems very friendly and, you know, Tom gets on with anybody.'

'Until he doesn't.'

Fred was thinking of the rows between Tom and some of the more traditional members of previous congregations. Proper 'up and downers', Don had called them. Don acknowledged the point.

'Aye well, until he scares them off with his politics, or whatever. But this guy seems happy enough. They talk a lot. He can offload a bit, I think.'

'I've always marvelled at how Tom and Pete manage not to fall out, what with their differences an' all.'

Don considered this.

'You mean church stuff?'

'Aye, but it's more deep-rooted, don't you think? Pete wants rules and boundaries, predictability, safety. Tom wants the opposite.'

'That's why he's married to Liza.'

'Exactly. The attraction of the rebel. The energy she gives off. Anne's got it all sussed, knows who she is, Liza's still working it out. Tom likes the idea that you're always trying work it out. Anything else is a trap.'

'You're very deep today, Fred. Must be the beer.'

'Yes, but I'm right, aren't I?'

'It makes sense, yes. But the church stuff! If one thinks one thing you can guarantee the other will take the opposite view. Still, doesn't seem to matter.'

'Allus been that way. But I think Liza and Anne help.'

'They both landed on their feet there all right.'

Don grinned. 'They did an' all. I worry about Liza though.'

'Do you? The rebel stuff?'

Don's worry was about Liza's suitability to be a vicar's wife. He was used to men of the cloth who were married to equally committed women, so the churches effectively got two for the price of one. Liza was not only uncommitted but frankly sceptical. Not only that but she was irreverent, sparky, and focussed on her own world. Don loved her for it, but worried that she, or Tom, would end up being hurt.

Fred was phlegmatic. Tom and Liza had now been together for the best part of 30 years. They had survived a number of parishes and life events, not to mention parenthood, so why worry now? And, in his view, they would now benefit from being only an hour away from London. Their children, now in their twenties, were both based in London and there was a good chance they would see more of their parents than in the last few years. Matt and Abi were good kids – difficult to believe that Don had grandchildren in their twenties – and seemed settled with their partners. There were no weddings in sight, but the world was a different place to the one Don and Fred had grown up in. And if there were difficulties for Liza, well Don reckoned the lass could look after herself – Tom too.

'Maybe, provided it doesn't drive a wedge between them.'

Fred tried a weak pun on wedges, bunkers and driving, which fell flat. The food arrived. Liza and Tom's situation faded as they focussed on sating the appetite built up during the morning.

*

Jancy Nower was on her way to meet her old friend Fenella, driving her battered 4 x 4 across the heath in driving rain. The radio was tuned to Heart FM, a station Jonny loathed, and she was singing along intermittently. She loved the rain, the heath, the old and mainly superficial songs on the radio, and she was looking forward to a good catch-up.

She also loved Micklebury Heath with its wooded areas broken up by ancient heathland and pasture. She loved the mix of oak and birch, beech and ash; the bracken and twitch grass and the paths and bridleways where you could spot bee orchids and a wealth of wild flowers. She had walked or ridden these paths and byways all her life and the two roads which snaked across the heath were where she had first learnt to drive. This was home.

Micklebury Heath straddled a chalk ridge and Jancy's route took her along the ridge to the west and then down a swooping and twisting lane to the village of Capley and a converted pub which was now a slightly twee tea room. It also involved avoiding cyclists, walkers and spatially challenged motorists. The rain today had deterred most of these, and she reached the tea rooms without mishap to find Fenella already ensconced reading *Hello!* magazine which she put down with a slightly guilty start when she saw Jancy arrive.

'Hello darling.' They kissed. 'Change of reading material?'

'It was on the table. It makes a change from *Horse and Hound*.'

'I bet it does.'

'All these glamorous lives, darling – the drama, what they go through!'

'It sounds terrible.'

'I'm sure you're better off with the *Church Times* darling.'

'A bit snippy today, Fenella?'

Fenella pulled a face. Where to start? She was having a bad week. First came the apology, then the diatribe. Her children were taking her for granted, her grandchildren were ill-behaved, her husband was never there, she had this huge house to look after, her car was playing up and, to cap it all, it was pouring down. Jancy listened, made sympathetic noises, avoided too much comment, and waited for the storm to wear itself out.

'Sounds like tea and cake is just what you need then.'

She ordered and they settled to the routine catch-up, exchanged news and views and sipped Earl Grey out of china cups. Once she had had time to vent, Fenella lost her snippy edge and relaxed a little.

When they had done the weather, compared the tea rooms favourably with the American coffee houses colonising the local high streets, and exchanged the latest news on grandchildren, Fenella turned to the subject of the Raistricks.

How was Jancy getting on with them? What was Tom like? She, Fenella, had been at a do and had bumped into Liza. She made quite an impression. She was not what you would expect from a vicar's wife. Very charming, of course, but really, those clothes. And her language! She'd caused quite a stir.

'So you don't approve?'

'I didn't say that...'

'Oh, I think you did. Wrong clothes, inappropriate language.'

Fenella collected herself. What she had meant was that others were offended. She, Fenella, had tried to take the poor thing under her wing. She was clearly out of her depth so someone had to.

Jancy smiled. She had yet to spend very much time with Liza but couldn't imagine her being out of her depth because a few Surrey ladies found her a little bohemian for their taste. She was curious to know how she had responded to being taken under Fenella's wing.

Fenella was unsure. On the one hand, Liza had seemed not to notice the helping hand being offered to her and had ploughed on regardless. On the other, she had been sweet and lovely to Fenella.

'You mean she didn't object to being patronised?'

'Oh you do twist things. I was not being patronising.'

'Sounds like it to me. So what's the verdict? You're not sure you approve but you rather like her?'

'Yes. I think that sums it up rather well. I think she's lovely. Talented, I shouldn't wonder, but not very steady – not a support for him.'

'I don't think modern vicars' wives are expected to devote their whole being to supporting their husbands.'

'You don't? No. Well, times change. But I would expect her to be more of a liability than a help, that's all.'

'A liability, darling?'

'Well, there he is, preaching away, trying to set the tone, encourage standards.'

'Is that what he's doing?'

'Of course it is, Jancy. What else?'

'I rather thought he was supposed to be preaching the word of God.'

'Now you're being difficult. It's the same thing. Anyway, all the time he's doing that she's drifting around in unsuitable clothes, swearing, and mixing with goodness knows who. And her paintings! Well.'

Jancy smiled. 'You've seen her paintings have you?'

'No, but I gather they're most unsuitable; naked men and things.'

'I bet you're dying to see them.'

'I don't think that's the point, dear.'

'They tell me they sell well. Not cheap either.'

'Is that supposed to make it better?'

Jancy tried another tack.

'Have you seen them together?'

'Who?'

'Tom and Liza.'

'The vicar and his wife? No. Why?'

'Because, Fenella darling, they're rather sweet. They're a very supportive couple.'

'Well I'm not sure a vicar should be supporting that kind of thing.'

On the way home, Jancy found herself wondering about the impact of Liza's arrival. Fenella would certainly not be the only one to be a little sniffy, a little disapproving. The expectations of the vicar's wife were rather different these days, but Liza was certainly on the edge, for a small, rural community at least. Her flamboyance, her art, and her disregard for convention, all told against her. On the other hand, she was tremendously likeable – warm, funny, attractive, and talented – qualities which would make her plenty of friends, but also enemies.

*

A few miles away, in Betcham, those qualities were doing exactly that. On her way to visit Anne, Liza had called into St Matthew's. Pete had been talking about the reordering of the church building on which he'd been working ever since moving there a couple of years before. Among the talk of getting faculties, canvassing opinions, and housekeeping details, he had mentioned a rather good triptych which had been uncovered, and Liza was keen to see it. Unfortunately, Liza walked into the middle of a full-blown argument between two pillars of the church – a doughty woman in tweeds and sensible shoes and a frailer-looking lady with an accent which could cut glass and an outfit which tended to the chic rather than the sensible. Sensible Shoes was arguing strongly that a large floral arrangement should be placed directly in front of what was clearly the triptych in question, while 'Posh Chic' was equally clear that the view of the triptych should not be obscured.

Her artistic sensibilities aroused, Liza could not resist the urge to weigh in. It was quite clear to her that it would be ludicrous to hide a newly rediscovered work of art. She said so, in no uncertain terms. Sensible Shoes suggested she mind her own business. Posh Chic suggested that the views of a visitor were very important. Sensible Shoes suggested that Church affairs should be left to people who understood the church. Liza informed them both that she had plenty of insight into church affairs as her husband and brother-in-law were both vicars. At that point Pete walked in.

'Liza! How nice to see you.'

'You know this woman?' This came from Sensible Shoes.

'This woman? Liza, you haven't been upsetting people again, have you?'

'I only said what I thought. This is a lovely piece of art, Pete.'

'I know. Let me introduce you. This is Beth, who runs the flower rota and makes sure the church is cleaned and in order. And this is Sarah, one of our churchwardens. Beth, Sarah, meet my favourite sister-in-law, Liza.'

'Your only sister-in-law.'

'You're still my favourite, even if you don't know when to keep quiet.'

'Nice to meet you,' said Beth. 'Got to get on.' And she bustled from the church.

'There are a few bridges to mend there.'

'I'm sorry Pete, have I upset the apple cart?'

'It's been upset before. We'll get over it.'

'It's just, well, it would be stupid to hide something like that just when you've rediscovered it – sacrilegious.'

There was a raised eyebrow from Pete.

'Perhaps I should assess whether it's sacrilegious.'

'Okay. I'll butt out. Sorry.'

Posh Chic came to Liza's aid.

'She made some very good points actually, Pete.'

'I'm sure she did Sarah, but how diplomatically?'

'Diplomacy doesn't work with philistines.'

'Liza! Perhaps we should get you out of here.'

'Oh, sorry Pete. That wasn't very…'

'Diplomatic?'

'Helpful, I was going to say.'

'Well no, it wasn't either. It's nice to see you though.'

'Really?'

'Always.'

'I was just on the way to see Anne. I thought I'd admire your triptych first, so to speak.'

'You'll get me into more trouble if you're not careful.'

'Does it work that way round?'

Pete turned to Sarah.

'Forgive us, Sarah, we were students together – old habits.'

'I envy you. I can't bear my brother-in-law.'

'Not everyone has a brother-in-law like Pete. He saved my life when we were students.'

'Really?'

'She exaggerates. I was a shoulder to cry on.'

'Before we all settled down. Well, better go and see my beloved sister. It was nice to meet you Sarah. Bye Pete.'

'See you.'

They embraced. As Liza left, Sarah turned to Pete and looked him up and down.

'Secrets from your past?'

'Not really. It was very complicated. Her husband's my oldest friend, my wife's her sister. When I first met Anne she was going out with Tom.'

'Your brother-in-law?'

'That's the one. Liza and I spent a lot of time making up foursomes with them before... Oh dear, it does sound complicated, doesn't it?'

'A little. But you all survived with relationships intact?'

'Oh yes. I love Liza to bits. Always have. My own sister is a bit, well you know.'

'No. I didn't know you had a sister.'

'Exactly.'

'She's very different from Anne. Liza I mean. You can see the family resemblance but...'

'She's more out there? Liza's the extrovert, the arty one. Anne's the thoughtful one. They're a formidable pair.'

The formidable pair in question were shortly to be found drinking tea and laughing. Liza was regaling her sister with the story of Sensible Shoes and Posh Chic and the triptych. Anne was pleasantly horrified.

'You upset Beth? Pete won't be happy.'

'He seemed okay about it.'

'Only because it's you, and you can do no wrong in his eyes, whereas he can do no right in Beth's.'

'Oh dear. He did tell me off a little bit. I wasn't trying to make his life difficult.'

'No, you were just being you. She drives him round the bend. He was probably pleased to see her taken down a peg or two. You didn't really tell her she was being stupid did you?'

'Not to her face. I think 'ludicrous' was the word I used to her.'

Anne spluttered into her tea.

'Priceless. Wish I'd been there.'

'Posh Chic seemed nice though.'

'That'd be Sarah.'

'That's right, Sarah.'

'Yes, she's nice. She's a great support to Pete. Beth makes her life a misery as well.'

'All these women in Pete's life – Tom's too – fawning over him.'

Anne stirred her tea, again, and looked across at Liza.

'Does it worry you?'

'A bit. No, not really. Tom's too absorbed in what he's doing to notice.'

'You think? He's still besotted with you though.'

'When he remembers. You don't worry about Pete though.'

'Oh, I think it's less a case of fawning over Pete than competing to mother him.'

There was a pause, while tea was sipped, before Anne asked how things were going in Molebridge.

'Oh. Tom's making a name for himself; stirring things up.'

'No change there then.'

Anne was right, this was all par for the course. Liza thought of the spring in Tom's step when he returned from Micklebury.

'I think he enjoys St Aidan's most.'

'I don't see him as a rural priest.'

'No, but he's less constrained there, left to his own devices. And he gets on with the people. It's a small church. Could have gone either way, I guess.'

'It always could. Being part of a team ministry not Tom's style then?'

'Well, you know Tom, the individualist. He does like to run things. And he seems to have found a friend and confidant at St Aidan's.'

'Oh?'

'Jonny Nower. One of the wardens. Terribly well connected. Bit of a maverick.'

'Nower? Wasn't that the local family?'

Liza pulled a face.

'Yes. St Aidan's was his family church, the estate church, but no more. Not that you can tell. It's a bit feudal out there.'

'So this Jonny Nower runs the place?'

'He encourages Tom to do so. He's spent most of his career running some City business. I think he's learned to delegate. Anyway, they're great buddies. He's always ready for a deep, philosophical discussion and it's certainly helping Tom to settle in. Jancy is nice too, Jonny's wife.'

'And you? How are you finding it?'

'Oh, you know, the usual. Suspicion and disapproval follow me round like a pair of Border collies. But the area's nice, and I've found some friends outside the church.'

'Jonny and Jancy no help there then?'

'No, to be fair, they're fine, friendly and understanding. And others too; a healthy minority. I don't have the vicar's wife touch that you have.'

Anne bridled slightly.

'I do work at it, you know.'

'And I don't? No, actually, I don't really. And I can't seem to talk the talk, you know. It's Tom's career, not mine. Oh, let's talk about something else.'

And the conversation turned to family, friends, and other subjects.

CHAPTER THREE
WALKING IN THE RAIN

On Bishopsgate the rain was abating a little, as Jonny walked to the office from London Bridge. As usual, he was enjoying the atmosphere of the city, soaking it in, in more ways than one. A countryman at heart, he still loved the feel of the City with its nooks and crannies, old buildings and new developments jostling for space. And he still valued the breathing space the walk gave him, a space between the crowded train and the demands of the office.

Reaching the office, he called Dave Pullman. It went to voicemail. He left a message – 'Let's catch up' – and then went for a wander around the offices.

When Jonny had started up, letters were typed by secretaries and lunches were long and liquid. Now it was all changed. Individual, idiosyncratic money managers had been replaced by teams, groups of people sitting at banks of desks cluttered with dual-screen computers, mementos of foreign trips and (still) paper reports.

Correspondence was electronic, almost nobody had a secretary, and lunches were, in the main, a sandwich snatched at the desk. Going for 'a wander' around the various teams and chatting about what was going on had become a key part of Jonny's day – a part he loved. Hearing the insights of these bright people, listening to their banter, supporting and encouraging; he filled a role which he had always filled – and which he saw nobody else taking on. In his view, the new world had created a lot of managers but fewer leaders. And senior staff, with days full of meetings and targets, tended to have little time to spare for walking the floor.

Jonny was deep in conversation with Hardeep, one of the younger portfolio managers, when Dave caught up with him.

'Is this a good time?'

'Yes. 'Scuse me Hardeep, duty calls.'

They headed for Jonny's office.

'Doing your man of the people thing?'

'It's not a 'thing', Dave, it's what I do. Chat. Keep involved.'

'Bright lad?'

'Hardeep? Yes. We've a good team there – him and Bill especially, if we can keep them.'

'You don't think we can?'

'I don't know, Dave. This is a big outfit now. It doesn't command loyalty quite like the old set-up. I do what I can, but it only needs a tempting offer.'

Jonny sometimes felt he was fighting a rearguard action. His old firm had been personal, a family, everyone had a role. Now it was part of a much bigger outfit, and while the senior people seemed to expect complete loyalty there seemed little to reward that loyalty; no family feel, no direct access to the top. These things were difficult to manage in a large house, Jonny knew that, and efforts were made, but they tended to backfire. Inclusivity programmes and values initiatives and the like probably played well in the States but were met with deep cynicism in London.

Dave never quite grasped this, or not completely, so he was perpetually surprised by the negative reactions to some of these initiatives. What he did understand was that Jonny was the glue which held all this together, and he had made that point clear to Junker many times.

'Well, don't go anywhere yourself any time soon, Jonny.'

'Me? Where would I go?'

'Oh, I don't know – trekking across Peru.'

'Peru? Why Peru?'

'It seems to be popular right now; among the young. You know, gap year stuff.'

'I'm hardly gap year material.'

'Well okay, not Peru. Digging wells in Africa maybe. Running a charity here. Or just tending your garden.'

'No, it's no good, you're not tempting me. I think I'll stay here and annoy Junker – much more fun.'

'I'll buy that. Let's talk Scafell.'

With that they headed into Jonny's office, and Dave relayed his lengthy conversation with Junker of the previous evening. Junker's view of Jonny was a little tarnished by the fact that Blue Island had paid top dollar for Nower Asset Management at the height of the market bubble caused by the enthusiastic purchase of technology, media and telecommunications stocks. Since then the TMT bubble had burst, dragging assets under management down. Since Nower's fees were a percentage of assets under management, it now looked as if they'd paid over the odds. It wasn't Jonny's fault, but Junker wasn't convinced.

'It wasn't easy, Jonny, I have to tell you. Getting Junker to give ground is like pulling teeth.'

'Especially to Dan Murphy?'

'Especially to you.'

'He's not giving ground to me. I'm protecting his interests.'

'Try telling him that.'

'So, what's the outcome?'

The outcome was that, after much argument and prevarication, Junker had agreed to everything put forward by Jonny ('But not before I'd convinced him most of it was his idea,' explained Dave). Essentially, Jonny was now to be central to everything that happened on Scafell. He would be the senior client executive, a member of the board for the dedicated company, and had carte blanche to talk with Dan Murphy (and Jim Ferguson) about whatever he felt appropriate, whenever he felt it appropriate, keeping Biff in the loop. The main sticking point was the fee issue. The way Junker saw it, Scafell were now getting special treatment from a senior man, access to all sorts of internal briefings and a seat on the board, and still wanted to pay less for the privilege. Jonny was not fazed by this.

'Let's just say to Jim that we need to see how the new arrangements work, and we'll review the fees in a year's time.'

'Think he'll go for that?'

'I've already set his expectations, and he's got everything else he wanted. He'll know we're fobbing him off, but it does leave the door open for a later discussion, and he knows that in a year's time we'll have invested a lot of time and prestige in the project so we'll not want to walk away even if he does push harder.'

'Okay, over to you, Jonny. Can you have a chat with Jim and keep Biff in the loop?'

'I'll ring Biff as soon as he's in, and try Jim now.'

'Good work. I'll leave you to it.'

Dave headed out, turning at the door to ask Jonny to drop him and Junker a note confirming the agreement when finalised.

'He'll probably want to sit in on a meeting when he's over next, of course.'

'Of course. We'll stage-manage something.'

Jonny proceeded to call Jim Ferguson. It was early afternoon by the time he had made contact, but the deal proved acceptable. Jim warned him that Dan would have the fee issue diarised for 12 months' time, but otherwise he was very happy, and was sure that Dan would be.

'Give Dan a ring, can you Jonny. Tell him what we've agreed. Fix a meeting for the three of us. Include Biff if you want. It'll be good to see you.'

Jonny duly rang Biff, brought him up to date, and apologised for stepping on his toes. Biff told him not to worry; he was only making Biff's life easier.

'Nice of you to say so, but now you have an extra job.'

'Which is?'

'Keeping me honest.'

'That doesn't sound too demanding, Jonny.'

'Maybe not, but I'm in danger of serving two masters here.'

'How do you mean?'

The way Jonny saw it, he was paid to represent the interests of Blue Island, but he also had a loyalty, arguably a much deeper one, to Jim Ferguson and to Dan Murphy. As Dan was an old sparring partner, their relationship had always been business and that made it a little easier, but there were family ties with the Fergusons over three generations. These ran deep. Biff was a company man, an outsider in all this, able to spot conflict and bias.

'Don't hesitate to call me on it, Biff. It's okay so long as the interests are aligned but once there's a conflict... Well, these people are like family. I'm instinctively on their side.'

'I'll do what I can.'

'Good man.'

*

In Molebridge, the rain had given way to a light mist and Liza was walking Rothko, the family Labrador, across the heath. The moisture was gathering on Rothko's yellow coat and in Liza's blonde hair, as they crossed a patch of open ground and found themselves in the woods again. They were not alone. Other dog walkers exchanged friendly greetings with Liza, and Rothko bounded through the undergrowth with a succession of collies, springers and labradoodles before they were far enough away from the car parks and houses for the dogs and walkers to thin out, leaving Liza free to think.

When she realised she was likely to spend her life away from the sea, Liza had worried about where she would find somewhere to walk and think. In some parishes this was a real problem, but here, with heath and woodland aplenty, she felt she could get away. It might lack the grandeur of the ocean, or Tom's native moors, but she found it stimulating in the nuanced greens and browns and the sounds of the wind in the trees and the birdsong. It was also reassuring and peaceful. Here she could feel something of the spiritual experience which both Tom and Pete seemed to regard as normal. Here she felt connected, herself, in a way she otherwise only felt when painting.

It was also here that she could find time to think, to clear her head. There had been another row that morning, and she was still feeling irritated with Tom. Actually, she was feeling irritated with a whole lot of people. The select bunch of friends he had made, as he always did, who were delighted to have a vicar who was good one-to-one, who had wider interests, and who was down to earth. Pete and Anne for being so bloody content. The church as a whole for taking up all his time. And, not least, the fan club in the congregation who thought he was a saint. They should try living with him, she thought, then they'd know what a bloody saint he was.

Today Tom was off on some parish activity, setting up a food bank or something. She hadn't really been listening. She found it easier to object to his constant external focus if she didn't think too closely about what he was actually doing. It was difficult to argue against spending time on such worthy causes without feeling selfish, mean, and uncaring. She envied people married to bankers. They might work all hours but at least their partners could moan about it without feeling they were depriving the ill, the bereaved and the starving.

Her reverie was cut short by the sound of barking, and she realised Rothko was nowhere to be seen.

'Rothko! Rothy! Come!'

No response. She tried again.

'Rothko! Rothy! Come!'

She tried whistling, not something she was good at, called again, and was rewarded by the unmistakeable sound of solid Labrador barrelling through the undergrowth.

'Good boy! Where have you been?'

Her question was answered by the appearance of a black Lab from the same direction, followed, on a more conventional path, by a man of about her own age carrying a lead and wearing rain gear and a grin.

'Sorry. Barney seemed very attracted by this one.'

'They seem to be having a good run.'

'How old is yours?'

'Rothy? He's two and still full of it.'

'A similar age then. Rothy? That's an unusual name.'

'It's short for Rothko. I'm an artist – of sorts.'

'You might have to unpick that for me.'

'Unpick?'

'Explain. Take it to pieces and explain the constituent parts. Sorry, bad habit.'

'What is?'

'Overanalysing, especially language. I'm Bob, by the way.'

'Nice to meet you. I'm Liza.'

'Well it's nice to meet you too – and Rothy. Hope to see you again.'

Bob made to move off.

'Don't you want to know about Rothko?'

'No. Yes. I was afraid of being presumptuous.'

'No, that's fine. Talking's good.'

'So, tell me about Rothko.'

'The dog or the artist?'

'The artist. I know dogs.'

'But not artists?'

'I could recognise a Picasso.'

Liza smiled. 'I can see I'm going to have my work cut out.'

For the next few weeks, they met regularly. The dogs ran around and the conversation moved from art to literature to engineering (Bob's field) and a bond grew. Liza found herself looking forward to these conversations. It was good to have someone's largely undivided attention, no phones going, no pressing issues to do with marriages, divorces, births or deaths, no church politics. Bob was from a different world, and she felt like some door had been opened and fresh air was wafting in.

She felt a little guilty about not telling Tom about her friendship. No need, she told herself, we're just talking. But if they were just talking, why was she being secretive? She barely hinted at the growing friendship even to Anne, although when she did let the odd comment slip Anne was quick to follow up.

'I hope you know what you're doing,' she remarked.

'What's that supposed to mean?'

'You know very well what I mean, an attractive man, listens...'

'I never said he was attractive.'

'You didn't have to. Attractive man, listens to you, notices you, no baggage. No churchy stuff. A breath of fresh air. It's easy to get carried away.'

'Tom notices me.'

'Really? When?'

'Oh. Now and then.'

'Exactly. You can't fool me. Tom has the same pressures as Pete, the same dedication. It's hard work attracting Pete's attention sometimes, believe me.'

Liza felt a little irritated. Her big sister was sticking her nose in. She wasn't doing anything wrong.

'I'm not doing anything wrong.'

'Tempted though, aren't you?'

'No. Maybe. I love Tom.'

'But he drives you round the bend.'

'Yes, sometimes.'
'Well, you be careful.'

*

Tom had also taken to tramping across the country, engaged in philosophical debate with Jonny Nower. Jonny no longer worked on a Friday and as this coincided with Tom's day off a long morning walk had become the order of the day. Tom was no morning person, but a 7.30 start had its own rewards, such as the mist rising from the valley, the sun breaking through, or the town revealed below them as they strode across the Downs or broke free from the woods. The aim was to finish by 10.30, have coffee, and leave the rest of the day free. Not that they always made it. Sometimes other pressures cut the walk short, and sometimes they just kept on till lunchtime; a rare feeling of freedom.

They were in the midst of one of these longer walks when Jonny surprised Tom by asking about the priesthood. What was it like? Tom considered. What was it like? He wished he knew, or could form a view with any consistency. Right now it felt like a weight round his neck, dragging him down. At other times, it felt like an awesome privilege. His response to Jonny was that he supposed it was like anything else, a curate's egg of bad and good. This failed to satisfy. What, specifically, were the rewards and downsides, Jonny wanted to know. How hard was it to get in? How tough the study? Tom stopped, wheeled round, and looked at his friend.

'Why?'

'Just thinking things through.'

'For you? You're not serious?'

'Why not? I'm a spare part at work. I've got to do something.'

'It doesn't sound like a calling.'

Jonny thought about this. Was it a 'calling'? He didn't honestly know.

To Tom he said, 'Well, I have a faith, I'm involved, and interested.'

'I'm not sure that does it. Anyway, I thought you were involved with rescuing major client relationships.'

'Oh, I can still add value, as they say, from time to time, but is it enough? I used to run the place. Now I'm a spare part, brought out of the cupboard every now and then. It's not working for me.'

'It was your choice, Jonny.'

'I know. It made sense. Still does. But I need something else.'

'Okay, but the ministry?'

'What other interests do I have?'

'Going into the ministry isn't an interest, it's a vocation. And I'm not sure I'd recommend it.'

'Really? But still, what else could I do? Really, Tom. What?'

'You're interested in lots of things; everything it seems to me.'

'Interested, yes, but involved? My old cronies from the City play golf, or go cycling, or they shoot or something. I'm cack-handed, not built for getting on a bike and, okay I can shoot, but frankly it's deadly boring.'

'So you need your mind occupying, that's what you're saying.'

They paused to greet two horse riders; the horses standing patiently, steam rising from their flanks, the riders looking fulfilled and at peace with the world. Jonny knew them both, exchanged news, sent his regards to their families and complimented them on the way the horses were looking. They moved on.

'You could ride.'

'I could ride Tom, but that's a vocation too.'

'It's hardly the same.'

'Well, you have to be up with the lark, you have to groom and fuss, feed, muck out. Riding's only a bit of it.'

'Can't you get someone to do that for you?'

'It's an expensive way of filling the odd hour, and it's still a commitment I don't want.'

'Okay. There must be something else though. Is ordination really the answer? To be honest, I'm not convinced, and I'm a pushover. The bishop will be tougher.'

'Oh well, just a thought.'

'Exactly.'

'But Tom, I'm just pew fodder at the moment, a spare part. Everywhere I look I'm a spare part.'

'Is that how you feel?'

'That's how I feel.'

'Okay, so how can you change it?'

'By running things – like I used to.'

'Have you thought about halfway houses?'

'Ex-cons or drug addicts?'

'No, Jonny, I'm thinking of you being neither the boss nor just pew fodder. Not that you are, but let's run with it for the moment. I'm talking of more involvement without going to the extreme.'

'So give me an example.'

'Well, in the church context you could become a lay reader, get involved with synod, all sorts of things. And outside the church, you could get involved with a charity, even start one. Or you could study or write.'

'That sounds more you than me.'

'Maybe. I dream of having time to think and write. Time to myself.'

'Time for Liza?'

'That too. We barely spend any time together these days. She's off painting, and I'm at the beck and call of half the county.'

'Your choice, Tom. Put in some boundaries.'

'I wish I knew how.'

'How does your mate do it? Pete.'

'Pete? He's worse than I am. He runs round with his bevy of admirers, sorts out everybody else's life, or fails to, tries to meet everybody else's expectations. The difference is that Anne is always there; patient, giving.'

'Still carrying a torch for her?'

'I told you about that did I? She's very dear to me. And, yes, I suppose I do carry a torch, but Liza is the one, no question. I made the right choice, or had it made for me. It's just not always easy.'

*

In Betcham, the Rev. Pete Ogden was thinking on similar lines. He had picked up a hint of dissatisfaction from Liza when they'd last chatted, and he knew he wasn't the most sensitive of men so the chances were that the 'hint' was in reality a huge flag with 'unhappy' scrawled across it.

Being aware of an issue was one thing, doing something about it quite another. Was it even his business? He supposed so; they were his two closest friends, and effectively his brother and sister by marriage. He knew they were both very attractive people, charismatic even. Not, he thought, in a churchy sense. Tom had never been one for strange tongues or falling over, and Liza would run a mile. But in the secular sense, they both certainly had charisma. It was probably a mixed blessing, both of them, he suspected, open to temptation from elsewhere if they were feeling insecure.

Pete was due for his fortnightly get-together with Tom, his fortnightly argument as he sometimes thought of it. Anne had tried to persuade them to stop talking theology, but it was no use. Her argument was that the two of them had held opposing views on almost everything to do with church or faith since they were teenagers, and it was pointless to keep on arguing about it since neither was about to change his mind. 'All you do,' she'd said to Pete, 'is strengthen his determination to hold on to his views, and he does the same to you'. She was probably right, but it was part of their relationship. Not the only part, not dominant, but he'd be lost without it. Probably they both would.

So, here he was, with Tom due any moment, unsure of whether to raise the Liza issue and knowing that Tom would come in with some church issue to debate. Maybe he should have talked with Anne. She probably knew her sister's mind. She was probably torn, as usual, between the two of them – as was he.

When Tom did arrive he seemed cheerful enough. Pete heard the door, heard Anne answer it, knew he had five minutes while Tom and Anne caught up, and used the time to think and pray about the coming conversation. Hearing footsteps approach, he sprang to his feet and moved to greet his old friend.

Tom entered the room as he entered most rooms – as if he owned it – an approach which could bring rooms to life or shatter the peace, depending on your point of view. In this instance, Pete was inclined towards the latter interpretation. Tom bounced in, talking. After five minutes of moans about church, worries about Liza, and enthusiasm about various initiatives Tom was leading, Pete called a halt.

'Tom. Tom. Draw breath.'

'Oh. Sorry, was I on a roll?'

'You could say.'

'Sorry, I'm a bit hyper today.'

Tom was pacing the room. Pete smiled.

'I noticed. What's the trigger?'

'The trigger? Oh, right, yeah. Liza. I'm worried about Liza.'

'Liza. Anything specific?'

'I don't know. Like what?'

'Well, she could be (a) distracted and absorbed in her work, (b) not interested in yours, (c) upsetting the congregation with her unorthodox views or (d) having an affair.'

'Thanks, Pete. Straight to the point as usual.'

'It's what I'm here for.'

'You really think she's having an affair?'

'I don't know. It's one of the possibilities. What do you think?'

'God, I don't know. What if she is?'

'Why are you worried about her?'

'We hardly communicate. She's distracted. I'm distracted. We barely touch. Our sex life…'

Pete jumped in. 'Please. Don't tell me about your sex life.'

'There's nothing to tell.'

'Tom, that's enough.'

'Sorry. Maybe it's because she's getting it elsewhere.'

'Tom!'

'Sorry.'

'So you're both busy and distracted and not finding time for each other?'

Tom confirmed this was the case.

'And are you having an affair?'

'Pete! Of course I'm not.'

'So why assume she is?'

'I hadn't thought of it until you put the idea in my mind.'

Pete was unabashed, and not about to let Tom off the hook.

'Well you need to talk to her, whatever.'

'She hasn't said anything to you?'

'Why would she?'

'Oh come on Pete, anything she's worried about, it's straight to you or Anne – or both.'

'She'd hardly tell me about an affair.'

'Maybe not, but anything else she would. And she hasn't?'

'Not to me, but I really think you should talk to her. If things are so bad that you're genuinely worried about an affair, it's time to start talking.'

Tom recognised the truth in this argument. It was a reluctant recognition. For some reason he couldn't identify, he was not eager to start talking to Liza. Maybe he was afraid of what might emerge. He did not want to get into that with Pete.

'True. Okay, I'll talk to her.'

'And listen.'

'What? Yes, and listen.'

'So, Liza aside, why are you distracted?'

'Back to first principles? You really want to hear? Of course you do, sorry. It's church stuff.'

'Naturally.'

'I seem to have a knack for upsetting the diehards.'

'St Peter's or St Aidan's?'

'Oh, St Peter's. They're a friendly lot up in Micklebury. Small church, village feel, used to rubbing along and catering for everybody.'

'And Molebridge is different?'

'My theory, Pete, is that it's to do with being in a town. There's a choice of churches and if you don't fit in, or it doesn't suit you, then you go to another one. So what happens then is you get a church dominated by a clique or a school of thought, or a particular approach to worship. The element of choice reinforces the insular focus. But if you're there professionally, one of the clergy team, you don't have that choice. And that's me. I open my mouth and upset somebody. Hear someone spouting nonsense, and I feel the need to say so.'

Pete grinned. He could imagine this only too well.

'Let me guess, you do that a lot.'

'There are so many people spouting nonsense, Pete – all the time.'

'And what about the rest of the team?'

Tom thought. He actually liked the others, just found them frustrating. Why?

'They're masters of avoiding confrontation, every one of them. They tell the congregation what they want to hear. They avoid criticising me, which is nice, I guess. They avoid even disagreeing, which is frustrating. And if things feel really difficult then they avoid me altogether.'

'Then what do you do?'

'What do I do? Oh, head for St Aidan's and a bit of sanity. Go for a walk with Jonny. Talk to the others up there. Clear my head.'

'How about Liza?'

'Oh, she's usually out and about somewhere, and bored with my church stuff. So, no, I don't really talk to Liza about it.'

'You should.'

'I know, Pete. I know.'

'I don't think she's happy, Tom.'

'How do you mean?'

'I'm not sure. Look, you know I'm not good at this stuff, relationships, emotion, reading the signs.'

Tom did know. Pete continued.

'But Liza's different, Tom. I think I understand her as much as I understand anyone, and I just get the feeling she's struggling.'

He paused, fiddled with the books on his desk, avoided Tom's eye. Tom shifted in his chair, stared into space, thought about all the signs he might have missed and mentally berated himself for being self-absorbed. Pete broke the silence.

'Say something, Tom.'

'Like what? I don't know, Pete. Thank you, I suppose, for alerting me. But how come you can spot it and I can't? I'm supposed to be the people person, not you.'

'Am I really telling you something you don't already know? Or just something you've been trying not to know?'

'It's difficult, you know, when the kids have gone; things change.'

'They've been gone a while now, Tom.'

'In a sense, yes, but, y'know, they kept coming back.'

'True, and now they seem settled, and it's really just the two of you.'

Tom felt bereaved by the loss of the children, the empty house, and the removal of one of his roles in life.

'I miss them – even the fights. And I know we should have more time for each other now, but... I don't know.'

'You also have more freedom to be out of the house.'

'I guess.'

'What do you advise your young couples?'

'Make time to talk. Date nights. Cherish the other.'

'Maybe you need to apply it.'

Tom nodded. Maybe he should. There was plenty to talk about – missing the children, feeling under attack at St Peter's, doubting his calling, wondering what purpose he served, and feeling less sure of himself. Unfortunately, he was feeling less sure of Liza as well.

CHAPTER FOUR

MATT AND ABI

'Are you guys ready yet? I'm on a double yellow.'

Matt was pacing anxiously on the pavement outside the Hammersmith terrace shared by his sister Abi and her partner Jamie, whose face now appeared at the open first floor window.

'Hi Matt. Almost there. Fifty per cent.'

'You mean one of you 's ready?'

'Yeah. Guess which one.'

The head withdrew, the window closed. Matt took out a packet of cigarettes, looked at them, put them back in his pocket. This was not the time to weaken. The wind blew some stray packaging down the road. A cat appeared at a window opposite and studied him. Otherwise nothing moved. An oasis of calm in a busy metropolis. Except Matt wasn't feeling calm. Patience was not his strong suit.

His sister appeared, clutching bags and flowers, which she spilled into his arms.

'Careful with the flowers. Jamie's on his way...'

With flowers and parcels stowed in the boot, Matt turned, and embraced his sister.

'We're going to be late.'

'Don't worry. You can blame me.'

'Oh I will.'

'Oh, I know. How are you?'

'Good. Knackered though.'

'No Issy?'

'She's working. Always working.'

'Well someone has to.'

'I guess.'

The door behind them shut with a bang, and they turned to see Jamie struggling with the key.

'Bloody lock. We need to get it fixed. No Issy?'

'She's working to keep Matt in beer.'

'Shall we go?'

'Sorry. Sensitive subject?'

'I'll tell you in the car.'

As they negotiated Hammersmith Bridge and the roads south, Abi grilled Matt on the true story behind Issy's non-appearance. Matt was a little defensive but had never been able to keep secrets from his sister. It seemed there had been a misunderstanding about the date, a row and an atmosphere. It seemed this was a regular occurrence. It was unclear who was to blame.

Abi and Jamie exchanged glances.

'So, she keeps ducking out of going anywhere with you?'

'And she's always working?'

'Yes and yes.'

'Has it occurred to you…?'

'Is she seeing someone else? Yes, it's occurred to me. I don't know. Maybe I should finish it. I thought we were really going somewhere though, you know.'

'What've you told Mum?'

'Nothing. Why?'

'So she's expecting her today?'

'Oh, I see. No. I texted her.'

'And you think Mum will have read her texts?'

'Fair point. Maybe you should ring her.'

'Maybe I should ring her? Nice one.'

'Well I'm driving.'

It was Liza's birthday and the family were getting together for lunch. Abi was the image of her mother but with her father's empathy; Matt combined his mother's artistic flair with his father's interest in ideas and appetite for argument; and Jamie was described by Tom as his ersatz son-in-law to overcome the mild embarrassment he felt that the vicar's daughter had chosen to cohabit rather than to marry. Pete and Anne would be there too; Pete adding to the opportunities for conflict and debate, Anne filling her normal family role of understanding aunt and general peacemaker. They were all looking forward to it, something which Issy could never understand, the combination of love, nurture and philosophical fireworks being outside her experience.

Abi sighed, took out her phone and called her mother. No answer. Just voicemail.

'Oh hi Mum, it's Abi. Just checking if you've read your texts this morning. There's one from Matt. We're on our way. See you soon. Lots of love. Byeee.'

She put the phone back in her pocket. It immediately rang. She dug it out.

'Hi Mum. Yes. I did... I left you a message... It said had you read your texts this morning... Yes. Your texts. You've got one from Matt... Thought not... Don't worry. It's Issy, she's not coming… Yes, I know, you've got special stuff in for her diet… Yes, Matt is a total plonker.'

Matt intervened. 'She didn't say that.'

'Matt doesn't believe you called him a total plonker… Well someone has to help you say what you really feel… Yes, we'll be there before long. The three of us… Bye… Love you.'

'What did she really say?'

'She said you're a total plonker, and I've always been her favourite child.'

'Right. And she hadn't read her texts?'

'Of course she hadn't read her texts. She hasn't worked out how to yet. But she now knows that Issy isn't going to be there… so, thank you Abi.'

'Thank you, Abi.'

'It's a pleasure. I'll teach you how to make a phone call one day. Like a grown-up. Don't you think that would be a good idea Jamie?'

Jamie shifted in his seat. 'Don't get me involved in this. This is strictly sibling stuff.'

'Well you're an honorary sibling.'

'Honorary siblings hold on to their status best when they keep quiet.'

'Coward. Watch out here Matt, they've put in cameras.'

They were now on the A3 heading south past New Malden and Kingston and down to the Tolworth junction, nearing the point where urban sprawl started to diminish. By the time they left the A3 and headed off for Molebridge, they had swapped the retail estates and busy junctions for fields, trees and the low hills of the North Downs. Jamie was enthusiastic.

'Why don't we get a place out here Abs?'

'Because I like it where we are.'

'But there's so much space out here; room to breathe.'

'Space to spend hours travelling through every day to get to work.'

'It takes me ages now.'

'And it would take you longer. It would be a drag.'

'Oh, I don't think so. What do you think Matt?'

Matt thought it was a great place to visit, or to settle down in, not so good for a single man wanting the bright lights of London. Jamie queried whether Matt was really a single man. Matt felt that it was starting to look that way. Abi expressed the view that Issy wasn't good enough for him. Jamie queried whether any girl would be good enough for Abi's brother. In the process, they arrived at their destination, a large Victorian terrace in a quiet, residential street in Molebridge.

'Not really my idea of a vicarage,' commented Jamie.

'They come in all shapes and sizes these days. I think St Peter's sold the original off years ago – too large and expensive to maintain. Here's Dad.'

And here indeed was Tom, beaming at them from the porch and restraining Rothko with his left leg, holding the door with one hand while unclipping his dog collar with the other. Rothko's desire to escape grew more pressing as they got out of the car and he knew who was arriving. Tom gave up the struggle, and he bounded up to Matt who was leading the way, leaving Tom to hug his daughter and exchange greetings with Jamie. Somehow they all bundled into the house, with presents and flowers, exchanged greetings, hugs and kisses and settled in the large conservatory at the back of the house with a view across fields to Micklebury Heath and the spire of St Aidan's poking through the trees.

'Drinks? Abi, glass of wine?'

'Not sure Dad. Jamie, are you driving back?'

'Yes, I'll just have a beer now and call that it.'

'Wine it is then. Beer for you too Matt? Abi, can you dig your mother out of the kitchen? I'll take over when I've done the drinks.'

Tom disappeared to the cellar where he kept the drinks, and Abi slipped into the kitchen to find Liza chopping cabbage.

'Dad says leave that to him. It's your birthday.'

'I'm just finishing this bit.'

'Come on. Come and sit with us.'

Liza smiled, put down the knife and turned.

'Apron off too.'

'Okay. It's good to see you.'

They hugged. Before heading into the conservatory Liza paused and turned to Abi.

'Can you try and keep Matt off Dad's case today. Just change the topic if they get on to church stuff. He's a bit unsettled at the moment and with Pete here I don't want a three-way ding-dong. You know how he likes to wind them up.'

This proved more difficult than it sounded. No sooner had Pete and Anne arrived than it started. Tom offered drinks. Pete asked for orange juice on the grounds that he had already had his fill of communion wine, and Jamie asked what he meant. Pete explained that it was incumbent on him ('as the incumbent' put in Tom) to finish off the communion bread and wine reverently after the service as it was sanctified. It wasn't usually a problem, but from time to time the likely numbers taking the Eucharist were misjudged, leaving a larger surplus for him to drink.

'Can't anyone help you?' asked Jamie.

'No,. It has to be me.'

Tom had to butt in here. 'That's not really true, Pete, is it? You can ask selected people. You can even reserve.'

It turned out that Pete's view was, not surprisingly, narrower than Tom's. He was not happy to select communicants to help him because that would mean choosing some above others and 'we are all equal in the sight of God'. He was not happy to 'reserve' the wine for the next Communion as this would mean it just lying around and it was sanctified. Predictably, Tom thought it was all nonsense, the symbolic nature of the bread and wine being relevant only in the service itself. Equally predictably, Matt was scathing about the whole procedure.

'You really believe this is the body and blood of Christ?'

'No, we believe it represents the body and blood. I think we're agreed on that Pete?'

'Represents, yes – for most people.'

'What about for you, Uncle Pete?'

'Yes, for me it represents. But that's not the point. The point is it's consecrated.'

Tom snorted. 'It's a symbol Pete, they're symbols. Feed what's left over to the dog, it wouldn't matter.'

Abi jumped in. 'Rothy's looking well on it. You must be walking him a lot.'

'Your mum's always off walking him. They're both super fit.'

That provoked a quizzical look from Anne, but Matt wasn't ready to let go.

'So you both persist in glorifying cannibalism?'

'What?'

'Eating the body, drinking the blood. Sounds like something out of the *Twilight* saga.'

'Now you're being silly.'

'I'm being silly? I'm not the one who has to believe six impossible things before breakfast.'

Pete laughed. 'You're your father's son all right.'

Liza jumped in. 'And mine, and it's my birthday, so just drop the arguments, okay?'

'Yes,' interjected Anne, 'don't you boys have some cooking to do? I want a chat with my niece and sister. Jamie, you're excused kitchen duties. You can drink beer and watch.'

'Why does he get excused?'

'Because he doesn't spend time picking fights like the rest of you. It was bad enough when it was just your dad and your Uncle Pete, without you joining in.'

'And you and Mum never argue?'

'You know we do, but not constantly. And only because she's spoilt.'

'Spoilt! I had a big sister bullying me.'

'I'm just trying to redress the balance. Off you go lads.'

With the quarrelling men gone, conversation moved away from theological argument, much to Jamie's relief. The relief was short-lived, however, as the three women began to catch up and reminisce. He excused himself and went to add to what was now an overmanned kitchen team.

No sooner had he gone than Abi turned to her mother and asked how she was.

'Fine. Why?'

'I sense an atmosphere with you and Dad. Are you okay?'

'Oh, you know, the job. He's always helping somebody out, or at a meeting somewhere, or responding to some crisis, when he isn't upsetting people with his unorthodox views. I hardly feature. That's nothing new.'

Anne sympathised. 'Vicar's wife syndrome. Pete's much the same, except he upsets people with his orthodox views.'

Abi smiled. 'They're an odd couple.'

'They've been as thick as thieves since they were small. They'd be lost without the arguments. But I'm concerned too, Liza. You will talk to me if you need to, won't you?'

'Haven't I always?'

'No, not always, that's what I'm worried about.'

*

The kitchen was not overlarge and was cluttered with stools, chairs and, right now, bodies. When Jamie joined them, Tom was busy with vegetables, the meat was resting on the side, and Matt was restraining an enthusiastic Labrador who thought it was all for him. Pete was lost in thought by the window. From experience, Jamie knew this was all typical of a meal at the Raistricks – and that what emerged from this chaos would be delicious.

And so it turned out. Pete was delegated to lay the table, a job he did with diligence, lining up each item of cutlery with precision. Matt was dispatched to open wine, pour water, and take drinks orders. Jamie was entrusted with draining veg, finding and warming dishes to serve them in, and making sure there were chairs to sit on. Meanwhile, Tom put the finishing touches to the gravy, produced perfect Yorkshires and carved the meat.

Conversation over the lunch table turned to weddings. St Aidan's was a popular choice for non-churchgoers who wanted a rural church and, predictably, Tom and Pete had very different views on the extent to which they should be accommodated. Anne wanted to know what the younger generation thought about it. Matt, for once, had no strong views.

'What about you Abi? Do you think you'll want a church wedding?'

'What makes you think I'll get married?'

'Oh, everybody gets married – eventually.'

Jamie jumped in. 'That may have been true once, but not now. It's outdated, irrelevant.'

'How can a public declaration of a lifetime commitment be irrelevant?'

'Why does it need to be public Auntie Anne? We know how we feel.'

Matt took a different line. 'It's a lot easier for tax, and benefits, and all those sorts of things.'

Tom smiled. 'That's a very practical view. It's not very romantic.'

'Well, these things matter. And you can do the romantic bit privately.'

Everyone laughed.

'You know what I mean. So, why go to church? Just slip off to the registry office with a couple of witnesses.'

Anne and Liza exchanged glances and spoke at the same time.

'No, I want to wear a hat.'

'And miss out on the party?'

'They could have a party as well.'

'You seem to be reinventing the wedding breakfast.'

'You all seem to be forgetting we're not getting married.'

'At least you can, not like some.' This came from Matt.

Anne jumped in. 'Can we not have the gay argument as well today?'

'It's important.'

'I don't deny it, but so is your mother's birthday.'

'No, it's okay Anne. Let him have his say.'

'Thanks Mum. It just really upsets me. My friends are second-class citizens, just because they love each other.'

'Who? Who's this?'

'You don't know them, Uncle Pete. Brad and Mark. They're friends from uni. They've lived together for ages. They're committed. But there's no recognition of their relationship by the Church, or the state, or anyone really, apart from their friends.'

Abi put in. 'Well, that's not quite true. They get some benefits and stuff now.'

'Not much. And the Church is awful. Full of hypocrites preaching love and practising hate.'

Pete and Tom both bridled at this. Pete spoke first.

'I don't hate anyone Matt, you know that.'

'Not personally maybe, but would you bless their union? Put them forward for the ministry? Let them have any leadership position? No, thought not. They're second-class citizens.'

'It's very difficult Matt. Leviticus…'

'Le-bloody-viticus! Hundreds of rules and you ignore most of them.'

'He has a point, Pete.'

'Which side are you on Tom? Biblical authority is biblical authority.'

Tom sighed. Sometimes he found himself on both sides of the argument at once. Trying to make things clear sometimes had the opposite effect.

'Let me try and explain. The Church has a view, partly based, as Pete says, on Leviticus. As priests we're obliged to respect that view. Personally, I find it a tough one to respect or, indeed, defend and that's only partly because of my reluctance to base my whole belief system on a selective interpretation of scripture.'

Abi groaned. This was going to be a long one. Tom felt he needed to explain.

'No, I promise not to be too long-winded, but Matt raises an important issue, which we're going to have to get to grips with.'

'It's not an issue Dad, it's people.'

'Exactly. That's why I say my finding it tough is only partly a scriptural thing. It's people. Try applying the letter of Leviticus when you've two guys like Matt's friends in front of you and then tell me how you feel.'

'I have,' said Pete. 'I felt a heel. But it's what we're taught, and it's a sin. But I can still love the sinner.'

'Not really. Not truly. Not when you're refusing to accept or respect the very basis of what they are, then it's just fine words Pete. It doesn't wash. You can't do both, and – no, let me finish...' (This was to Matt who was bursting to get in.) 'Let me finish, this is important. If it's the very basis of what they are, it can't be a sin, it's just who they are. Deal with it.'

'Well said, Dad. Maybe there's hope for you yet.'

'Okay, time to change the subject. I was allowed to marry the love of my life and don't regret it even though she got a bit older today.'

Liza stuck out her tongue.

'And even though she still hasn't grown up. So a toast to the birthday girl. Liza...'

'Liza!'

CHAPTER FIVE

CHANGES

Tom's study was his sanctuary, book lined, with a CD tower, long unplayed vinyl and a dusty guitar competing for space beside his desk and red leather armchair. He was in that leather armchair, deep in thought, when the phone rang. It was Jonny Nower, wanting to talk, preferably face-to-face. Tom thought it sounded serious. Jonny was quick to reassure – nothing dramatic but life-changing, he said. Intrigued, Tom agreed to meet for coffee later that morning at Betty Latty's.

Betty Latty's was the latest independent coffee house in Molebridge. Its real name of 'Better Latte than Never' being more than either man could cope with, Tom had come up with a suitable alternative which seemed to be acquiring wider currency. The two men settled with an Americano each and exchanged pleasantries for several minutes before Tom asked to be put out of his misery.

Jonny had been thinking over their previous conversation, had reached some conclusions and, he said, taken some action. Impressed, Tom asked for more specifics. Jonny stirred several sachets of brown sugar into his coffee before leaning back and announcing that he'd resigned.

'Resigned? From Nower Asset Management?'

'Soon to be renamed Blue Island Investments.'

'Really?'

'I think they were just waiting for me to jump.'

'So. A clean break?'

'Yes, a few client conversations to have, but basically Junker can't wait to see the back of me – which he won't entirely achieve.'

'Why's that?'

'You remember I told you about the Scafell issue? My old friends Jim Ferguson and Dan Murphy?'

Tom did remember.

'The big client? Demanding. You poured oil on troubled waters.'

'That's them. They've asked me to join their board. So Bob Junker will have me as a client. He'll have to be nice to me.'

The irony had not escaped Tom. Nor had the possibility that Jonny was going to enjoy being the client. Jonny promised to try not to enjoy it too much. Anyway, that would just be a few days a year. For the most part, he wanted to do something completely different. What, he was not yet sure. This was where he needed Tom's help. Tom was keen to help. Helping was what he did. Where to start? Jonny pondered, took a sip of coffee, and hesitated.

'Well. I think, if you don't mind, we start at the beginning.'

'The beginning?'

'My life, my upbringing, the things that made me. I've been on autopilot y'see? Feels that way sometimes.'

'Well I'm comfortable, there's a supply of coffee, so I'm all ears.'

'I've time on my hands. Don't want to assume you have.'

'What's the issue?'

'I was born into St Aidan's in a way; the Nower family church. When we had estates it was literally ours. The congregation was our workers, in the main. It'd all changed by my day, of course, but the past doesn't go away, not in a church like St Aidan's, not in Micklebury. So I grew up special, was humoured, treated with a mix of respect and resentment, I felt so anyway. I was made to feel like the church belonged to me, and I played along. Still do in a way. I've been churchwarden for years. The maximum terms were immediately rejected by the parish when they came in. People can't envisage not having a Nower as warden. Some people anyway. They're going to have to some time. The next generation are not interested. And not in the area. I go every Sunday, read the lesson, y'know, but what do I believe? Interesting one that.'

Tom smiled, moved the Kilner jar which housed the sugar cubes out of the way, and leant forward. This was right up his street.

'You were thinking of ordination not long ago. That suggests a faith.'

'Maybe I was just moving down the same track. I've been thinking about it since we chatted. You know Tom, it's not my church, not my responsibility, not really. And this whole thing of playing a role in the community... I don't know. Isn't it a bit... patronising?'

Tom thought not. Jonny was prepared to park that thought.

'Okay. But what do I actually believe, Tom? I've sat there, week after week, in the family pew – another throwback – and listened to vicars, curates, bishops, lay readers, visiting missionaries, you name it. I've been charmed, cajoled, frightened, bullied, persuaded and encouraged to believe. I've heard about sin and redemption, the saving grace of God, the Prophets, the Apostles, the children of Israel, Adam and Eve. I've sat there and listened. Sometimes. Other times I've been lost in thought. There's sin for you; not listening to the sermon. Sometimes, over lunch, Jancy will ask what I thought of the sermon, and I have to admit I've no idea what was said, not a clue. But I've listened enough. I've got it, the basic theology, the idea of the Cross and the defeat of death, dying to sin – all that. But what do I believe? Really believe. I don't honestly know. And I need to work it out.'

Tom wondered whether Jonny thought he could work it out and then stick with it. That, he felt, was his own predicament. This was a new thought to Jonny, but he imagined he could. Did Tom think he was likely to change again?

Tom moved the sugar again.

'If we stop growing and changing it's a kind of death, don't you think?'

'Maybe. Maybe that's been my problem. But lots of people don't seem interested, you know? In church, faith, anything of that sort; doesn't seem relevant. It might be true, it might be a load of nonsense, but it doesn't seem to matter either way – think I'm weird for caring.'

'They think you're weird or you think you're weird?'

'They do. Me too sometimes. I keep coming back to it though. What do I believe? It's a big question. I'm not sure what I'm going to do now I've left the firm, but maybe I need to sort this first.'

'That could be a long process. Maybe things will become clearer as you work it through. More coffee?'

Tom threaded his way through the tables to order refills, returned with a flapjack each and sat down. They were home-made flapjacks, and his excuse was that Jonny would like them. Jonny raised an eyebrow.

'They're home-made. I thought you might like one.'

Jonny grinned.

'Know my weak spots. Where was I?'

'Being weird, I think. No, working things through.'

'Yes. See, here I am, pillar of the community, pillar of the church. Used to be the same thing. Still is, to some extent, in Micklebury. I think of myself as a Christian, but do I believe in the Garden of Eden, the Flood, the parting of the waters, the burning bush? No, not really.'

This was one of the reasons Tom felt so comfortable with Jonny. There was always the possibility of sensible discussion about issues that interested him. He tried to reassure Jonny.

'You're in the majority on most of that; creation myths, allegories, poetic language.'

'Okay, but the Virgin Birth, the Resurrection? I don't know. I really don't know.'

Tom questioned whether this really mattered. Like many people, Jonny saw it as fairly central to the Christian faith. Tom's point was that it could be symbolic, a metaphor, and could still represent an important truth. Jonny was unsure.

'I'm a simple man, Tom. I want to feel that it happened or it didn't happen.'

'I can't help you there, I'm afraid.'

'I know. Just need time to think, read perhaps. See, I'm not sure what I've done with my life. Have I wasted it?'

'Not from where I'm sitting. How do you mean?'

'Well, look around you. Look at the world. There are problems everywhere. Famine, disease, poverty, wars. Y'know. And here am I, born with a silver spoon, y'know. What have I done? Made more money. God, even the fact that I have time to worry about this stuff is down to affluence. Most men my age are still working hard to support themselves. And that's just in this country. In Africa they might be dead.'

Tom felt it was time to challenge.

'What about Micklebury, Jonny?'

'What about it?'

'You've kept that church going, I know you have. You've been there for people when they needed help. You're trusted, respected, loved even. It doesn't happen by accident.'

'But is it enough, Tom? Is it enough?'

'It's more than a lot can say. And what about the firm?'

'Looking after money for rich people?'

'Oh, come on. It's more than that, Jonny – way more. There's training and mentoring youngsters, caring for clients, demonstrating integrity, modelling good behaviour in an industry that needs good role models. Counts for something.'

'Maybe.'

'And I'm hardly the one to mount a spirited defence of capitalism, you know that, but it's the system we have and without people like you it wouldn't function. Think on that.'

'I need to think on a lot of things, Tom. That's why we're here. I need help – suggestions for reading. Get me started. Might go on a retreat – what do you think?'

'It can't hurt. I can make suggestions. Perhaps we can catch up every week or so. See where you've got to. What does Jancy think?'

'I think she thinks I'm making a big thing of it. Just do what you can, help where you can and it's all okay is her view.'

'There's something to be said for that, Jonny.'

'Yes, but how do I know when I'm doing what I can? When is it enough?'

'You'll know when you know.'

'Maybe. Thanks for this, Tom. Appreciate it. Know you're busy.'

'I can always find time.'

This gave Jonny an opening for something else on his mind; Tom and Liza. Perhaps, he suggested, Tom had too much time for too many people. Tom was a little defensive, arguing that there was never enough time. Jonny took a sip of coffee, pulled a face and put the cup down. It was now cold. He queried whether Tom was spending enough time with Liza.

'Liza? Probably not. Why do you ask?'

'None of my business, Tom. Tell me to butt out, but I never see you together these days. Saw her in Waitrose last week and got the impression you weren't top of the pops.'

'I'm probably not. It's vicar's wife syndrome. She's at the end of the queue.'

'She deserves more than that.'

'I know. You're right. Pete keeps telling me the same thing.'

'Okay, enough lecturing. Will you email me some reading suggestions?'

'And possible retreats, yes.'

'Great. I feel a lot better for the chat. Thanks Tom.'

'Any time.'

Tom got up to go, hesitated and turned back to Jonny.

'Tell me, Jonny, why all this interest in Liza and me all of a sudden?'

'Interest?'

'You, Pete. Both asking how things are. Is there something I should know?'

Jonny looked uncomfortable.

'I don't know what Pete's heard, but there are rumours.'

'Go on.'

'Tom, I don't like tittle-tattle. There may be nothing in it.'

'But…'

'But Liza has apparently been seen with some guy. Quite a bit. Walking. In pubs.'

'In pubs? That's a bit public for an affair. If that's what…'

'Not Molebridge pubs, more out of area. I don't know, Tom. Might be a load of nonsense.'

Tom was visibly shaken. He sat down.

'I'm scared, Jonny. If Pete's worried too.'

'Not the most observant of men I hear.'

'No, but Anne may well have caught wind of something. Shit. I need to talk to her.'

'Anne?'

'No. Only make things worse. Liza. Thanks Jonny.'

'You know where I am.'

And they parted.

*

Liza was on the heath again, waiting to meet Bob and Barney for the daily walk which had become a key part of her day. Daily life at the vicarage had become tedious, lonely even. One of the joys of the very different milieus in which she and Tom worked was the different perspectives they brought to each other when they caught up. These days they rarely caught up, and when they did Tom was tired out, grumpy, and taciturn. By contrast, Bob was energised, new, interested and tempting. They had already progressed from occasional walks to daily ones and from that to meeting for lunch. Bob was pressing for more – much more.

'Tom doesn't even notice you' was his argument. 'Takes you for granted. I wouldn't do that. Leave him. Make a new life with me. I love you, Liza. Really. I'm a bit besotted to be honest. We could have a great life together, you and me. You know you want to.'

The trouble was she did want to, but the idea of leaving Tom was terrifying. And the repercussions didn't bear thinking about. Nonetheless, over the weeks she had felt herself weakening. Every time church stuff got in the way, every time Tom gave priority to somebody else's marriage, or their sick child, or took a call from the bishop when they were having a rare five minutes peace and quiet, she got a little closer to going – or threatening to at least. Now, as she waited for Bob, her phone went. It was Tom, on the vicarage phone.

'Hi Tom.'

'Where are you? We need to talk.'

'I'm out with the dog.'

'Where? I'll join you.'

'No need. I'll be back soon.'

'Liza, I need to talk to you.'

'So talk.'

'Not on the phone. Face-to-face.'

'Is something wrong?'

'I don't know. You tell me.'

Liza caught her breath. He knew something. What to do?

'I'll come home. Don't go anywhere.'

Her mind racing, she rang Bob. It went to voicemail. She hated leaving messages. She left one that she hoped wasn't too garbled, along the lines of 'Have to cry off today. Showdown with Tom looming. Don't do anything. Wait for my call.' And she went home, driving on automatic pilot, her mind numb, close to tears, and shaking.

She walked into the kitchen of the vicarage to find Tom standing staring out of the window. He turned. She looked at him and saw all their life together; the early passion, the laughter, the relief when he split with Anne, the sheer magnetism, the children. God, the children. She saw the essential honesty of the man she'd married and broke down in tears. He stepped forward and held her.

'So it's true then?'

'Tom, I'm sorry. I don't know what you've heard but I think it's over.'

'Over?'

'This. You and me. I think we're...'

'Over? You and me? No. It can't be. We can recover. Whatever you've done, I can forgive you.'

That was the wrong thing to say. She sprang away from him.

'Forgive me? Well thank you! Can I forgive you?'

'I'm not the one who's having an affair.'

'Technically, neither am I – yet. But I am the one at the back of the queue for your time. I'm the one who's been frozen out of this marriage. I'm not feeling like the guilty party here.'

'Liza, I've been true to you. You're the centre of my world. But you… You've been seen all over the place with some loser and his dog.'

'Loser! Bob's not a loser.'

'So he's got a name then, this Lothario.'

'He's a decent man who listens to me, cares about me…'

'Not my definition of decent, going after a married woman.'

'That's not how it was. And this isn't about Bob.'

'No?'

'No. It's about a marriage that's dead on its feet because you don't have time for it. For me.'

'Me not have time? You're never here!'

'And why's that do you think? Because there's nothing to be here for, that's why.'

'So what do we do?'

'What are you going to do?'

'Me?'

'Yes, you. Are you going to change? Give up some committees, say no to some demands from your congregation?'

'You make it sound easy.'

'Oh, it's easy. A straight choice. Your marriage or your flock.'

'My flock?'

'That's what you are, isn't it? A shepherd, with all these poor, helpless sheep bleating after you.'

'That's unfair.'

'No it isn't. So, them or me?'

'You know that's not a choice I can make.'

'Well it's a choice I can make. I'm leaving.'

'Liza, no. We can work this out.'

'No Tom, I don't think we can. Not unless you change.'

'My wife has an affair and I'm in the wrong.'

'Don't.'

Liza charged upstairs, sobbing, filled a bag with a few essentials, looked round the bedroom without really seeing it, and went down the stairs again. Tom hadn't moved. He looked like he was going to throw up.

'Where are you going?'

'To Bob. I'll get the rest of my things later.'

'Liza...'

'Bye Tom.'

And she was gone.

PART THREE

CHAPTER ONE

TOM AND JONNY

Bowling into St Aidan's on a cold Monday morning, Tom nearly sent Jonny Nower flying.

'Tom! Didn't expect to see you today.'

'Sorry Jonny, I wasn't looking. Church day?'

'I've done enough thinking for one week. Needed to do something.'

'Feeling drained?'

'A bit.'

'Me too. Coffee?'

'I'll put the heater on in the vestry. Not that it'll have much effect.'

Tom fiddled with kettles and cafetières. Jonny tried to point the inadequate fan heater towards the battered chairs at one end of the vestry, and moved a couple of piles of *Hymns Ancient and Modern* out of the way, before settling himself.

Tom half turned, and said over his shoulder, 'No milk, I'm afraid.' Jonny was unperturbed.

'Black's fine. Just add a bit more sugar. Take the edge off.'

'There you go. There are biscuits somewhere.'

'I think Nick finished them. I meant to get some more.'

'Never mind. So. At a loose end?'

'I've no responsibilities any more, Tom.'

Tom took a moment to find a chair, started to loosen his scarf, but thought better of it, before responding.

'And needing a break from thinking.'

'And me from reading. That list of books you gave me… Fascinating. But hard going, some of them.'

'You don't need to do it all at once, you know.'

A shaft of sunlight through the small, leaded window lit Tom's face. Jonny was studying the dust motes dancing in the light.

'Trying to find my… I don't know Tom, role? Position? Feels urgent.'

'Now that you're no longer the physical embodiment of Nower Asset Management?'

'Something like that. I mattered to people then.'

'You matter to people now.'

'I suppose so, but in a more restricted circle. At work, people had to trust us. Trust me. People give you their money to look after, their wealth. They have to believe they belong, have to trust you. Have to believe in you.'

'Sounds like the Church.'

'Very like. And the chairman becomes a godlike figure; caring, reassuring.'

'A bit remote?'

'Yes, but you get to break bread with him every now and then.'

'Very godlike.'

'The thing is, old boy, since the takeover that's all there was to the role. And now I've left, I've not even that.'

'There's Jim Ferguson's lot.'

'It's a meeting once a quarter. Interesting enough, but…'

He let the sentence hang. Neither spoke. The heater was having no effect and both men clutched their coffee mugs for warmth. The irony of two men with heated houses taking refuge in a cold church vestry escaped them. Jonny broke the silence.

'Strange. I moaned at the Americans. Felt I had no power, couldn't interfere. I was just a listening ear.'

'You could argue that's a bit godlike too.'

'Is that what's eating you?'

'Something like that.'

'Do share.'

Tom grimaced, struggled to articulate the issue.

'I don't know, it's just… Well, I'm surrounded by people who all know exactly what God's thinking, what he wants for them.'

'And you don't?'

'I think that's claiming to know the unknowable. It's not a popular position.'

'Hardly a novel one.'

'It's an acceptable position for a theologian, not for the vicar of an evangelical church.'

Jonny got up and moved around, passed the rack of blue and white cassocks, the piles of prayer books and the large, old King James Bible.

'So move on.'

'Don't tempt me.'

'We don't have those expectations here you know.'

'I know. St Aidan's is an oasis of calm for me.'

'It's a bit cold for an oasis.'

'There is that.'

Jonny hesitated before making a tentative offer.

'Well, if you do decide to move on, let me know. I might have a role for you.'

'Who might?'

'The Nower Trust – my charity. I've been syphoning money into it for years; bonuses, that sort of thing. Then when I sold the business, I put a load of the proceeds in; millions. I'd no need for the money. Wanted to have a pot I could use for other stuff. Y'know, grants to other charities, supporting good works; old-fashioned philanthropy.'

Tom was interested.

'And where would I come in?'

'Man of your skills? Writing. Lecturing,. Validating projects. All sorts... I'd sort something out if it became relevant. Bear it in mind.'

'I don't know what to say.'

'Say nothing. Tuck the idea behind your ear. Like a ciggy, for later.'

Jonny made a decision.

'Got boots with you?'

'In this parish? Of course.'

'Why don't we walk? Better for us. And warmer.'

They left the church by the back entrance, locking it behind them. Outside the graveyard was peaceful, showing signs of recent restoration work. A few headstones were carefully stacked on the mown grass, daffodils bent over worn inscriptions, and a wheelbarrow was propped against an elm. As they made their way through the lychgate, a cyclist raised a hand in greeting before disappearing into the trees. Jonny grumbled.

'Can never work out if it's someone I know or not with those helmets on.'

'It's sensible to wear one though.'

'Off-road, yes.'

'Just off-road?'

'All those tree roots and poor surfaces, much more likely to come a cropper.'

Their cars were parked opposite; Tom's beaten up Honda dwarfed by Jonny's Range Rover. Perched on the tailgates, they pulled on wellingtons and headed down a muddy track, through the wood, with beech and ash competing to throw shadows on the ground.

'So what's on your mind, Tom?'

'I'm not Bible-based enough for some of my congregation.'

'Okay.'

'And my own feeling is that I'm too Bible-based if anything.'

'Too Bible-based? In an evangelical church?'

'Exactly.'

'This can't be a new issue.'

'No. It looks like it's coming to a head though. I've had a delegation.'

'Really?'

'Three concerned friends, pillars of the Church, wanting change.'

'Awkward. How did you deal with that?'

They paused to cross a country road before emerging at the top of an escarpment. Below them stretched fields and woodland, with the town of Molebridge clustered in the valley.

'Look, Jonny. Isn't that beautiful? How lucky am I to live, and work in Molebridge?'

'So you shouldn't grumble?'

'Something like that.'

'And the deputation?'

'Oh, I listened. Gave them tea. They went off friendly enough,. But frustrated I expect.'

'Will it end there?'

'Don't know. They could take it further.'

'What does the bishop think?'

'I don't suppose he'll be too worried. He tends to see these things as growing opportunities. I don't know how much he knows. I've spoken with the archdeacon of course.'

'And?'

'Oh, he's supportive. But he's an Anglo-Catholic, so he sees things from a rather different perspective.'

'Usefully so?'

'On the whole. I think my stock is quite high with him, and the bishop.'

'That sounds good.'

'Well, yes, it is – but they're not the people I'm with day-to-day. I don't know, Jonny. I'm not sure I'm doing much good at the moment.'

'Don't be so hard on yourself. Three people are not the whole congregation.'

'True, but they do represent a sizeable group. And there is general discomfort at my marital status.'

'Not your fault Liza ran off.'

Tom snorted.

'That's not the way she sees it. And you did make the point yourself, as I recall. Was I neglecting my marriage? And it seems you were right.'

Jonny let that pass. Tom continued.

'But, y'know, I think people expect the vicar to have a conventional home life. They don't care whose fault it is. They never took to Liza, she was too much of a free spirit, but they did expect us to stay married – so did I.'

They paused to admire the view, Highland cattle dotting the field below them. Jonny dug a cap out of his pocket before replying to this.

'So they're glad to see the back of her?'

'I'm not sure I'd put it like that, but they saw her as a drawback when she was around, and they see her absence as a black mark now she's gone. Me, I'd trade the lot of them for another chance.'

'Getting any support?'

'Nothing formal. Pete and Anne, you know. The children appear and hover helplessly from time to time. I'm off to Pete and Anne's tomorrow.'

'Must be good to have that mutual understanding.'

'Because of the vicar thing or the length of the friendship?'

'Both. I know Pete's churchmanship is a bit different to yours, but...'

'That doesn't really matter. We've argued about that stuff for 40 years. He's like a brother to me. And Anne, well it's a bit complicated with her being Liza's sister, and with our past relationship, but it's good. I feel held.'

'Any chance of a reconciliation?'

'I don't know, Jonny. I really don't know.'

*

In practise, the delegation Tom had received had been a little more formal than he had told Jonny, a sign that he was not yet able to face the fact yet perhaps. Not only had there been an uncomfortable conversation, but he also now had, in his pocket, a letter, one that accused him of scant respect for tradition (guilty as charged), insufficient adherence to scripture, and a general woolliness. He understood that a copy, or a similar letter, had gone to the bishop.

Tom was surprised by his own reaction. He did not feel unfairly accused. He was a little scornful of tradition, somewhat impatient with the literalist tendencies of some of his flock where scripture was concerned, and as for woolliness, well, that merely meant he wasn't arrogant and exclusive. So he agreed with the letter in a way. He just felt these were all virtues rather than vices. Trying to say that to the triumvirate of Bert Smith, Jim Jenkins and Iris Murgatroyd had been difficult though. Bert, in his plain-speaking way, had told him he was a disgrace. Jim had been more conciliatory but clearly agreed. Iris had kept referring back to some old grievance about the non-use of preaching bands.

Tom was left with a feeling of frustration and despair. As a younger man, he would have stood up on Sunday morning and brought it all out into the open, declared himself. But now he was more cautious, anxious about the danger of creating a rift in the congregation; hence the frustration. Talking about it helped, but not having Liza to confide in hit him hard. He knew he needed to go and see Anne and Pete, but first there was the bishop to face. He had been asked to 'pop in for a chat' and was not looking forward to it.

CHAPTER TWO

PETE AND TOM

Pete was in his study; a vicar's study. Two slightly scruffy easy chairs, a desk and an old bureau. By the desk, a swivel office chair from IKEA and behind that a coffee table. And books – books everywhere. Pete had just returned, still humming (the hymn 'Blessed Assurance', the tune, 'Assurance'), still with cycle clips on his trousers, dog collar, middle-aged. It irritated Anne, this habit of humming snatches of hymns when thinking or when there was a lull in conversation, but he still did it. He put the Bible on the desk, fiddled with the other books, took off his jacket, looked for somewhere to put it, put it back on again, and settled in his chair to read. The doorbell rang. Pete ignored it, engrossed in his book.

If he had been listening, he would have heard Anne greeting Tom, telling him Pete was in the study. She called through.

'Pete! Tom's here. Pete! Oh, just go through Tom. He'll have his head in a book. Tell him the kettle's on.'

The door opened and Tom appeared, wearing his normal uniform of chinos and open-necked shirt. The contrast with Pete's dog collar and cycle clips was marked. As usual, his energy level was high. The two men greeted each other. Tom looked for somewhere to sit, picked up a pile of books from one of the chairs, and looked for somewhere to put them.

'Been tidying up I see.'

'No. Oh, joke. Just put them on the floor. I'll sort them later.'

Tom took in Pete's garb.

'Doing the rounds on the bike?'

Pete looked puzzled.

'You've still got your clips on.'

Pete looked down, took the clips off, and put them on the desk, before asking, 'So how are things?'

'Oh, you know. Anne said the kettle's on if you want tea.'

'She's not making then?'

'I think she may have other things to do.'

Pete had to digest this information, and its implications, before offering to make tea for Tom. Tom's response was a negative.

'Not for me, thanks. I'm tea'd out. Eight cups so far this morning I think.'

Pete was amused.

'Do you accept every cup that's offered you?'

'Yes, until I can take no more. I feel obliged.'

'Obliged?'

'The vicar comes round, you offer him a cup of tea. It's rude of him to refuse.'

Pete wasn't sure why. Tom explained.

'It's an important ritual. The giving and taking of tea establishes a mutual relationship; breaks down the barriers a little, makes it safe to have a strange man in the house, especially for a woman.'

To Pete's argument that Tom was not a strange man, Tom responded that all vicars were strange men. To Pete's logical mind that seemed untrue and he argued that he, Pete, was not a strange man.

'Yes, you are,' said Tom.

'In what way?' asked Pete.

'Well,' said Tom, 'you go round humming hymns and clutching your Bible. You wear cycle clips and forget to take them off. You wear your collar back to front...'

'That's part of the job.'

'You don't have to wear it all the time.'

'People expect it.'

'People expect me to drink their tea.'

'You seem to think vicars are a breed apart.'

Tom grinned.

'Vicars are a breed apart. When they try not to be, they just look like prats.'

Pete felt that the separateness of vicars, the apartness, was largely a thing of the past. Members of the congregation addressed him by his Christian name, only his barber called him 'Vicar', and he was able to go out and about wearing jeans (Tom: 'Jeans? You? When?'). Ignoring Tom, he warmed to his theme. When he first went to church, people were scandalised if the vicar was seen without his dog collar, or if others were too familiar. Now, it was all different. No separation. No respect. Tom argued that the only differences were in outward form, people were still a little wary of the clergy, and the clergy were still keen to encourage that.

Pete had to think about this.

'Maybe you're right. There is a degree of separation, a barrier, even with people I know quite well. I can't seem to break through it.'

Tom argued that Pete had no desire to break through it. If he did, he'd take off the dog collar, and stop wearing a dress every Sunday.

Pete was taken aback.

'Robes and dog collar are traditional.'

'If you don't want to be different, don't wear the uniform.'

'It's part of what I am.'

'Which is what?'

'A vicar.'

'And strange, different.'

Tom thought he'd won that one, but Pete was comfortable.

'I am what I am.'

'Sounds like Jehovah. Or Popeye.'

Pete was puzzled.

'Popeye?'

Tom grinned.

'Don't ever change.'

'Oh, I aspire to change.'

'No you don't.'

'Of course I do. We all do.'

Tom was unconvinced, leaned back in his chair and surveyed the chaos around him. Pete continued.

'Don't we all want to be more Christlike?'

'No. Not really.'

'But that's what we're supposed to want. That's God's plan for us, isn't it? His desire for us.'

Tom took issue with this, one of his bugbears.

'I don't think God wants you to be more Christlike. No. Let me finish. Want to know what I think? I think he wants you to be more Petelike.'

'More Petelike?'

'More Petelike. Think about it. If he wanted you to be Jesus, he'd have made you Jesus. He didn't. He made you Pete Ogden. So I reckon what he most wants is for you to be more fully Pete Ogden. That's the potential you have to realise.'

Pete countered that he didn't even like Pete Ogden. So, responded Tom, there was the first challenge. Learn to love yourself. Pete studied the dust motes in the light from the study window before admitting that that was a real challenge. He looked at himself and saw hatred, anger and bitterness. Easier to look outside, aim for an external role model. Tom's concern, expressed in different ways over the years, was that much of the hatred, anger, and bitterness was directed at him. Pete was very patient.

'None of it's for you, Tom. You're my best friend.'

'And rival.'

'Come on, Tom. I got the girl in the end, right? You very helpfully fell for her sister.'

'You're not second best, Pete.'

'Oh, I think I might be.'

'No! No. Anne dumped me for you.'

'She dumped you, Tom, because you were making a play for her sister.'

Tom grimaced. The idea still hurt.

'She dumped me because she prefers you – sensible girl.'

'Oh thanks. Now I'm the sensible choice.'

'See, resentment and bitterness.'

Pete had a theory, a set of rules to live by. One of these was not to stir things up. There was stuff in the past. Stuff that was best left there. He said as much – not for the first time. Tom's response was, on the surface at least, flippant.

'So stick to a little light flirting and we're okay?'

'It's what you do best.'

'Ouch. So no bitterness then?'

'Only towards myself. I can't measure up.'

'To what?'

'To the man God wants me to be.'

This was another of Tom's bugbears. Was Pete put on this world to wind him up, he wondered? He had listened to so many people beating themselves up, struggling to see any virtue, any merit in themselves and it was all down to the Church. 'Look on me a miserable sinner'. 'I am not worthy so much as to gather up the crumbs from your table'. And all the rest of it. He frowned, sighed, and remonstrated.

'The damage we do! You're full of empathy, love, and a sense of what's right.'

'That's just my job. I'm called to love others.'

'You can't begin to love others until you love yourself.'

'Oh Tom, of course you can.'

'Not really. Not properly. Not genuinely.'

'There you are, you see. I'm a fake as well.'

This was a familiar response. One requiring patience and forbearance.

'No, Pete, you're not. You're just disadvantaged.'

'Disadvantaged?'

'Yes, because you find it a struggle to love yourself. If you could get past all this sinful man full of hatred rubbish you'd be, you'd be… way more effective.'

Pete fell back on an old argument. He was conscious that these debates could become a little like a game of chess between two old adversaries, playing for position, for advantage. The difference being that in this game nobody ever won, and both players felt what they were playing for was key to their existence. Pete knew what he had to say next.

'But we are all full of sin.'

'I'm not.'

'Yes you are, Tom. That's why we need saving.'

'We don't need saving. We need fulfilling.'

'Tom! 'The wages of sin is death'. Romans 6:23.'

This moved the discussion into different territory, the authority of the Bible. Tom's reaction and Pete's riposte were equally predictable.

'Pete, you have to think beyond the Bible or you'll never get anywhere.'

Pete still managed to be shocked by this. His friend was getting more liberal as he aged. Pete had hoped for the opposite.

'Think beyond the Bible?'

'Exactly.'

'What happened to you?'

'I grew up.'

A storm was brewing outside. Rain lashed the windows, and the curtains proved the lack of draughtproofing on the windows by knocking papers on to the floor. Rescuing them and securing them gave Pete time to think but didn't temper his reaction, which was to protest strongly that the Bible was central, 'what it was all about' as he put it. Tom disagreed. God, in his view, was what it was all about – our relationship with him, our relationships with our fellow men. The Bible was just a guide. Pete picked up his dog-eared New International Version and waved it at Tom before pointing out that it was God's word.

'Infallible, is it?' asked Tom.

To Pete's answer that it was essentially, but not literally, infallible, Tom countered that Pete based his arguments on an understanding of the Bible as literally true. Challenged on this, he pointed out that Pete had often preached on the Gospels as true. That, maintained Pete, was different. The Gospels were eyewitness accounts. Including the gospel of Thomas, asked Tom. The gospel of Thomas was clearly a different case, was the response, and was beside the point as it wasn't in the Bible.

So why, wondered Tom, was it not in the Bible? Because men had decided to exclude it. Holy men, suggested Pete. Political men, was Tom's view. At which point the argument moved to the letters of Paul and the degree to which Christianity, as they knew it, was a Pauline concoction rather than a true reflection of the identity and work of Jesus Christ. It was Tom who moved the conversation on to broader issues.

'So, here we are,' he said, grinning at his old friend, 'two clergymen in the same church and we could argue all day about this stuff.'

'Is that a problem?'

'It is in that as soon as we get on to the Bible we don't illuminate, we confuse. Look, we could trade texts all day and not get anywhere. Sometimes that's exactly what we do. It's almost a game, one we've been playing for years.'

Pete felt that the game had changed. In his mind, he had been consistent, and faithful, while his old friend had moved from political activism based on a solid faith to a liberal view of the world based on vague cultural concepts. Tom, of course, had had teenage, and now adult, children to influence him. Pete and Anne had been unable to have children. Maybe that made the difference. Nonetheless, as he matured he became stronger, more certain. As Tom matured, he seemed to go in the opposite direction. He was prepared to concede that sometimes they could both be right. Different views could both be true because the context was important.

Tom's view was that context was everything. Pete was not prepared to go quite that far.

'Why not?' Tom wanted to know. 'What makes sense out of context?'

That seemed like an easy one to Pete.

'Absolute truths.'

To Tom's riposte that there was no such thing, Pete pointed out that that was a statement he couldn't make. Why not? Because it was a statement of absolute truth. Trying to get away from this potentially circular argument, Pete stated his view that there were such things as absolute truths. The sanctity of human life for a start ('a principle, not a truth' according to Tom); God is love ('You believe that, but you could be wrong'); Jesus saves (same response); killing is wrong.

'Back to your first example,' said Tom, 'but better put. Who says it's wrong?'

'All the major religions, civilised society, moral codes; everybody.'

'In all circumstances?'

'Of course.'

'Really? In wartime? If someone's attacking Anne with a knife?'

Pete sighed.

'Okay. It's an absolute truth except in certain circumstances.'

'So it's relative.'

'I think it's time I made that tea. You make my head spin sometimes, Tom. It's all so complicated.'

'But we are complicated, Pete.'

Pete was having none of that.

'I'm not. I'm a simple man, Tom. I know what I believe. I have my calling. I just get on with it.'

'What you mean is you choose not to think too much.'

'How do you make that out? I do my Bible study, I write sermons, prepare study notes. I can't do that without thinking.'

Tom disagreed. 'Do you think outside the box?' he wanted to know. 'Try to get out of the box even? Challenge yourself?'

'Every time I write a sermon I'm challenged.'

To Tom's cynical reaction, Pete responded with some passion.

'I do a sermon on God's love and I'm reminded how little love I show; I do a sermon on prayer and I realise how little I pray; I do a sermon on forgiveness and I think of all the grudges I bear.'

'That's not being challenged, that's being demonised. No. Think about it. What do those three examples tell us? You don't show enough love; you don't pray enough; you don't forgive enough.'

That made Pete feel a bit of a failure, not what Tom had intended. In Tom's view, it simply made him a man who struggled to love himself. Who couldn't see his own good qualities. The two of them had been friends since childhood, and what did he see when he looked at Pete, after all these years? Apart from the grey hair? He saw someone loving, caring, and forgiving – a man of prayer. There was an objection from Pete.

'You said I couldn't love, earlier.'

'I said you were at a disadvantage. Not the same thing. And why are you at a disadvantage? Because you don't love yourself. Because you're too busy telling yourself that you're a horrible, miserable sinner when you could be seeing yourself as a reflection of God.'

This hit home. Pete maintained that he was trying – trying hard. Tom was not prepared to let him off the hook.

'It's not about trying, Pete. It's about accepting, building, allowing, forgiving.'

'Meaning?'

'Accepting who you are. What you are. Building on that. Allowing your natural talents to come through, your natural interests, your natural instincts.'

'And forgiving?'

'Forgiving your father for the weight of expectation. Forgiving yourself for not being your father.'

There was a pause before Pete asked the big question.

'And where does God come in?'

'Where do you think you got your talents and interests from? Isn't He interested in you as you are?'

'I don't know, Tom. I think He wants me to repent and be saved.'

'Perhaps,' said Tom, 'He wants you to repent of the sin of doing yourself down all the time. He wants you to give yourself permission to grow.'

Pete looked a little hurt. Tom ignored this and pressed home his point. What useful purpose did the Church serve? Shouldn't it be to enable faith, to broaden minds, encourage spiritual experience? To help people fulfil their potential? How could it do that when it had become a set of rules and regulations, creeds to which people must adhere, a bastion of religiosity? Pete fiddled with his bicycle clips, unconvinced.

Tom switched tack, asking if Pete believed in a miserable, vengeful, killjoy God? Of course Pete didn't. So why, wondered Tom, was he acting as if he did, saying he was a failure, couldn't measure up, was full of sin, and needed to repent?

'I'm saying that despite all that He still loves me and will forgive me.'

'It's very negative.'

'No it's not, it's very positive.'

'So why are you so miserable about it?'

At that point, the doorbell rang. Pete looked relieved, made for the door.

'I should get that.'

'Anne's there. You're avoiding the question.'

'It's probably Gill Brown for me. Sorry, Tom, I really need to see her.'

'Not right now you don't. You're allowed Pete time, you know.'

The doorbell rang again. Tom observed that if it was Gill Brown, she wasn't very patient. Pete affirmed that that would be a good assessment of her character. Anne called from the kitchen that she would get the door and could then be heard greeting Gill. There were indistinct murmurs of conversation. Anne was clearly trying to deal with the visitor. Pete looked resigned.

'She won't take no for an answer.'

Anne's head appeared round the door.

'She won't take no for an answer.'

'I just told Tom that.'

Tom suggested that there was a need to put in boundaries. No-one disagreed. Putting the principle into practice, it seemed, was more difficult.

'Sorry Pete, you know what she's like. She says she really needs to see you. I told her you had company, but she's in a state. She's also in the lounge; waiting for you.'

'It's okay. I was just telling Tom I'd need to break off. I'll go. Sorry Tom.'

Tom was in no hurry, and was perfectly happy to spend some time on his day off with Anne. They had some catching up to do.

*

Pete was both annoyed and relieved. His times with Tom were special, an opportunity to really be himself and to share his worries and concerns, but sometimes the theological arguments became a bit much. He always had the feeling that Tom would have an answer to any argument he could muster and it was exhausting.

On this occasion, it probably didn't help that he was painfully aware that Gill Brown was someone with whom he had been quite unable to put in any really meaningful boundaries. She called unannounced on a regular basis, refused or ignored all his suggestions of people better qualified to help her, and appeared constitutionally incapable of taking no for an answer. She had had a tough time with her family and with her health, she was struggling to cope, the list went on. He was sympathetic, empathic, he listened, but he knew he was doing her no favours. There were people available who could do all that as well as, or better than him. The church had a team of trained pastoral assistants, Gill's doctor had offered to refer her to a counsellor, various strategies had been suggested but no, it had to be Pete. And it had to be what he thought of as 'Pete on demand'. He needed to get tough, for her sake as well as his. This time he was going to do it. No more prevaricating. Taking a deep breath, he went into the lounge.

'Gill, what can I do for you?'

She burst into tears. Not a good start. He felt his resolve weaken. He was going to have to listen to this.

CHAPTER THREE

TOM AND ANNE

As Pete steamed out of the room looking relieved, Anne settled in a chair and watched him go before suggesting that Tom might have been giving him a hard time. To Tom's protestation of innocence, she pointed out that Pete had seemed glad of the excuse to leave the room. Just eager to minister to his parishioners was Tom's response, greeted with a laugh and the suggestion that Pete was not normally keen to minister to this particular parishioner. 'Difficult' would be an understatement, was Anne's view. Tom ventured a guess, a suggested profile. Gill Brown, he suggested, would be insistent, have tunnel vision, and be unwilling to talk to anyone except the vicar. She'd be Pete's fiercest critic but completely dependent on him.

Anne acknowledged it wasn't a bad character profile and challenged Tom to predict what would happen next.

'I predict he'll agree to see her again in, oh, two or three days' time. Say Monday afternoon.'

'And that's a bad thing?'

'Only in the sense that he isn't able to say no when he may need to.'

'You should know, Tom.'

'He can't be everywhere for everybody all the time. He can't rescue her, whatever her issues. She has to do some of the work.'

Anne's view was that Pete was incapable of stepping back, was driven to help, always trying to save people. She also felt that Pete was not alone in this. Tom pushed back; not a trap he, Tom, fell into.

'Really? What were you doing with him just then?'

'We were just chatting.'

'You were trying to save him from himself.'

'I'm a minister of religion. That's what we do.'

'Which kind of proves my point.'

This was the point at which the conversation changed. Anne wanted to know how Tom had been, and why he had not been to see them in weeks. Chatting to Pete over the phone, which was a regular occurrence, did not count. He could talk to her, any time, about anything.

'I know. We were close once.'

'We're close now, Tom.'

'Not in that way. I miss you, Anne, now that I'm on my own.'

'I'm still here, silly. I'm not going anywhere.'

Tom grimaced.

'You know what I mean.'

Anne got up, moved to the window.

'I'm ignoring what you mean. So we don't both regret it. We made our choices. You chose Liza, I chose Pete.'

'You don't ever think you chose the wrong man?'

'I chose the man to love and I love the man I chose. Don't complicate life, Tom. Be my wonderful brother-in-law. I love you that way.'

Tom pulled a face.

'And don't play with fire, Tom. It's Liza you're missing really. You know that.'

'I miss her like mad, but I can't help wondering what might have been. Don't you?'

Anne moved to stand in front of him, and studied him, before responding.

'Yes, I wonder, Tom, when Pete's too distracted to notice me, when there's no romance, when I feel taken for granted.'

For a moment there was something in the air, a sense of possibility. Then Anne broke away.

'And then I remember that Liza felt the same. You're no different from him.'

'Cut from the same cloth, two men of the cloth.'

'Exactly. And I still love him, okay. Still love you too. If you can remember you're my brother-in-law. If I can remember you're my brother-in-law. And I'm here for you, believe me.'

Tom knew that, acknowledged it as true, but pointed out that Anne had enough on her plate being there for Liza, and, as he put it, 'you're married to one turbulent priest, you don't need two.'

Anne's assessment was that Pete was not turbulent, just driven, a striver with a highly developed sense of his own inadequacy. Tom, on the other hand, was more of a troublemaker, even if his charm hid the fact. Tom's instincts, it seemed to her, were to say what he thought, and get away with it by taking a real interest in the other. Pete, on the other hand, was a natural rule follower who felt less, if any, need to challenge authority. Pete accepted the authority of the hierarchy, Tom didn't. Pete felt that boats were for steadying,

Tom felt they were for rocking. Pete had found the answers that he could live with, Tom was still searching. Poor Tom.

'No. Lucky Tom. Don't pity me. Pity people who've given up the search. Don't you see? The search is the point. If you're not searching, you're not really alive. Why does the Church fail? Because it's full of people who think they've found the answer.'

'And haven't they?'

'No! The answer's always round the corner. We're not meant to find it. If we did, we'd atrophy, vegetate, fossilise.'

'So what's the point in looking?'

'It's how we grow, mature, realise our potential. It's like sport. Look, you play tennis, right? Why? What's the point?'

'I enjoy it, it keeps me fit, nice crowd of people. And it's somewhere I can be me, not the vicar's wife.'

Tom leant forward, in his stride now.

'You didn't mention winning. And you're competitive; I know that, still got the bruises. So yes, you play to win, but that's not actually the point of playing. The point is to improve, to learn, to share and to enjoy yourself, right? Well, searching is the same. I'm searching for the truth, for the Divine, for that perfect intersection between philosophy, quantum physics, and the human soul. I make progress, improve my understanding. I enjoy the process, build my spiritual and intellectual muscles, share the journey with my friends. So searching's good. But there are no winners. What happens if I find the answer?'

'I thought there wasn't an answer.'

'Bear with me. If I believe I've found the answer, I stop looking. I get boring, rigid, unforgiving. I get judgemental. I think everyone who hasn't found the answer is in error. I probably tell them so. I think everyone who thinks they've found a different answer is in real trouble. I tell them so. I get arrogant. I upset people, damage people, impose burdens of guilt and shame on them. I divide families and friends. Some people think I'm right, a prophet, a guru, whatever. Some people think I'm an idiot, a charlatan. I started off searching for truth, and I end up creating hurt and conflict.'

Anne smiled. She loved his passion.

'A bit like the Church.'

'Exactly. Exactly like the Church.'

'So why do you stick with it?'

'Because the Church is also about the search. Because the search is beautiful, challenging, redemptive. Because it's a journey, and I like travelling companions. And because I can't leave the Church to the Pharisees. The Pharisees. The factions who think they have all the answers, who distrust all the other factions. You know. The people who try to overcome their own insecurities by insisting everybody else does it their way.'

Anne's observation was that the Church was full of people exactly like that. All the churches were. Exclusive Brethren refusing to eat with anyone else. Catholics insisting Anglican orders are absolutely null and utterly void. It was all arrogant claptrap, according to Tom. Anne found it had to disagree. It seemed to her that all the churches needed their 'Toms'.

'Nice of you to say so, but of course they do. Take the Catholic Church. It's full of wonderful, sensitive, caring people who are searching. What would I do if I was a Catholic priest? What I'm doing within the C of E I suppose, refuse to abandon the mother church and leave it to the Pharisees. Be a thorn in the side.'

'Pete looks up to you, you know. Defends you when people criticise you.'

'It's mutual, believe me. He's a fellow searcher. He's just too bogged down in pastoral issues to give it the time it needs.'

Pete's voice could be heard dimly from the next room, a low, sympathetic murmur below a higher pitched flow of sound. It seemed he was busy being bogged down even as they spoke. His job, as he saw it. Working all hours to meet an inexhaustible stream of demands from people who thought he had nothing else to do. Fitting meetings and sermon writing in among, somehow. Putting in an appearance domestically when he could. Anne's concern that he would exhaust himself was mixed up with her frustration and resentment at never seeing him, being bottom of the queue, and while his times with Tom were also a demand on time that could have been hers, she felt they were oases of sanity which he desperately needed. She just felt so angry for him sometimes; run ragged, no real thanks but lots of criticism, nobody seeming to notice what he did, but everybody noticing what he didn't do. Tom, as always was a sympathetic listener. He wanted to know how she felt. How she felt was squeezed out, angry. Guilty for feeling angry. And angry again for being in that position.

'Clergy marriages!'

'Tell me about it.'

'I'm sorry, Tom, that was insensitive.'

'No, it was real. I fell into all the traps. Everything you just listed.'

'In my diatribe?'

'It's all true though, isn't it? All the traps. And now I've got the perfect storm; Church in turmoil, bishop wanting decisions, Liza gone. Time to show what I'm made of.'

'Time to grow up.'

'I just said something similar to Pete. But I have grown up, Anne, matured, thought things through. That's part of the problem.'

'So now you get to show your maturity, use your wisdom, be the man you want to b. Show them all what you're like under pressure.'

A pause, the rain was subsiding and a shaft of sunlight lit the room. Anne spoke again.

'I spoke with Liza yesterday.'

Tom just looked at her, waiting.

'I think she misses you.' She paused. 'The grass wasn't greener.'

'It never is.'

'You try and remember that.'

'I will. I'm sorry.'

'Would you consider a reconciliation?'

'With you?'

'With Liza.'

Tom got up, walked across the room, and fiddled with some of the clutter on Pete's desk before responding, with a question.

'Is that what she asked you?'

No, Liza had not raised this. Anne was reading between the lines. Tom was the love of Liza's life even if she had temporarily lost sight of the fact. Tom was magnanimous. How could he not forgive her?

'It's what I do.'

Anne thought he was missing the point. She hadn't said Liza wanted forgiveness.

'She ran off with another man. How can we reconcile if I don't forgive?'

'If you forgive her, nothing changes, same old power structure; everything revolving around you.' Tom looked confused. 'Oh, Tom. Understanding is what she wants. What you need too. Maybe she's able to give you that now. What about you?' Tom gave a perplexed shake of the head and a look of raw pain. 'If you can't understand, how can you forgive?'

Tom felt on safer ground here.

'They're totally different concepts.' It was Anne's turn to look confused. 'Forgiveness comes from the heart, understanding from the head.'

'True understanding implies a degree of empathy, surely.'

'How can I empathise with her running off with another man?'

Anne snorted. 'You could try getting over your male pride and empathising with her position as a vicar's wife; like you just did with me. She was in the same position. You could see it in me. Why not in her?'

'That's different.'

'No it isn't. Come on, Tom. Liza hasn't stopped loving you. She just felt left out, ignored, taken for granted, and at the bottom of the pile. And yes, I know you love her, but how did you show it? By attending church meetings, ministers' fraternals, and, and, and governors' meetings. By studying and writing all hours of the day and night. By having an open-door policy for every waif and stray with a personal problem. By asking her to help out occasionally and getting the PCC secretary to give her a bunch of flowers at the annual meeting. No wonder she left.'

Tom looked chastened.

'But I've changed.'

'It's not good enough. Understand what I've just said, take it to heart, empathise. Make a connection between all that and your new-found ability to delegate. Ask her forgiveness.'

This felt like a bridge too far for Tom. Why should he ask forgiveness? He was the injured party. Anne was frustrated. How could he not see? It was a two-way street. His unavailability to Liza, his neglect of his marriage, was a key factor in what had happened so, yes, he had some need of forgiveness. And Liza needed to know he recognised that fact.

So, she concluded, 'If you ask her to forgive you, genuinely, sincerely, whatever the words are you use about confessing, same principle, if you can do that, then you'll have earned the right to forgive her.'

'I should have stuck to theology, it's easier.'

'You want to know what I think? This is theology, Tom. It's all about realising your God-given potential, being what you're called to be - and helping Liza to do the same.'

'Hoist with my own petard.'

'You can't go on about it as much as you do without applying it to yourself, Tom.'

'Touché.'

The lounge door could be heard opening. The voices got louder and more distinct, Pete's bright and reassuring.

'Well, I hope that's been helpful,' he was saying. 'We'll talk again on Monday.'

Tom nudged Anne. 'Told you.'

'Or just give me a call,' Pete continued.

Anne looked at Tom. 'Why does he say that?'

'Any time.'

'Pete, no,' muttered Anne.

'Bye now. Bye.'

The front door slammed shut. Pete entered, humming 'Assurance' and wanting to know what he'd missed. 'Marriage guidance' was Tom's answer. Pete's reaction was one of hope – 'It's not all over then?' Anne thought this was a bit negative. 'Why would it be?' she asked. 'Well, there was that other chap' was the slightly embarrassed response.

'Which Tom is man enough to get over.'

'Good. Forgive and forget?'

'It's a little more complex than that.'

'Still…' Pete shuffled some books. 'Good. I miss Liza.'

'Do you think I don't?'

'No. Course not. I just… Sorry, foot in mouth.'

'And you still see her anyway.'

'Yes, but not, you know, properly. Not with you.'

Anne was amused.

'I hope you're not like this with your parishioners.'

'No, just, you know, family… Did you make tea?'

'No, I didn't. Did you? No tea for Gill?'

She gave in to the inevitable, and went off to make three teas. Pete shrugged. Making tea for Gill would only encourage her and while he was unable to be as tough as he should be, he could at least withhold tea. Aware of his own weakness, he apologised to Tom – 'Insistent woman', he explained. Gill, not Anne. Tom suggested gently that perhaps Anne wasn't insistent enough. Pete looked up from the papers he was fiddling with at this.

'How do you mean?'

'She was just giving me a pretty clear picture of Liza's frustrations with me. It struck me there could be parallels.'

'There but for the grace of God?'

'Exactly. Liza was married to a husband who was focussed on his church, his flock, his sermons, his meeting commitments. Everyone thought they owned a piece of him, and she was at the end of the queue. Ring any bells?'

Pete groaned. He could see himself in the description more than Tom. And Tom was the one with the broken marriage. Could he learn from Tom's mistakes, he asked himself. He wasn't sure. He asked Tom. Tom wasn't sure either. Rather, he held himself up as an example to learn from. Pete was worried about Anne, whether she was likely to say 'enough' and walk out, as Liza had done.

Tom didn't help by commenting that she was an attractive woman (not to him, he hastened to add, or not in an active way, anyway) with a social circle of her own, so if she became frustrated 'beyond all endurance', then what? Pete felt frustration was not a problem. Tom responded that he wasn't talking about their sex life,. He was talking about time, attention, fun, talking, all the things Liza was starved of. Along comes someone who treats her as if she is the centre of the world, someone with no parish, no flock, no ridiculous expectations, - What would happen then?

Pete shifted in his chair, had a mental image of Anne packing her bags and leaving. decided it wouldn't happen, and didn't quite manage to convince himself. His particular insecurity had always been the residual feelings between Anne and Tom, not threats from elsewhere, and as time went on this insecurity, and the guilt that went with it, had receded. His main concern now was for Tom and Liza. He couldn't help but feel that everybody would be happier if they just got back together. He certainly would. Tom was dubious, regarding Anne's optimism as wishful thinking. Pete digested this.

'In the meantime, I'm in danger of failing in my marriage.'

'I didn't say that.'

'No, but it sounds like I need to try harder.'

'I think you need to try less, Pete. You try hard at everything. Chill out a bit and let the real Pete come through.'

Chilling out was a new concept to Pete. He was unsure what it actually meant. Tom tried to elucidate.

'Stop striving. What was that hymn you were humming as I came in?'

Pete thought, hummed a few bars, and searched his memory.

' 'Assurance'. 'Blessed Assurance'. Why?'

'Think about it. What do the words say? "Blessed assurance, Jesus is mine; Oh what a foretaste of glory divine". You believe that, right? Well you don't look very happy about it.'

Pete looked doubtful. 'You're not going to preach at me again are you?'

'Preach? No. All I'm saying is stop worrying and trying to work your way into heaven. Enjoy yourself a bit.'

Pete objected to this. He was not trying to work his way into heaven. He just had to help everybody else get to the same place. He felt responsible.

CHAPTER FOUR

RESPONSIBILITY

I've lost count of the hours I've spent doing what I was doing that day. Since I was a youngster. Standing at the bar of The Fleece, trying to catch the eye of a barman who seems more interested in chatting to the group of young women on their lunch hour than serving other customers. The Fleece is, I suppose, my local though, to be honest, I rarely visit. I've never really frequented pubs much, coming from a temperance background. My parents regarded them as evil personified. But I enjoy the odd pint, always have, and he keeps his beer well does Bob.

I suppose it was the younger generation's influence that got me dropping in for a pint a bit more often. My boy Tom was never out of the pub when he were a lad. Him and Pete, putting the world to rights, or arguing about what needed doing more like. Never known anything like those two for an argument. Still at it even now, when they should know better. Well, I'm a fine one to talk.

Any road, I managed to catch the barman's eye, ordered two pints of bitter, the Tetley's, and some crisps, felt some mild irritation when the young lad had to enter everything laboriously in the computerised till, and waited for the top-up once the beer had settled. Then I went back to the corner table where Fred Ogden was sitting. I had to have a moan of course.

'I could've told him how much I owed before he'd finished pouring. Why do they need to rely on those daft machines?'

Fred grinned. 'Grumpy old man.'

'Well, 'appen I am, but really! Slows down the whole process. If he learned some mental arithmetic he'd have more time to chat up those birds.'

' 'Appen you should tell 'im.'

'I don't suppose it's down to him. It's anti-fraud, fancy stock control. World's gone mad.'

I've known Fred vaguely most of my life, but we found ourselves spending more time together when the boys palled up, and when they left home and got married we started meeting for a regular catch-up. We played a lot of golf, but Fred's legs aren't what they were so we play less now, and only a few holes when we do. We have the odd curry and, more often, an evening in the local. It's not bad, The Fleece, still a proper pub, despite the computerised tills. And that's another thing that drives me round the bend, bar staff who can't add up – have to key everything in, after serving you the drinks. They can't even do it as they go along for some reason; slows them down. As I said to Fred, I know how much it's going to be before they've finishing pulling the pints. It's hardly rocket science. Why can't they do it?

Anyway, the pub. They've renovated, of course, but there's no stripped pine, or white leather sofas. It's not become a restaurant in disguise, and you can feel comfortable here even if you're over 25 and not obsessed with the footie, as you can tell when you look round you. There's plenty of familiar faces of all ages.

On this occasion, once we'd settled the ills of the world, disagreed about Europe, the government of the day, and Yorkshire's chances at the county championship, talk inevitably turned to Tom and Pete, their families and their careers. It always did, to be fair. Fred worries about Pete and Anne's childlessness ('Not my business of course, might be their decision, but still.'). I worry about Tom's proclivity for controversy and Liza's unsuitability as a vicar's wife. Not that I'm knocking her, you know. I love her to bits, but it must make it difficult – for both of them. Both of us have always been mildly amused that we're 'sort of related'. Fred delights in getting people to ask us to explain exactly how. 'Go on, Don,' he'll say, 'You tell 'em.'

'Our boys married sisters, you know,' I'll say, 'so I'm his daughter-in-law's sister's father-in-law. With me so far?'

'And I reckon,' Fred will put in, 'that that's a relationship by marriage so we're stepbrothers-in-law.'

'No, I think you'll find we're brothers-in-law by marriage.'

'I think you'll find,' someone might chip in at this point, 'that you two could pick a fight over anything.'

'Much like your boys,' someone else will add and the argument finishes with laughter and more beer.

The day I'm thinking about though, the concern was about Tom and Liza's marriage. I was very upset at the break-up, Fred hardly less so. Liza is a charmer, I've always said so, a bobby-dazzler. She's sweetness and light. I know not everyone sees her that way, but I'm finding it hard to see her now as the guilty party in the break-up, almost harder than if it had been Tom. Fred's comment that nobody had a monopoly of guilt helped a bit, but only a bit. You have to understand, for me marriage is a lifetime commitment and adultery is a sin.

If Tom's been guilty of being a bit distracted, or even self-obsessed, that doesn't weigh in the scales very much.

We tossed these ideas around a bit as we sank our pints. Fred's background was a bit different, so he could take a broader view. I can't deny that helped. We were approaching the bottom of the glass when Fred asked if it would really have been easier to blame Tom. Tom had always been the golden-headed boy, the son destined to succeed, in Fred's view. The drinking, womanising and skirmishes with the law over sit-ins and demos had only added a touch of glamour, while Pete trailed in his shadow. Fred felt both relieved and envious. A touch of glamour was always welcome, if a little dangerous, and Liza had only added to that. There was no denying that Anne was a great daughter-in-law, but she didn't quite add the danger that Liza added. He supposed he was grateful for that, but he was not sure.

I wasn't sure how to take this, so I reminded Fred whose round it was. It gave me time to think. Fred picked up the empty glasses and headed for the bar. He didn't trust the newfangled way of serving beer in newly washed glasses, it only made it flat. He preferred his second pint in the same glass and had a debate with the barman whenever he bought anything other than the first drink. This time he won and returned triumphant with two pints of bitter.

'They don't seem to do mild any more,' he said as he sat down.

'What?'

'Look at those pumps. Three bitters, two pale ales, Guinness, cider, four lagers, but no mild.'

'And the lagers all taste the same.'

'Aye, they taste of nowt. In my day it was one bitter, one mild, Guinness and maybe a lager. Don't know why it's gone out of fashion.'

'Well that's easy. It's gone out of fashion because they spend all their money advertising lager. It's easier to make money out of. They nearly killed bitter too, you know. And mild was always a minority taste.'

'They used to say they put all the rubbish in it. Still…'

We both took a pull at our beer; the second one as good as the first. Fred wanted to know what I thought of what he'd said. I wasn't sure. Tom and Pete seemed two sides of a coin, complementary, to me. They helped define each other. Maybe Tom was more charismatic, though I'm not sure that's a good thing. And, yes, Anne was maybe a bit steadier than Liza, less volatile, but as to whether that was less 'dangerous' as he put it, I didn't know. I think probably not, now. They're a pair, those two, that's for sure. Know their own minds. Very similar, but very different. You see the similarities when they're together; family get-togethers, that sort of thing. When they're apart it's easy to focus on the differences.

With Tom and Pete it's different. They're so different that it's easy to forget what they've got in common. Which I was hoping would see Tom through this particular crisis. That and Anne's support, although I've not forgotten how smitten Tom was with Anne in the early days. My wife tells me to worry less, but I'm not sure I really worry more than she does. She's a bit less doe-eyed about her daughter-in-law, I suppose.

*

Back in Betcham, Tom was arguing that Pete, despite all his instincts, was not responsible for everybody else. They were each responsible for themselves, their own health, their own security, their own salvation. And they might each take a different route to those ends; even salvation. Different routes to salvation – a concept Pete found difficult. Not everyone finds salvation through the Church was Tom's view. Not everyone finds salvation, was Pete's. More than you'd think, was the response, but Tom's list of other ways of finding salvation caused a raised eyebrow. These included searching, praying, meditating, caring, giving, sharing, music, nature, and reading. It was a long list.

A long list, but were they Church substitutes? All ways to God. On their own? Tom's view, clearly not shared by Pete, was that the Church was not a way to God on its own either. Pete saw a clear differentiator. The Church had the truth. Which church and which truth, Tom wanted to know – the Anglican? The Catholic? The Baptist? The Methodist? There were essential shared elements but was this enough? And the synagogue, the temple, the mosque all had shared truths too.

It was while they were arguing about the nature of truth, and the claims of the major religions, that Tom came to the crux of what was really bugging him. Pete had just accused him of sounding more Buddhist than seemed appropriate for an Anglican priest, when Tom took an envelope from his pocket. It seemed that that was an accusation that had been made by others. It was okay for Pete to accuse him of almost anything, their relationship was based on the cut and thrust of open debate and disagreement, but for others to use his views to undermine him, that was a different matter altogether. Pete took the proffered letter and started to read.

' "Dear Tom, we feel compelled to write…" Oh dear, never a good start…' He scanned down – ' "We the undersigned…" Never a good finish.'

'My personal team of critics. Look what they have to say. Read it.'

Pete scanned down… ' "Unbiblical… Scant regard for tradition… Lack of focus on the need for forgiveness; lack of emphasis on the redeeming power of repentance". No lack of lacks apparently.'

'A lack of any sense.'

Pete read on, finished the letter, looked up at Tom with some concern, and went back to the letter.

'Not comfortable reading.'

'Why am I wasting my time on these people? No, don't tell me. Because I feel called to. Actually, I feel called to punch one or two of them on the nose right now. I know, not very Christian, but I wore myself out for these people, I sacrificed my marriage to hear their problems, I pray for their ills, marry their children, bury their aged parents; and what thanks do I get? A knife in the back. They've written to the bishop for Pete's sake. I'm just doing my job, following my conscience. What am I supposed to do?'

'Maybe respect tradition a bit more.'

Tom snorted. 'Tradition!'

'What's wrong with tradition?'

'Nothing, provided it's not used to justify anything. Oh don't look like that, Pete. You know what I mean – "We've been beating our wives for three hundred years, so it would be wrong to stop now". The last refuge of the idiot and the charlatan!'

Pete, who loved his traditions, chose to ignore this. Instead, he suggested that maybe Tom could be less confusing. Tom himself looked confused at this.

'These people,' Pete explained, 'are trying to hang on to their certainties and here are you telling them to let go.'

Tom looked agitated. 'It's my job to help them on their spiritual journey, not to preach stuff I don't believe.'

'It's your job to teach the 39 Articles. You're an Anglican priest.'

'Stuff the 39 Articles. This is more important than antiquated dogma.'

It was Pete's turn to be upset. He was talking about the foundations on which the Anglican Church was built. Tom, on the other hand, felt he was talking about his life, and everything he'd worked for. Pete accused him of being melodramatic. Tom disagreed.

'I've carried these people, Pete, almost physically. I've put them first. I've shared my love, my insights, my knowledge.'

'Your doubts.'

There was no dissent from Tom.

'Maybe that's the problem.'

Tom did not take kindly to this.

'Problem?' he exploded. 'What are they, toddlers that they can't cope with doubts!'

'Maybe they are. Maybe they don't need your doubts.'

'I would be no good as a priest without my doubts, Pete.'

'You may be no good with them. Have you thought of that? We all have our blind spots. Maybe mine's blind faith. Maybe yours is the lack of it. You intellectualise everything, worry at it till there's nothing left. Everything's relative, everything's a maybe. Every point of view is valid. People don't know what to think. You're a leader, Tom. For Christ's sake, lead.'

There was a shocked pause. Tom seemed to freeze in mid pace. Pete swallowed hard. He'd gone too far. The two men looked at each other, appalled. At that moment, Anne walked in, looked round and wanted to know what was going on. Pete tried to apologise. Tom called him 'Judas'. Pete apologised again. Anne was still confused. What had Pete done? What had he said? Tom looked at her bitterly.

'My wife deserted me; my congregation deserted me. Now Pete.'

Pete leapt to his own defence.

'All I meant was that your doubts may have had a demoralising effect.'

Tom exploded again.

'Demoralising! Doubt's essential. How can we test what we believe if we never doubt it? How can we grow?'

Anne was unsure how to answer this question – which didn't matter because Tom had his answer ready.

'We can't, that's the truth. Without doubt we stay locked in a sixteenth century time warp, small-minded, straitjacketed, rule-bound.'

Anne relaxed.

'Oh, I see, you're not getting it all your own way.' Tom looked affronted but she carried on. 'That's what this is all about. Typical bloody man. A bit of criticism and you want to take your ball home. You have to be the leader, Tom. Very upset at the merest hint of mutiny.'

Pete pointed out that Tom had just been saying how mature he was, to which Anne countered that modesty had never been his strong point. Tom listened to his friends dissecting him before reminding them that he was in the room.

'Yes,' was Anne's rejoinder, 'with your friends. Friends who will tell it like it is. Yes, and support you too, before you ask, but with our eyes wide open. You know the problem? No, I'll tell you. You're talented, clever, a leader, but you're also impatient, a little arrogant, and you expect people to fall in line with your new ideas. But they can't. We can't. We can't all keep up. What do you do all day? No, don't answer that, I know. You go to meetings, make visits, take services, advise, support, do admin, write sermons – all that. But all the time your mind's working away, isn't it? Gnawing away at the problem of faith and belief, worrying about metaphysical stuff, trying to make sense of doctrine and reality, conducting an ongoing dialogue, right?'

'Like everybody does, I guess.'

'No, not like everybody does. Most people have some inner dialogue going on while they get on with their lives, but it's about mundane things. Will they catch the train, what's for tea, will West Ham win on Saturday, that sort of thing. Or it's about work, the new boss, the awkward colleague, the tricky client, whatever. Yes, they might think about faith and stuff every now and then. If they're devout, or disciplined, they might make regular time for it. More likely they mumble the odd prayer and leave the rest to Sunday morning. They don't have time to mature, Tom. Not like you.'

This calmed the atmosphere down a bit but left Tom back in argumentative mode. Anyone could make time, if they wanted to, he argued. They have time to write to the bishop. 'Because they're desperately clinging to what they've always believed' was Anne's response. 'And you're stamping on their fingers. They think they're going to fall.'

'Fall? They'd soar.'

'Maybe, but clinging on is easier.'

Tom looked downcast. How could he challenge, lead, help, if this was the reaction he could expect from his parishioners? And no, it wasn't about criticism. He could take criticism ('Really?' from Anne). But now it was different. This time his job was on the line. This was news to the others. The bishop wanted a chat, he explained – that afternoon.

Anne looked up at that.

'Hence the histrionics? Calling Pete a Judas, collapsing in tears, all this wounded soldier stuff.'

'No. That's about lack of support. Lack of appreciation. Feeling deserted.'

'It's about your wife running off with another man.'

'That's a completely different issue.'

'Is it? That's a betrayal too, isn't it? And it robs you of all the support she used to give you. Oh Tom, open your eyes. What would you have done if you'd got this letter a year ago? You'd have talked it through with Liza, right? Thought so. And you can't do that now.'

'But I'm talking it through with you.'

Pete jumped in.

'You'd have done that as well. And you were in a better place then. Less defensive, more self-confident.'

'Yes, well. She's gone. Can't do much about that now.'

'Not true,' said Anne. 'Reach out to her. Stop being so bloody hurt and proud and reach out to her.'

'Why can't she reach out to me?'

'Don't you think she has? By talking to me?'

'No, I don't. She'd talk to you anyway. You're her sister.'

'But she clearly wanted to see if there was a way back. Why don't you give it some thought?'

Tom agreed to think about it. In the meantime, he had the morning services to look forward to. Perhaps fortunately he was not down to preach, but he was due to take the service, and Communion. That got Pete's sympathy.

'So you're facing the bishop today and your critics tomorrow? Come to lunch after,. You might need some moral support, and we can talk again then.

'Thank you. Yes. I need time to think, to regroup.'

'Shall we pray before you go?'

They bowed their heads as Pete led them.

'Oh Lord, we just ask you that you watch over your servant Tom. Bless him as he seeks to serve the truth, to divine the truth and to support his church and parish. Give him peace as he is criticised for saying what he thinks, give him wisdom as he works out what to do, and make him aware of our love for him and of your love for him. Amen.'

There were hugs all round, Tom already focussing on what the bishop might say. He left them looking at each other in some relief. As his footsteps receded they both sighed, stepped together, and embraced; a familiar, comforting, homecoming hug. Pete was the first to break the silence.

'Thank God I've still got you. I do still have you, don't I? By some miracle? What? What's wrong?'

'I shouldn't need to tell you.'

'Sorry, but you do. I'm a thick, insensitive man. I need help through this stuff.'

' "Thick, insensitive man"! You're not thick and insensitive when Gill comes round, are you? Oh no. You're all compassion and understanding. You're not thick and insensitive when some woman in the congregation's lost her husband, some couple's lost their baby, somebody's lost their job. You're all sympathy and understanding when someone's ill, or depressed, or worried sick about their kids. Not thick and insensitive then are you? Are you, Pete?'

Pete looked uncomfortable.

'No. In fact the only time you are thick and insensitive is when it comes to me. Then you can do thick and insensitive. Why is that do you think?'

'You're going to have to help me.'

Anne snorted. 'Our life in microcosm!'

Pete was struggling, wishing that life was simpler. His conviction was that Liza left Tom because she found someone else. Anne was more interested in why Liza had been open to finding someone else. Because there was mutual attraction and she gave in to temptation was not, apparently, a sufficient answer. The fault appeared to be Tom's, in Anne's view. Pete struggled with this. Tom, apparently, was insufficiently interested in Liza, despite adoring her. He had a very funny way of showing interest, always out, never available when he was in, always busy with somebody else's problems, always tired. Anne seemed to think that should ring some bells.

The light began to dawn. She wasn't only talking about Tom and Liza. He wished she wouldn't do that; talk about one thing when apparently talking about something else altogether. And she was important to him; how could she not be? Anne seemed to require proof, a demonstration of importance of some sort. Pete still needed help on that one. He tried her patience just a little more by admitting this.

'For goodness' sake, Pete! Promote me to the top of the queue for a change. Show me the old Pete, the one I married.

The man who wanted to spend time with me, who made me feel important, who had energy. Now I get what's left after everyone else has sucked you dry.'

'Have you any idea of the demands on me? Do you know how many people are out there saying I don't do enough? I don't need it at home as well.'

'Your choice, Pete. Happy congregation or stay married. Which do you want?'

'If I have to even make that choice, I've failed.'

'If you learn to delegate you don't need to fail.'

Pete sat down heavily. He found delegation appealing as a concept, but frightening in practice. He was far from sure that he could really delegate. She was asking him to be something alien to his nature. Not for the first time, he tried to explain this to her. Anne's response was not encouraging. It was something along the lines of there being a choice between delegation, sharing the load, having time for his marriage on the one hand and being on his own on the other. If he had been frightened before, he was terrified now. How would he cope?

'No problem,' was the response. 'You could hire someone to do all the cooking and cleaning. Nice and easy. No emotional demands.'

Pete's response that they already had someone to do the cleaning was a mistake (A couple of hours a week. Do you really think that's all there is?) as was his claim that he 'did his bit'. (You wash up. Let's not even get started on who pulls their weight round here. Just be thankful I'm a primary teacher.)

This started a whole new line of discussion. Pete had never considered Anne's job as a particular blessing, but it seemed that a staffroom of women and a general lack of attractive, available men was a differentiator between Anne and Liza.

'Think about it,' said Anne. 'In her job she meets attractive, available men. So when she's really had it up to here with Tom, when she despairs of ever getting any of his time or attention, and someone says "Why not come out for a drink?" she thinks *Wow, someone noticed me!* and she goes. And maybe there's no harm in it. But if someone keeps on listening to her and acting like she's important… well, she's not getting that at home. It's probably not all she's not getting at home either.'

'You mean sex.'

'Yes, sex. But not just sex. Attention. Interest. Sharing. Doing things together. Which is where we came in.'

Pete threw his hands up. He was trying. He really was. He was facing so many demands. And he was very tired.

That was a more contentious statement than he had intended. Anne pointed out, strongly, that after 40 years of women's lib she had a responsible job, did virtually all the housework, and her husband was still the one who was tired.

'And we're still together. That's the miracle. And yes, I know, there's no escape from the job. But you won't put up defences. No day off. No, listen, I know you have one in theory, but what happens? You publicise the day off and then ignore it as soon as there's a cry for help. It can't go on, Pete. It's very close to being your job or your marriage.'

Pete did not feel he could make that choice, which Anne felt was, in fact, making a choice – the wrong one. And she was not mollified by his assertion that Tom would have been as bad, she already knew that. And it wasn't Tom's time and attention she was competing for. It was Pete's.

Feeling like he was drowning, Pete tried again. He pointed out how much he loved her, how she was everything to him. He told her she knew the truth of what he was saying. She exploded again.

'Do I? How? Because I'm always right there on your 'to-do' list. Easy to spot – right at the bottom, after everything else; spend time with Anne. Well I've had enough. I want attention, support, love.'

Pete tried to rescue the situation by promising they would spend time together that week; make a new start. Anne suggested Monday, after school. Pete couldn't do that, he was seeing Gill.

'Bloody Gill. That's fine, Pete. She's clearly more important than I am. I hope you're very happy together.'

Anne headed for the door, fighting back the tears. Pete tried to stop her. She resisted.

'Just think about it, Pete – very carefully.'

Pete was left staring at the slammed door, unsure of what to do, or how to respond.

CHAPTER FIVE

RECONCILIATION

Sunday morning after church was normally a peaceful time. Not today. Pete was feeling irritable. His space had been invaded, his books were all over the place, and a barrage of instructions were coming from Anne. They were tidying up. His protestations fell on deaf ears. This might be his inner sanctum, his personal empire, where he did his thinking, his praying, his work, but since the rest of the house had been colonised by Sunday school equipment, they had to use what space was left. Pete felt this argument was exaggerated. 'Colonised' was a bit strong, it wasn't the whole house, and it was only for a while. And it was playgroup equipment, not Sunday school. And yes, he would concede, it was Sunday school equipment in the spare room; playgroup in the lounge. But, and this was the important point, he would never be able to find anything now. Yes, of course he could normally find things. References, books he needed, visual aids; he had a system.

He admitted that he rarely used visual aids, but that was hardly the point. The point was that his working life was dependent on this still space which was now being systematically destroyed. He acknowledged Anne's counter that her space was non-existent, crowded out by playgroup and Sunday school equipment but, in truth, was not convinced of her need for space. She had space at work – in the staffroom. Well, on the way to work maybe.

And did they really need to have pre-lunch drinks in here? Why not the lounge? They could use the playgroup equipment as tables. Well, the dining room then. No room because they'd be extending the dining table. Really? Why? Because this was a special lunch and important. And did they really need a suitcase by the door just where it would trip him up? Yes, they did. It was a visual aid. A reminder that suitcases could be packed, people could move on, things could change. A warning? If that's how he chose to see it. Look at Tom, was the underlying message. No, Tom would not spot the suitcase, and what if he did? Pete was apparently more bothered about what Tom thought than about how Anne felt – about what anybody thought. At which point the doorbell rang, signalling Tom's arrival.

The first thing he noticed was the suitcase, prompting an inappropriate joke about Anne getting ready to run away with him. At another time, that might have gone down better. The second thing he noticed was the room. He suggested getting professional help if they were intending to decorate and was amused to hear that Pete was, in Anne's words, 'graciously allowing us to use this space'. If we can find it, was his response.

Pete was drawn into defending his territory again, explaining how he knew where everything was, how he referred to all these books constantly. Tom proceeded to hamper proceedings by picking up books at random and teasing Pete about their relevance. *The search for unity – A challenge for the 1990s* (Still relevant, according to Pete). *Our Archbishop* (Rowan's a very interesting man; 'Yes, but this is about George Carey'). Pete broke free by offering drinks.

Tom declined the traditional pre-lunch sherry in favour of a beer. His morning, it seemed, demanded nothing less. Pete was halfway to the kitchen before Anne reminded him she would like a drink as well. Pete knew that, he responded, a glass of white. Tom and Anne exchanged glances; Anne unsure as to whether that counted as being taken for granted or touching anticipation of her needs. Tom gave her a shrewd look.

'Do I detect a touch of tension?'

'I reminded Pete that I existed, that's all.'

'Not well received?'

'He's scared, poor love. Can't quite see the way ahead. He's finding it tough.'

'But not as tough as coming home to find you gone.'

'Exactly. Which could happen yet, if he's not careful – if we're not careful. That was tactless. Sorry.'

Tom reassured her there was no need to be sorry. He should have seen it coming, spotted the packed suitcase. The whole thing was a mess of his own making, and a wake-up call for his friends maybe – the ones he had left. The atmosphere in church that morning had been a little on the chilly side. Anne wanted to park that subject until Pete returned and to explain something about the suitcase, but at that moment Pete backed through the door, juggling with a beer and two glasses of wine. Anne rushed to hold the door.

'Pete! Why don't you use a tray?'

'This is easier.'

'Yes, it looks it. Let me help.'

She relieved him of two of the drinks, gave Tom his beer, and raised her glass.

'There. Cheers.'

'Cheers.'

'So, Tom, we're agog. What happened? How did it go?'

'Give him a chance to drink his beer, Anne. He might not want to share.'

'Shut up, Pete. Of course he does.'

Tom took a pull at the beer, grinned and spoke.

'If you two can stop bickering for a minute, I'll bring you up to date. Church was interesting; quite a mix. Half the congregation don't know anything's going on, the other half are all ears and eyes. And as for the plotters, well Bert Smith told me straight out he thought I ought to go. Not one to mince his words; honest at least.'

'You're too soft. What did you say to him?'

'I thanked him for his honesty. He looked a bit taken aback; I think he was expecting a fight. The others were all different. Jim Jenkins shook my hand but couldn't look me in the eye; Iris Murgatroyd slipped past while I was talking to somebody else, and the rest weren't there. Terry Johns saw something was up and asked me outright; another plain speaker – a rather more sympathetic one – but I'm afraid I fobbed him off rather.'

Pete looked up.

'Perhaps you need to be more open.'

'I don't want to cause a rift.'

'It's already there. You're just pretending it isn't.'

'How Anglican of me.'

Pete suggested preaching about it, but Tom felt that was tantamount to attacking members of the congregation from the pulpit, not that he used the pulpit any longer.

Pete argued that he wouldn't be attacking them, he'd be addressing the issues they themselves had raised. No need to make it personal, he said, just set out your stall, review the other points of view, challenge the congregation. Be explicit – and detailed. Tom felt that would get him into all sorts of trouble. More than he was already in? Maybe. But, in answer to their questions, what he really wanted, what was important to him right now, was what?

'Well, I want to share my faith, share my journey. I know that sounds a bit trite, but it's how I see it. I want to engage in constructive dialogue, get people talking and exploring, take the blinkers off. ... and... I want to get Liza back. Most of all, I want to get Liza back.'

Anne asked why.

'Why? Because I love her. Because I screwed up and blamed her. Because we should be doing all this together. And yes, I know, people break up – all the time. I know, I've seen plenty. And sometimes it's for the best. But sometimes you just know they're making a huge mistake. And we're in the second category. She's my soulmate. We will regret it the rest of our lives if we part now.'

'So why not call her? It's not a difficult concept, Tom. You take the phone and dial the number.'

'Easy for you to say, Anne. But what would I say?'

'I don't know. Sorry? Come home? I love you? It's up to you.'

Tom appeared unsure that he'd still have a home if his congregation had anything to do with it. Pete was more sanguine, pointing out how difficult it was for a PCC to remove an incumbent, always assuming that there was a majority in the first place. Not for the first time, Pete was taking Tom too literally. Tom's point was that the situation was uncomfortable, rather than that he would actually be out of a job and a home. Pete did, however, verbalise thoughts that had been running through Tom's head for weeks which were thoughts of escape. Maybe Tom wanted out. He had been in the job for years. He was frustrated, and a bit burnt out. He had ideas to share and felt constrained. If he moved on, he could write the book, lecture, and lead retreats. There was, however, another complication; the bishop.

Unlike some of his parishioners, the bishop was a supporter. He liked Tom's clear-thinking, his willingness to put himself in the firing line and valued his abilities as an organiser, a motivator and a thinker. To the bishop, Tom was an asset who could be put to wider use, especially if he wasn't hampered by a traditionalist congregation. The bishop looked at Tom's responsibilities and saw much good work at St Peter's, aside from the theological controversies. He also saw what a strong, positive influence Tom was at St Aidan's. He knew Jonny and Jancy Nower, and they spoke enthusiastically about the way he had galvanised their small congregation. His instinct, therefore, was to find him a larger role, one in which he could inspire, support, challenge and motivate. There was a role for a new archdeacon, and he wanted Tom to fill it.

Reactions to this news varied. Pete saw it as an obvious way out, taking the bishop's line that this would be a good way of using Tom's talents while removing him from a difficult situation. Anne was more nuanced in her reaction, seeing pros and cons, but also feeling he should consult Liza. Tom was unsure which way to jump but wanted to make the decision before talking to Liza – get the baggage out of the way first, clear the decks. That would be a big mistake, was

Anne's reaction. The last thing Liza would want was to be presented with a fait accompli. Pete reminded Tom that he was a man of the cloth, with a calling. What did he think God would want him to do?

Tom grimaced at this.

'When I was a young man I had a sense of calling. It was very easy. But now… Now I no longer see things in black and white.'

'You mean you knew what God wanted from you and now you don't?'

'Now I distrust people who are sure what God wants. It tends to be an excuse for doing what they wanted to do anyway. And it's arrogant. Who am I to say what God wants?'

'But you do feel a calling. That's how it looks to me. You feel called to explore faith, the link with the Divine, truth. You're passionate about this stuff. That's a calling isn't it?'

Tom drained his beer before answering this one. Yes, it was a calling, but he could explore faith, the link with the Divine, all that, in any number of ways; as a vicar, as an archdeacon, or outside the Church hierarchy altogether. In fact, he would have more time for thinking, writing and sharing as a freelance writer; fewer constraints. The same books would be open to him, the same people would be ready to talk, he would even be able to contribute to church life as a visitor or stand-in. The only things missing would be money, accommodation, food. The Church paid him and he lived in a vicarage.

Pete suggested that the accommodation problem could be resolved by a move to Yorkshire. Tom and Liza had bought a bolthole in the Dales a few years before and the position, just outside Pateley Bridge, was ideal for a thinker and writer.

It was, of course, some distance from Liza and her art studio, and some distance from the children and Tom's own support network. He was less helpful on the money front, which was when Tom remembered Jonny's offer. It involved some kind of salary for doing a range of things which, if he recalled correctly, included writing. Clearly he would need a proper conversation with Jonny, but he felt sure they could make something work.

Anne listened to all this and suggested his next step was to talk not to Jonny but to Liza. Tom felt he needed to think things through before calling Liza; be clear what he was going to do. Back to the 'fait accompli' – Anne was exasperated.

'You've learnt nothing, have you? If you want her back, you need to involve her in the planning, don't you think? It does impact her. You've got an ideal opportunity to plan your future together. Don't squander it – talk to her.'

Tom agreed, a bit reluctantly, to call Liza first; in fact, to call her that same evening. No need, was the reply, she's here. And like a magician pulling a rabbit out of a hat, Anne produced Liza, who had been waiting in the lounge.

There was a stunned, and slightly awkward, silence. Pete tried to indicate to Tom that this was Anne's idea, not his; Anne was trying to edge Pete out of the room. Tom and Liza looked at each other slightly awkwardly. Pete broke the silence.

'More beer, Tom?'

Anne latched on to this idea.

'We'll go and get it.'

And she bustled Pete out of the room, leaving Tom and Liza alone. They moved together, a little awkwardly, embraced, separated. Tom was the first to speak.

'God, it's good to see you.'

'You too.'

They sat, a little apart, leaning forward from time to time to clasp hands. It felt a little like a very awkward first date with someone you were very keen on – for both of them. There was a lot of catching up to do. How much did Liza know of what had been going on? Quite a lot, it seemed. Anne had kept her up to date. Tom felt he had messed things up. He apologised. There was a lot of apologising. Could they start again? Liza was unsure.

'When I went off, I thought it would all be different, romantic, no hassles, no arguments, no playing second fiddle to the PCC. It wasn't like that at all, Tom. I just missed you.'

So far so good. But, she went on to say, she couldn't live the way they did. Tom was quick to deal with that one.

'You don't need to. I need to make changes, I know.'

'But will you make them?'

There was no doubting Tom's wish to make changes. Even Liza saw that. She was also painfully aware that he was struggling to work out what those changes should be, not in general, that was clear enough, but the specifics. The question running through her mind was simple enough too. How much should she help him, how much did he need to work it out for himself? Right now, Tom was saying they needed to make changes together but seemed unable to share his decision-making with her. She moved closer to him, looked into his eyes, saw the trouble there, and tried to help.

'What happened to that loving man who always put me first, us first? That's what I need to see.'

'I'm still here. You've always been top of my list.'

'After the PCC, the bishop, the staff team, and any and every waif and stray who came calling.'

'You were top of my personal list. The rest came with the job; I had no choice.'

Liza felt the old irritation growing.

'Don't give me that crap, Tom. You made a choice every day. Every time the men's group came calling, or the youth fellowship, or the Mothers' sodding Union – or anyone else come to that. There was me, back of the bloody queue as usual. It's not good enough.'

Tom reached for a lifeline.

'Well, there's good news there; the bishop wants to promote me – archdeacon, away from all that parish stuff.'

To his surprise, Liza was unimpressed – unimpressed and unenthusiastic. She regarded a move to the archidiaconate as a retrograde step. Tom struggled to understand why.

'Why? Because it's a more senior job with even more potential to feed your ego and your workaholism. Because you'd just get a better class of waif and stray. Because it's the same job as you've been doing all these years but with a better skirt.'

'It's a cassock. And it's my job, Liza. It's what I do.'

Not enough. Liza moved away, presented him with a choice. Start putting her first – their marriage first – or stick with the committees, the fellowships, the Church hierarchy and maybe she'd send him a card at Christmas.

'It's them or me, Tom.'

Tom's face was a picture. She wanted to hug him but stayed clear. Could they find a way through this? For his part, Tom was just confused. He thought she wanted to start over. She said she did. But her terms seemed unreasonable. Well, maybe not unreasonable, but unreal, impractical. Liza reassured him, in part. Yes, she wanted to start over, but not to repeat the same mistakes. She was pleading now, pleading with him not to screw it up. She came to Pete and Anne's feeling sorry, contrite. She had hurt him. She was angry. Then she was confused. Then she was sorry. But now he was starting to wind her up again, and she was beginning to be sorry she came.

From all this, Tom gleaned a nugget.

'So you're ready to try again?'

'That's what today was all about.'

'Thank God.'

'Don't thank him yet, you're not out of the woods. And I'm not coming back to an archdeacon.'

Tom was near tears now.

'I want you back so much.'

'So use your brain, Tom. Get your act together.'

As they clung to each other, she whispered, 'I want you back too, you know.'

Apologies followed. Tom apologised for neglecting her, neglecting them, about expecting her to be happy about the archdeacon offer. Liza almost apologised for walking out, for Bob, but not quite. It was Tom's moment to reflect. Almost thinking aloud, he mentioned Pete's suggestion that he should give it all up, write the book, lead the odd retreat. It was, he admitted, an attractive idea. Liza's response was encouraging.

'So think about it. Think about us; the book and us, the retreats and us. Then we can talk again. Do some planning, and decide if we have a future.'

Tom was emphatic. They did have a future.

'So show me. Convince me. In the meantime, we have a drink with Pete and Anne. We have lunch. We talk again.

Look, Tom, I've made mistakes too, but now, my suitcase is ready. I'm ready. Are you?'

'Whatever it takes.'

'Well then. Come here.'

This time the embrace was a little less tentative, and felt a little more like coming home, held a little more promise. When they parted, Liza mopped the corner of her eye with a tissue before setting off to see where the others had got to with the drinks.

Tom collapsed into Pete's chair, swivelled round to face the window and let out a sigh. He was conscious of feeling more tentative than he might have hoped, despite the reunion having gone well, so far. Where did they go from here? His thoughts were interrupted by the arrival of the others with a tray of drinks. Pete was full of enthusiasm.

'Great news. Great news,' he kept saying.

Liza tried to bring him back to earth. Not great news yet, was the message. We're still working on it – keep praying. Tom wanted to thank Anne and Pete for spending the time to make this happen. Anne deflected, pointing out that it was a family matter and therefore her responsibility to do what she could and adding, a little tartly, that Pete had plenty of time because he now had a day off each week – in theory, unless Gill Brown came running, or someone else. Anyone else actually. But all this was going to change. Wasn't it?

Pete was hesitant. It felt a bit like rubbing salt in the wound to say they were trying to avoid making the same mistakes as Tom and Liza, but that was what it amounted to. And the positive for him was the possibility that their struggles could help him not to lose Anne, if they could overcome the disagreements, the difficulties. He still felt that the vicarage lounge was an entirely appropriate place to store playgroup equipment, that when a parishioner called he should automatically be available and that his 'calling' meant putting himself low on the priority list. He knew that Anne disagreed strongly on all these issues, that putting himself last also meant putting her last in some way, and that these were going to be difficult issues to resolve. Even his attempts to articulate this to Tom and Liza felt fraught with danger. At any moment, he felt, he might say the wrong thing and enrage Anne. Liza rescued him by talking about a process and about fences taking time to mend.

Pete assured them he was working on it.

'We,' interposed Anne. 'We are working on it. We'll get there when Pete learns to say no, and to delegate when he has to say yes. Wouldn't you say that was the secret, Tom?'

Tom did agree, and added that a little more support from the archdeacon would help, always assuming they got the right man for the job. There was some debate about who that might be, with Liza very clear about who it should not be. Pete moved the discussion on, from what felt like tricky ground, by adding that he also needed to be clearer about what Anne wanted. This was a mistake. Anne felt it was very clear what she wanted, even to Pete. Liza suggested they were, as she put it, 'all emotioned out', and that they had reached the point where another glass of wine might go down better than more talk.

Anne moved into action mode. There were vegetables to finish off, there was wine to pour; that was her and Pete, in that order, despite Pete's offer to do both. Pete's lack of kitchen skills were legendary. As Anne put it, he was the only one in the house she would not allow near the cooking. He was, on the other hand, a dab hand at washing up and clearing, running the whole process like a military operation. Tom's offer to help was gratefully received, and Pete and Liza were left alone in the study. Pete was very happy to have some time to talk with Liza and wasted no time in seeking her advice.

The question, as Pete saw it, was simple. The answer less so since it involved keeping Anne happy and everybody else; the church family, the PCC, the wardens, the bishop, everybody. Speaking from experience, Liza summed up the answer in one word; prioritise. Easy for her to say, thought Pete. Liza was having none of that.

'I've lived through this, Pete. It's a parallel. Do you think it was easy, deciding, leaving, thinking about coming back?'

'You are going to get back together though?'

'It might not work, Pete. I don't know. Will he change or just piss me off again? Sorry. It's a risk.'

So, not easy, any part of it, but worth trying. And no, she did not think it was too late. Pete was seriously rattled by the fact that Anne had a suitcase packed and ready. Liza laughed. It was her suitcase, she was staying over. Anne was relying on him not recognising their own suitcases to make a point about how easy it would be to pack up and go.

'Except you said it wasn't easy.'

'The problem is, love, that she won't really know how difficult it is until she's on the way out of the door.'

Pete started moving piles of books back to their original positions, while Liza watched him, amused. Creating chaos out of order was the phrase she challenged him with.

'So I need to change?'

'No. You both need to change. Just you changing won't make any difference. The issue is how you operate together.

Listen Pete, Tom had to realise that I needed to forgive him just as much as he needed to forgive me, right? Hear me out. It's always a two-way street is what I'm saying. You can't treat Anne as more important than all the other stuff in your life unless she lets you. She has to change as well. You have to do it together. That way you can get through this.'

'So there's hope.'

'There's always hope. You know that. Just stop being a pillock. Put this room back together. Fight for your marriage. It's not too late. Trust me. I wouldn't lie to you. I love you Pete, you know that, and Anne, obviously. I'm here for you. Now, I'm going to check up on my husband and your wife. See you in a minute.'

Left to himself, Pete was able to focus on putting his study back together again. This pile of books on a chair, this one on the desk, crucial notes and 'Post-its' where he could see them. It looked like chaos to the untrained eye, but he knew exactly where everything was, and needed everything to be in place. He hummed as he worked – the tune, 'Assurance', the words to which were running through his head. *Blessed Assurance, Jesus is mine; Oh what a foretaste of glory divine; Heir of salvation, purchase of God; Born of his Spirit, washed in his blood.* And the chorus, which always aroused such strong emotions in him, making him switch from humming to song. *This is my story, this is my song; praising my Saviour all the day long.* And repeat. He was just starting on the second verse when Liza came back to call him through for lunch.

*

While Liza was supporting Pete, Anne and Tom were chatting over the meal preparation. Tom was at the sink, washing knives and pans, while Anne put the finishing touches to the meal. Anne was naturally curious about what progress Tom and Liza had made, and Tom confessed that he feared he might have blown his chances of reconciliation by assuming Liza would be pleased with the archdeacon option. Clearly she wasn't, and he felt it had sounded like a fait accompli. He now knew he should have listened to Anne, who had correctly predicted this. In fact, Tom was feeling that he had never paid Anne enough attention. Anne was keen to deflect this.

'Don't start that again.'

'Well, I messed up, didn't I? Big time.'

'In neglecting your marriage, yes.'

'Not what I meant.'

'I know what you meant, and no, you didn't. We both ended up with the people who were right for us.'

At this, Tom turned from the sink and asked the question which was on his mind – what if he and Anne were right for each other all along? Anne felt he was just confused. Confused and scared, was his response. He looked forlorn. Anne put her arms round him.

'It'll be all right.'

They held each other. At that moment Liza walked in, took in the scene, and asked, a little too brightly, whether lunch was ready.

CHAPTER SIX

REALITY

Anne put the phone down in despair. She'd had four calls that morning and all unsatisfactory. First, her head teacher had rung, which was unusual for a weekend. Problems in the staffroom were coming to a head, and she wanted to talk through some options with Anne – none of them were appealing. Next, one of the churchwardens had rung with some issue for Pete which he insisted on explaining in great detail, despite Anne's repeated promise to get Pete to call him. Then Pete himself had called to say he was going to be later than expected returning home because he was dealing with a domestic crisis somewhere in the parish. It was his day off – switching it to a Saturday had been a hard-fought battle. They were supposed to be driving to the coast for a relaxing walk along the shore and a meal, but the chances of this were receding as fast as Anne's patience. This was the third week in a row that he had fouled up their time together.

While Anne was talking to Pete on the landline, Liza rang on the mobile, so Anne went straight from hearing Pete's excuses to listening to Liza moan about Tom. According to Liza the chances of a proper reconciliation were dwindling.

'It's over,' she had said. 'I do believe it's over.'

And no, Anne couldn't help; she needed to wallow in her own grief. Anne saw this as Liza in full diva mode, and her irritation competed for the upper hand with her upset. And Liza, understandably, had no time to listen to what she regarded as Anne's minor moans.

Anne headed for the kettle. Coffee was what she needed. Except, in this case, it failed to soothe her. The routine of filling the cafetière, waiting, depressing the plunger and pouring simply made her impatient, and the coffee tasted bitter on her tongue. The seascapes on the lounge wall only reminded her of how circumscribed her life had become. She felt hemmed in.

She tried hoovering. Maybe physical activity would help. It didn't. She toyed with the idea of going to the tennis club but there was a tournament on. A tournament she had not entered because it would clash with Pete's day off. Pete rang. He had to go and meet someone in Guildford. He was sorry, but he would see her that evening. Anne was sorry they no longer had a phone with a cradle she could literally slam it down on. She rang Tom.

Tom was also struggling. He was in the throes of disentangling himself from the Church and had not expected it to be so painful. At St Peter's, his critics were still carping, while the rest of the congregation just seemed puzzled. There was an endless round of goodbyes, explanations, and handovers and very little constructive work. At St Aidan's there was a general feeling of regret. He remained popular there, well thought of, and valued. He was sorry to be leaving. And at home, there was housing to think of. They were okay in the vicarage for a while and had enough put by for a deposit, largely from the sale of Liza's work, but there were decisions to be made. At the same time, just when he needed support from Liza, she was absent. Not physically – physically she was very much there – but emotionally. She had a tendency to dismiss the antagonisms at St Peter's, the sorrow at St Aidan's, and Tom's own mixed emotions, as details which carried no weight. Tom should be happy. He had come to a crossroads and chosen the right route, made a decision he should have made years ago, got his life back, and got his wife back. Why regret anything? Be pleased, was her attitude. Be pleased and come to bed.

Tom was not pleased though – or not yet. He needed to grieve the life he was leaving, to process the animosities at St Peter's, to reassure the flock at St Aidan's. And those needs were stronger, more pressing, than the positives at this moment. The results were constant miscommunication, misunderstandings, arguments, and doubts about whether either of them had in fact made the right decision. Matters had come to a head the previous evening when Liza had told him, somewhat sharply, to stop wallowing and 'get a grip'. He had accused her of not caring. She had accused him of being self-centred. He had pointed out that it was Liza who had been self-centred enough to seek a relationship outside their marriage. She reminded him that he had driven her to it. Ignoring the traditional advice not to let the sun go down on their anger, they had each seethed through the night and carried on arguing through the morning. Liza had called Anne to let off steam, but Anne was insufficiently sympathetic, and Tom was still there when the call ended, looking hurt, angry and ready to pick another fight. Liza could take no more.

'I need a break from this,' she announced. 'I'm off to Goring, to spend some time with someone who really loves me.'

'Run off to Mummy then,' responded Tom. 'You're never too old.'

'Don't expect me back in a hurry.'

And she was off. Tom made himself coffee; didn't drink it. He fiddled around on his laptop, picked up a book, put it down again. The phone rang. It was Anne – in tears. Not something he was equipped to resist. It seemed she had had enough of Pete, nothing was working for her. She needed a shoulder to cry on. Tom did not hesitate to offer his.

'Liza's stormed off,' he said. 'Left me, I think. Gone to your mother's.'

'I'm sorry, Tom.'

'It's all going pear-shaped, isn't it? Where shall we meet?'

'I need to get out of here. Shall I come to yours?'

'I'll put the kettle on.'

'Haven't you got anything stronger?'

'I'll see what I can do.'

The call over, Anne went into the downstairs cloakroom, saw a puffy, tear-stained face and decide remedial work was called for. She headed upstairs to wash and change, squirted a little perfume behind her ears and set off. Tom meanwhile set to tidying up the debris of breakfast, making the place presentable, calming down, plumping cushions, finding the corkscrew.

Somewhere near Horsham it dawned on Liza that she might have overreacted. Maybe she had been a little insensitive? They were both on edge, unsure of each other, the old certainties gone. She considered turning back, struggled to make a decision. By the time she had decided it would be a sensible thing to do she was at the Findon roundabout, much nearer Goring than Molebridge. It would feel wrong not to see her mother now. Maybe she could just spend a few hours there, an overnight stay perhaps. Tom had been insensitive too. Let him sweat.

Pete was happily engaged in a deep discussion with the vicar of St Saviour's, unaware of how unhappy his wife was. He had a vague feeling that he needed to make it up to her, but it was his day off he was sacrificing, not hers, and this was a key meeting.

It was a 20-minute drive from Anne's house to Tom's. Anne was so eager to escape that, despite washing and changing, she made it in 35. Tom was texting Liza when she arrived – Have you taken Rothy? I can't find him. As he headed for the door, the reply came – 'My dog is with me.' So that's how things stood. He opened the door.

'Anne! Come in.'

Anne came in; to the house and to his arms.

'Thank God you were here, Tom. I'm so miserable.'

'Don't. It's okay.'

They stood there a while, just holding each other, before Tom suggested they sit down.

'Do you want something to eat? Drink?'

'A large glass of white wine please. That's what I'd like.'

'Coming up.'

Anne collapsed on to the sofa, kicked her shoes off, and closed her eyes. Tom reappeared bearing two glasses of wine, handed her one, and looked at her as she took it.

'You are beautiful, you know.'

'Thank you, and you're a dream, but that's not why I'm here. We had that chance. And blew it.'

'We had some good times though. So, what's going on?'

Nothing was going on – that was the problem. Anne's life had become a round of school, marking, TV and sleep.

She had a lonely life with an absent or obsessed husband. Pete's lack of awareness only exacerbated an already fraught situation. She felt unloved, unappreciated, neglected and trapped in a pointless marriage. This took a few minutes to relate. Tom spent less time reporting that his marriage appeared to be over. Anne wanted more detail. Tom reported on last night's row and the morning's reprise, Liza's exit, and her response regarding the dog.

'She's taken the dog?'

'Yes.'

'God, she does mean it.'

'Exactly.'

They had more wine, talked about old times. Tom sat at the other end of the sofa and absent-mindedly caressed her feet. He reassured her that she was loved, not least by him. His hand moved to her calf.

'If you're going to do that, Tom Raistrick, I won't be responsible for my actions.'

He jumped.

'God, sorry. I didn't mean to.'

'I didn't say stop. I need some physical contact right now.'

The caressing resumed. They continued talking and finished the bottle. His finger traced her calf muscle to her knee. She moved her other foot into his lap. He shifted slightly so his other hand could reach her hair, as she bent to kiss him.

'We shouldn't be doing this,' he murmured, undoing her blouse.

'No,' her fingers went to his belt, 'we shouldn't.' But they did; tenderly, passionately, enthusiastically, expressing the pent-up desires of 30 years, remembering familiar bodies.

Afterwards they lay semi-naked on the sofa and dozed.

Anne came to first, looked around her and groaned. Tom's trousers were draped over the armchair, her knickers on the table, and a stray sock by the fireplace. She freed her arm from Tom's weight and stood. She seemed to be half wearing her blouse but that was all. Tom lay there quite naked. She found a blanket and draped it over him, gathered her clothes and headed for the bathroom. Looking in the mirror at her flushed face, she was reminded of the first time she had slept with Tom, all those years ago. She had retreated to the bathroom then too, but her feelings then had been excitement, satisfaction, and contentment. Now she was more concerned with propriety, betrayal and consequences. Life had seemed much simpler at 19. She washed, dressed, touched up her make-up, and headed for the kitchen and the kettle. Tom was on the phone. She could hear his voice rumbling in the background but could not make out the words. She took tea through to the lounge. Tom raised his finger to his lips and mouthed 'Liza'. Anne retreated to the kitchen.

Liza had arrived at her mother's house in a confused state; unsure of herself, unsure of her actions, and needing to get her head clear. One positive was that she knew her mum would listen and help clarify without judging; Mary had had years of experience. Over coffee and a walk along the seafront, Liza poured her heart out, explained her frustrations, her longings and her guilt. She had not previously discussed her affair with Mary, and it was perhaps significant that she had never taken Bob to Goring. Now she tried to explain what had led to the break-up and to the reconciliation, and explore her feelings about it in the process. Mary felt that Liza maybe could look at the areas of unfinished business between herself and Tom. Had she gone back to him without any real change?

'He's giving up the Church, Mum. That's quite a change!'

'Yes, but it's still in the process. There are bound to be strains until it's done. Are you being patient with each other?'

Liza looked out at the grey waves breaking over the groynes and remembered walking along the seafront with Anne and Tom all those years ago, when Tom had been off limits as Anne's boyfriend. That had felt very complicated, but seemed straightforward compared to their current relationship. Maybe she had been hasty. She decided to ring Tom and try to put things right – again. In the meantime, Mary wanted to talk about Anne and Pete. She had been picking up signs of unhappiness on her weekly phone calls with Anne. The dutiful daughter, thought Liza, conscientious, every week. Liza was able to fill her in on this, on Anne's particular experience of what she thought of as vicar's wife syndrome. Mary was not convinced that the experience was limited to vicars' wives. Living with any obsessive, any addictive personality, was difficult in her view. The only difference for a vicar was the number of people who thought they had unfettered rights to his time. Or her time nowadays, she supposed.

So, did she see Tom and Pete as addictive or obsessive? Obsessive, in both cases, was the answer. Maybe Pete was a bit more of a workaholic than Tom, but they both became quickly immersed in whatever they were doing. Manage your expectations of this change in Tom's life was one of the messages coming across. He was quite capable of burying himself in his books. What was worrying Mary more was the lack of interests shared by Pete and Anne, what they did on their days off. Liza laughed.

'I think Pete works on his day off. That's part of the problem.'

'Exactly. And you?'

'We tramp the countryside with Rothy – used to anyway. Read. Listen to music. Go to the theatre.'

'So, there's something to build on then.'

'Yes Mum, you're right. And we can involve Anne and Pete too sometimes. We used to have great times, the four of us, until… well, until quite recently really.'

Liza was not aware of precisely how Pete and Anne, specifically Anne, were spending this day off and would have been mortified to know that, when she spoke to Tom over the phone a little later, he was standing naked in their lounge while Anne brought him tea. Nor was she aware of the struggle for Tom to respond to her peace-making overtures, though she did detect more of a reserve in his answers than she would have expected. Nonetheless, she came off the phone having agreed that she would return the following day, and they would seek to repair the damage. Not as satisfactory as she could have hoped, but she supposed it was a start.

Back in Molebridge, Tom put the phone down and grimaced. Now what? Anne suggested the first thing to do was put some trousers on, then he could update her.

'It's very off-putting, you wandering around with nothing on.'

Tom collected his clothes, putting them on as he talked. He was in turmoil. He had thought Liza gone for good, and now it seemed he was wrong, but what had he, they, done? Messed up. Made a mistake. Complicated everything. Hurt Liza and Pete. Idiot!

Anne was not impressed by his gallantry. So, she was a big mistake was she? A poor substitute about to be cast aside? No, not a poor substitute, was the reply. Tom could only think of one woman in the whole world who he would put ahead of Anne; Liza. That, for Anne, was rather the point. But she did see that this was not a tenable situation. Pete and Liza must never know what had happened. They had found comfort in each other at a low ebb, but it must be their secret. What the other two did not know could not hurt them. She needed to get back before Pete got home, and Tom needed to make sure there was no evidence of her being there – dispose of the wine bottle, wash the mugs and glasses.

'God, I'm sorry, this was all my fault.'

'Don't be daft. We're both to blame. And we should both know better. Now, make sure you tidy well. Just plant a decorous kiss on the cheek as I go out, in case the neighbours are watching. Love you.'

'Me too. I don't want to lose you Anne.'

'Back to where we were. Close but friends?'

'If we can.'

'We don't have a choice. Not if we're to keep our marriages.'

And she was gone.

She made it home half an hour before Pete, who arrived full of news of his day, his meetings, and his ideas. The advantage of being married to an obsessive, she thought, he notices nothing. Though, come to think of it, that was also what had driven her into Tom's arms in the first place.

Tom, whose arms were now empty, spent the evening thinking, reliving, regretting. Maybe if he hadn't opened the wine? Maybe if he had been more patient with Liza earlier? He could still sense Anne there with him, a pleasant sensation, but at what cost? He was tempted to head for Goring but felt he might be more ready to face Liza when he had had a night's sleep. Also, the reconciliation scene might be better played out without Mary as an audience, much as he loved her. Trying to take his mind off it, he dipped into various books, tried a range of music from Dylan to Coltrane, and made himself a complicated supper before settling down in front of an old film on the TV; Bruce Willis in *Die Hard*, running barefoot through glass, which was not dissimilar to the way Tom felt. Eventually he took himself off to bed, where he slept better than he had expected and woke to what he felt was going to be a tricky Sunday.

He was on duty that morning, taking Communion at 8 o'clock and leading the 10.30, not preaching, thankfully. Only a few more weeks of regular vicarly duties and then he would be free. That also meant only a few more weeks of living in the vicarage of course, although it had been made clear to him that he wouldn't be expected to vacate with unseemly speed. By the time he got home it was after 12. Liza had enjoyed a leisurely breakfast in Goring and had walked the dog as far as Ferring before returning home, but even so she had just beaten him to it, so the first thing he was aware of on his return was the enthusiastic greeting from Rothko who, it seemed, had really missed him. He spent some time making a fuss of the dog until Liza spoke from the kitchen doorway.

'I've missed you too, you know.'

'Yes, sorry. Me too.'

They hugged and both started apologising at once. Liza put her hand on his lips.

'Let's have coffee and talk. Kettle's on.'

A few minutes later, they were installed in the lounge with a cafetière, mugs and chocolate. Liza insisted on speaking first. She had been thinking about their rows, about what had been said, about the resentments. Her conclusion was that they were both hurting and both needed time. But, and this was important, their marriage was worth fighting for, their relationship was worth fighting for. She remained convinced that Tom was her soulmate and would fight tooth and claw to make things work.

'Wow, you're fierce this morning.'

'Tom, I'm serious. I know you think you've made the decision I wanted and I should be happy, but it takes time, you know.'

Tom did know. He agreed they needed to give each other time, not rush their fences. They did have to talk about some practicalities though; where they were going to live for one thing. Liza sensed that he was avoiding emotion but was unsure why. Was he just hurt? He seemed uncomfortable, kept scratching his left ear, a sure sign of tension. Tom assured her he was okay, but did not entirely alleviate her suspicion that there was something he was not telling her. To Tom's relief, she decided this was not the time to pursue it, and let the matter drop. He hardly dared hope that meant he was off the hook, but it was looking that way. Liza had moved on. She had been thinking, and knew what she wanted now. She wanted a proper discussion of their new arrangements. Yes, including housing, but also how he envisaged spending his time, and where; how that would fit with her work; how much time they would spend together. She wanted more time with Tom, or more uninterrupted time anyway, but also space. She did need her space. And Tom?

Tom was on safer ground now, could agree with what Liza was saying, could even see a way ahead that might work. If only he and Anne could keep their secret. On practical matters, he had identified that their savings would suffice for a deposit, provided they were not too demanding in their space requirements, and his new salary, together with her earnings, would mean they could get a mortgage. He suggested that they consider moving away from Molebridge to somewhere slightly less expensive. Liza leapt on this. They could move back to the coast. She had always yearned for the sea, and the light would be good for her painting. They settled on somewhere in the Ferring/East Preston area. Somewhere with an outbuilding, or room for one, that could serve as a studio for Liza. They would start looking straight away. Trouble averted, they celebrated surviving this latest crisis with a takeaway and a romantic film.

PART FOUR

CHAPTER ONE

CHANGE

Pete

Three reasons why change is difficult. One, you have to adjust; two, the old ways were comfortable; and three, it's very difficult to remember how you're supposed to behave. I've changed, but then I haven't. I've made myself a checklist of new behaviours to help. These are:

1. before offering to do something stop and think about the ramifications
2. think about the impact on Anne
3. keep the vicarage as 'our' space – within reason
4. observe my day off
5. help around the house
6. try not to think of it as 'helping'. Remember, Anne works too
7. delegate more church work
8. try not to get upset and take over when the delegatees (is that a word?) get it wrong, or do it differently
9. ask for support when needed.

I don't do all this really, but I'm trying. Anne is being very understanding about it, which is helpful. Tom and Liza have been a bit distant which makes number 9 more difficult. It would have been good to have had Tom as the archdeacon; the new guy is not to my taste, and the rural dean is struggling as much as I am.

Tom seems to be back around a bit more now, but we seem to meet on neutral territory most of the time which takes more organising – another change. It's odd, he used to be so close to Anne. Liza is keeping her distance. I suppose she's busy with her art. I miss her.

I miss my arguments with Tom as well. I've got nobody to bounce things off. Tom has gone all mystic. He seems to regard all the old theological stuff as irrelevant. I'm feeling a bit lonely, to be honest.

Anne

What an idiot. Me, I mean. I'm a soft touch for Tom Raistrick – always have been. And after all those years of distrusting Liza, based on teenage betrayals, it turns out that I'm the one you shouldn't leave alone with your husband. Okay, that's a little harsh. I'm just the one who can't be left alone with Tom Raistrick. A bit of comfort, some tenderness and before you know it the years have rolled away and we're getting hot and steamy on the sofa. He's my brother-in-law for God's sake; Pete's best friend. And I love my husband. I chose between them. I chose Pete. Now it's all a mess. I'm convinced Liza knows, but she's not saying anything. She's barely speaking to me actually, that's why I think she knows, you can't normally shut her up. Tom's hiding away in Yorkshire, so we can't deal with the aftermath like grown-ups. And Pete, he's the only one who has no idea. Poor Pete. He's trying so hard to make this marriage work, and has no idea that I've been undermining it.

It was a close escape though. Looking back, it feels like I was that close to doing something really stupid; running off with Tom. It wouldn't have solved anything, just created a whole new world of pain and recrimination. Fortunately, I held back, tried to recover some balance. Now I'm in a bit of a strange place. In limbo, I suppose. There's a bit of a barrier between Pete and me, all of my own doing. Tom avoids me. Liza is distant. I'm feeling a bit lonely, to be honest.

Liza

What an idiot, Tom, thinking I can't work out what's been going on – Anne too. A pair of prize idiots. I am not stupid. I can smell my sister's perfume, recognise that 'cat's got the cream' smirk. Yes, and that guilty look; pleased with himself and deeply ashamed all at the same time. And Anne's avoiding me. Well, that's probably the sensible thing to do. Bitch. Husband stealer. I should never have trusted either of them. I'm bloody incandescent – still. I'm not sure how long that feeling will last. You should see the vivid, angry reds in my work these last few months. It looks good actually. A silver lining, I guess.

Tom's hiding too – in Yorkshire. Nidderdale for Christ's sake. The middle of nowhere. Oh, it's very scenic, friendly people, and all that, but it's miles away. It takes forever to drive. I've been up a couple of times, but it's his space really and such a pain to get to – which he knows. This is not how it was supposed to be; good start at the reconciliation. Tom's switch to writing promised a more balanced life, more time for us. And getting away from the church? My bloody chains fell off. Then we had a couple of hiccups, a bit of rowing about Bob, some territory disputes and he runs off to Anne, his first bloody love. Not sure how we're going to make this work, but we've got to – somehow. Some bloody how.

Truth is, I love him. I did my running off and realised what a bad idea it was; the attractive other. It seemed like a good idea at the time. Actually, it was monumentally stupid. Bob and I got on fine, but really he was just a friend. Oh, I don't mean there was no sex. There was, if I'm honest, and it was fine, but he wasn't Tom. We didn't fit, spark, whatever. I guess my worry now is that Tom didn't go for the beautiful other. I could probably have coped with that, and known he'd come back. But no, he went for the familiar, for the woman he loved before me, lived with before me; my sister. God, I hate, love, hate her. What a bloody mess. The thing is, this is when we're supposed to grow, right? In times of pain. It just feels like marinating in shit. I mean, what now?

Is that it? One moment? Or do I have to watch them like a bloody hawk for the rest of my life? Right now, I'm waiting – which is not my strong point – waiting for Tom to sort himself out, talking when I can, and steering clear of Anne. I can't handle that at the moment. It means missing Pete too. Poor Pete, I bet he has no idea. I need to act – throw something, stir the pot, something – because this can't go on. We're all bloody miserable. It's stupid.

Jonny

Tom seems to think he needs some balance for this project of his, this backstory, the complicated relationships of Pete, Tom, and the Stewart sisters. He asked me to commit my thoughts to paper. What do you think? Right man for the job? I've been Tom's confidant. It's unfair on the others, rather, but Tom is insistent, persuasive, as Anne apparently found.

Thing is, I think the others are already providing the balance, jotting down memories, scribbling away. I'm not sure what that says about trust, assuming I'm correct, but they know he's writing his version of events and they are just a little worried about how they'll come out of it. Anyway, we've reached a difficult stage. There are four strong characters, with interconnected loves and loyalties. They all seemed settled – four people as happy as Larry – but it's a bit different now; abuses of trust, betrayals. They're painful subjects.

The way I see it, they've reached a crossroads. Tom has chosen his route – away from the church; ironic as I seem to be moving in the opposite direction. Liza seems to have chosen hers – to stick with Tom. Rebuild. Then, just as the lights change, the engine stalls and there's a contretemps of some sort. Words are exchanged. Tom runs off to Anne. Anne happens to be a bit pissed off with Pete – not sure why precisely, but no doubt he's tricky to live with. They end up… well, no need to spell it out. So now Pete and Anne are stuck as well. Pete's doing what he does best; ignoring reality and looking after his waifs and strays. Anne? I'm not sure, just kicking herself I think.

So, where do I come in? Father confessor? To Tom I suppose. A trusted friend to Liza, but she's not saying much.

My relationship with the other two is much less intense, which is probably for the best. I'll do what I can, of course. I think Tom and Liza belong, you know. They need to bury the hatchet, put it behind them. And given they've already forgiven each other for the past, it can't be that much of a stretch to get past this. Of course, the sister thing is tricky. Bob got excised; never seen, never spoken of. They can't do that with Anne.

Often wondered why bad things happen to good people. A theological question, I suppose,. Which means it's incapable of a cogent answer; can't spreadsheet it. Now I wonder why sensible people do stupid things. Liza, Anne, Tom, Pete, four of the brightest people I know – all round I mean, they have emotional intelligence and what have you. But look at the mess they're in. All largely of their own making. Can't spreadsheet that either.

Jancy says I expect too much. Maybe so. Still, it'd be good to help, as opposed to whinging on the sidelines which seems to be my main occupation. I went up to Nidderdale for a couple of days with Tom. Lovely place,. An old farm cottage, in the middle of nowhere. You wake to the sound of sheep. There's a desk set up overlooking fields, with hills in the distance. Don't know how he gets any work done. I'd be staring out of the window, musing. Anyway, not much work was done while I was there; lots of walking though. We tramped the Nidderdale Way, some of it anyway, crossed the moors, lunched in Pateley Bridge, and talked, listened, and talked again. Sat down over a glass of wine and talked more, well into the night. Cracked open the malt. Talked even more. About all of Tom's concerns, aims, uncertainties; Anne, Liza, Pete, Liza again. The sun shines when she smiles, apparently.

There's not been much in the way of smiles of late though, so he's in the dark; miserable. I couldn't think of any solutions so just listened. I hope it helped. I came home knackered.

Mary Stewart

The tide was in, breakers washing on the pebbles, as Mary Stewart made her way along the path between Goring Greensward and the beach. It was a walk she had enjoyed for many years, with Brian and the girls, with Brian after the girls left, and now on her own or with friends. Today she was heading to the Sea Lane Café to meet her friend Liz for coffee and a chat, and looking forward to sharing her worries.

She had set off early to give herself some space to clear her head. She was concerned about her girls, and found the sea strangely reassuring. There was something permanent and, ironically, solid about it which put her worries in perspective. She had been worried for a while since Liza and Anne seemed to be hardly speaking and this had been going on for a few months. Now, as autumn started to give way to winter, she had the added anxiety of Christmas planning. She knew this was unimportant in the grand scheme of things but, since Brian had died, her Christmas visits to one or other of her daughters had become more and more important to her. The fact that they lived close together, and were married to such close friends, had the added benefit of meaning she could spend time with both of them, even with the complications of services to be taken at two or three churches. Now, communication seemed so limited that she was unsure of what was in store. Nor was she very clear as to the source of the problem since both were tight-lipped about it. How could she help if they were unwilling to acknowledge there was a problem?

She had tried calling Tom. Experience told her he was always happy to chat and tended to over, more than under, communication. Not on this occasion though, which worried her even more. She decided not to ring Pete. If Tom wasn't talking about it, Pete wouldn't either.

She stood by the little headland next to the café, feeling the wind cut through her, and absorbed in the sea and her thoughts until there was a voice behind her calling her name. Liz had arrived.

'Penny for them.'

'Once we're inside. You can give me the benefit of your wisdom.'

'That won't take long. You get a table, my turn to get the coffees. Want a cake?'

The housekeeping agreed, Mary settled into a table overlooking the sea. At weekends and holiday times this place was packed. Today it was only half full, and they had space to themselves and a choice of seating. Liz reappeared with coffee and cake.

'What's to do, Mary?'

'Oh, I don't know. It's the girls. There's something between them, and I don't know what. They won't tell. Even Tom's clammed up. I don't like it when they don't get on. They're usually as thick as thieves, the four of them.'

'Four?'

'Them and their husbands. What with them being childhood friends and everything.'

Liz was a good listener, only commenting when helpful, making few suggestions, and Mary started to feel calmer, even though she was no nearer an answer. Liz did ask what Anne and Liza normally quarrelled about.

'That's the thing. They don't normally quarrel. I mean, they did when they were teenagers, over boys mostly, but not in recent years. They even seemed to cope with switching partners when they married.'

'How do you mean?'

'Well, it was Tom and Anne to start with, you know, and when she brought him home you could see Liza was smitten, but she steered clear, and then somehow, at some point, Anne dropped Tom and Liza wasted no time. Then, of course, Anne took up with Pete, and they seemed to become inseparable; four against the world.'

'Sounds a bit intense. Could someone have stirred it up?'

'Maybe. Tom and Liza had a bit of trouble, parted for a while, but seem to be back together now. He's left the church, you know...'

The conversation turned to Liz's daughter who was moving house to be nearer her grandchildren. Liz was concerned that she would be leaving behind all her friends. No solutions were found, but both women felt better than when they arrived. One thing they both agreed on was that worrying about the children seems to last a lifetime.

Abi

Time to sort her dad out was how Abi justified her few days away from London, Jamie and work. In fact, she also needed a break, time to think. London could get oppressive at times, work was stressful, and Jamie seemed to have decided that marriage would be a good thing after all, just when her parents appeared to be demonstrating the opposite. She needed time to think, and talk. Talk with someone who wasn't Jamie.

Her confusion was, in part at least, down to a number of shifts in perspective. These included her parents and their new semi-separate existence, Jamie and his sudden interest in marriage, and her own feeling that it might be time to move out of London. Only a few months ago all three of these things would have seemed highly improbable. It had been Jamie who was anti marriage and her who was fixed on the London existence. She had always been pretty laid-back about the whole marriage thing. She agreed their commitment to each other was already there but was not unduly opposed to a public declaration, the party that went with it, and the terminology of husband and wife. Those of her friends who had married after living together for a while were divided on the impact of the change in status. Some said it made no difference, others that it did; in a good way. And the London thing was partly a matter of swallowing her pride and changing her mind gracefully. And work? Maybe she could work outside London, avoid the commute. Plenty to talk through with Tom in Nidderdale.

Of course, the other reason for being there was concern about her parents, who had reconciled but now seemed to be drifting apart. On this side of things she was making less headway. Tom seemed disinclined to talk about it, determined to pretend there was no problem, focussing on his writing.

'Abi darling,' he'd said one night over dinner, 'you don't need to worry about your mum and me. We're not going to drift apart. We love each other far too much. We're just entering another phase of life, that's all, where we're able to focus on our creativity separately. When we get together we're like newly-weds, I promise you, can't keep our hands...'

'No. No sex details, please. You're my parents.'

This was hissed over the table as they were sitting in Olley's, Pateley Bridge's Italian restaurant. It had bare brick walls, carefully selected art and a mirror which had the effect of making the small side bar seem much bigger than it was. There was a good buzz of background noise to cover their conversation, but Abi was always ready to be embarrassed by Tom's propensity to forget to lower his voice. The place was packed, as it tended to be, and everybody was focussed on their friends and the food, so her caution was probably unnecessary. Tom had been greeted like an old friend when they arrived, and Abi deduced that he had been making regular visits. He was always one to sniff out a good eating place.

She was more successful on her own issues. Tom listened well, interjected here and there, and helped her to get things straight in her mind. Had Jamie actually proposed, he wanted to know. No he hadn't, things didn't really work like that any longer, Abi thought. Tom was unconvinced.

'I know you've been together for a long time, but if he's talking about marriage as a desirable thing, he will propose, just as soon as he thinks you'll say yes. It's in his conditioning.'

'You don't make it sound very romantic.'

'I thought you were too modern for that sort of thing. Do you love him?'

'You know I do.'

'Well then.'

'What if it doesn't work out?'

'Then you split up. Which is what would happen anyway. But I think you'll work at it, and if you're committed long term, why not? I know you think I'm biased as a clergyman, but if you want to know what I really think, I think you're effectively married already in the eyes of God. You've made the commitment. The rest of it is about public statements, parties and secular laws.'

On moving out of London he was a little less helpful. He had never understood why anyone would want to live in London in the first place so, clearly, moving out was the sensible thing to do. He did reassure her about job changing though, and that was, in itself, very attractive.

The other subject exercising Abi's mind was the precise nature of the dispute between her dad and some of his church members. She hadn't paid much attention to this initially but, now that it had prompted his exit from the Church, she felt she needed to know more. She'd tried talking it through with Matt, who was normally more focussed on this side of life, but he was no help, so she had decided to ask Tom straight out. Tom's vague answer about mutual incompatibility did not satisfy her – 'sounds more like a relationship break-up' was her comment. Well, Tom explained, that was precisely what it was, the end of a lifelong relationship. The Church, in his view, was no longer able to accommodate his beliefs and ideas. Why not? Because of a slavish adherence to the Bible, a literalness, a tendency to shrink God. The irony was that those of his parishioners who had disagreed with him felt that he was moving too far from God. In fact, he felt the opposite to be true. Abi needed more explanation.

'Well, think about like this. If there is a God, a divine being, as the Church teaches, omnipotent, omniscient, omnipresent, all that. If he, she, it exists then he's so much more than anything we can imagine, okay? So much more than our minds can comprehend or our language can express. So the moment we start to talk about God we are distorting the picture, because we don't have the capability of doing anything else. And the more we talk in terms of human characteristics, the more we diminish him. I'm doing it now. God isn't him, or her, or even it. Just God. So what do we do? We talk about God being angry, pleased, loving, jealous, or needing worship. Every one of those things is a human thing – the God we talk about is more like a benevolent dictator than anything else. And we ask him to intercede on our behalf – with illness, the weather, wars – like some kind of celestial policeman. And we know that others are busy asking him for the opposite – rain for the crops against sun for the garden party, victory for their side in a war. None of it makes sense. And it can't.'

'So you don't believe in God any more?'

'That's one route to go down, but not for me. I believe in God, something divine, something we can reach out to, but not something we can limit – a mystery, approachable through meditation, quiet prayer, good living. Something outside us and something within.'

'Sounds Buddhist.'

'It's a tradition in all the main religions; mystic, thoughtful, non-prescriptive. It's been rather out of fashion in Christianity for a very long time, but it's still there. And I'm trying to describe it, reconcile it to mainstream Christianity, today's mainstream, that's all.'

'And what does Uncle Pete think?'

'He thinks I've lost the plot. Pete likes rules and tidiness. This is unruly and untidy; not for him. But I'm not saying it's wrong to go down that path. It's just limiting – to you as well as to God. And I really don't agree with telling other people they should believe a given list of things, worship in a certain way, or pray in a certain way. Some of this is not new, but some of it, well, it's a significant shift, an unburdening, liberating. But that's a bit difficult at the moment. I'm afraid a lot of people don't understand me.'

'Mum?'

'Oh, she's closer to understanding, but she does doesn't see it as important. What about you?'

'I think it makes more sense than all the stuff we learnt at Sunday school. I'm not sure how central it should be to my life though.'

'It's central to me. How much time and thought you give to it is entirely down to you. Thank you for listening though. You're an angel.'

On the matter of his relationships with Liza, Tom, and Anne, however, he was less ready to talk.

After three days of walking, talking and eating, Abi felt ready to face the world again, ready to make some decisions. She just wished she felt better about her parents, that she could reassure her grandparents a little more. Tom tried to send her off with a positive message which she half believed. She just knew there was something being held back.

The Fleece

I don't know how long I've been standing here, but it's too long,. A man could die of thirst. My round again. Fred's sitting snugly at a corner table. I'm planning a trip up the Dales to see Tom. Not sure whether to take Fred. He'd want to see the lad, of course, but I've a feeling it might be handy to have a bit of father and son time. I can't make it out, you see. He and Liza get back together, all forgiven and forgotten apparently, and a good thing too, but then he takes himself off to Nidderdale and hides away with his books. I'd have thought he'd be focussed on rebuilding the marriage.

Relations between him and Pete seem a bit distant too. Don't know why. Fred thinks happen Pete disapproves of him not being with Liza. He could be right. I think Tom and Liza's relationship is pretty important to Pete, and he can be a bit black and white. Oh, I know, pot and kettle. Still. Ah, here we go.

'Two pints o' bitter please. And some peanuts. Ready salted, none of that other rubbish. Thanks. There you go.'

Steady, I've been accused of spilling more than I drink before. Best come clean with Fred I guess.

'Get that down you, it'll put hairs on your chest.'

'A bit late for that,' he says. 'What's to do?'

'How do you mean?'

'Don't give me that Don Raistrick. Something's eating at you, I can see. Is it your lad?'

'Aye.'

'Well, get up there and have a word, just the two of you. Don't worry, I know what you're thinking, I can forgo the pleasure. This is father and son time.'

'Thanks Fred. He'll be getting a complex, but still.'

'A complex? Why?'

'Our Abigail's just been up to see him, now it's me. We're all trying to sort him out.'

'And Matt?'

'Oh, I think Abi was a delegate. Matt's always on the phone to his dad though.'

'He'll feel loved and cherished. He should, any road.'

So that's settled. Perhaps he'll take me to that nice Italian, or we could have fish and chips, there's a good place in Pateley. It's always good to talk over food. Maybe I can draw him out. He doesn't seem short of people ready to listen, if only he'd talk. Thing is, some of this seems to be relationship stuff and some of it theology. I'm not sure where to start. I'll play it by ear, I guess.

Tom

Ripples in the pond. I make a lifestyle change and everyone else starts to worry. I've been lucky. I've managed to transition from Church to freelance with a minimal amount of pain. The decision we made all those years ago to have a property of our own so we had somewhere to go once the vicarage years were over has paid off. Liza moans about accessibility, of course, but she's generally moany at the moment. And my concern about income has proved to be ill-founded. Jonny's trust pays me just as well, or badly, as the Church. He wanted to pay me more, but the other trustees were less sure.

Dan Murphy was the toughest. Old City contact of Jonny's, an East End boy who takes no prisoners. I like him, we have a natural rapport, and he makes sensible suggestions. It was his idea to link the initial salary to my old stipend, otherwise, he suggested, it would look like we were 'taking the piss'. I had to agree, especially considering the workload is very light – Jonny wants to get into publishing with my books and count the writing as part of the workload, but we managed to persuade him it doesn't work like that.

So here I am, doing what I dreamt of doing, in a place I love, and everyone's worried. Mainly, I have to admit, because Liza and I are not together much, and that is an issue we need to address. I think it will take time to get back to full normality, whatever that is. We've bruised each other a bit. Thank goodness she doesn't know about the Anne incident. I think she suspects, and I'm not sure how to deal with that.

Meanwhile, Abi seems concerned about my faith – ironic given her habitual scepticism – my dad too. Liza's mum knows something's up, she's been on the phone. Pete and Anne are keeping their distance. I guess it will all settle down in time. In the meantime, I'm writing, giving talks, leading workshops, and doing my bit for the Nower Trust. And I'm finding time to tramp the hills. If I could make it right with Liza, all would be well. I've a new life which suits me,. And it could suit her. It feels like everything has changed, but I still need Liza.

CHAPTER TWO
FIVE YEARS ON

Tom

I don't know why it happened, I wish it hadn't. Neither of those statements is strictly true of course. I do know why it happened; deep-seated attraction, familiarity, loneliness, need, opportunity, all those things. And I don't wish it hadn't, not really. I enjoyed it, felt better for it, felt closer to Anne, felt loved. What I wish is that the consequences hadn't happened. Consequences like Liza's suspicion, Anne's guilt, Pete's studied myopia, and the break-up of our mutual support system. Five years of hardly seeing Pete, of Anne avoiding me, and Liza on edge. If I thought life was tricky before, well, I found a way of making it worse.

My other support system has been the Church, of course, and I cut myself loose from that as well. Not that I lost all my friends, Jonny and Jancy have been towers of strength. Ironic, given that Jonny has embraced the Church just as I've been distancing myself from it. And interesting to see how he has made the transition from the City to the clergy; how easily, how effectively.

I've adjusted too – had to. I've become a writer, a thinker, a speaker at conferences, and a leader of weekend retreats, helping people examine their faith, their beliefs, their callings and their lifestyles – another irony. A therapist introduced me to the concept of the 'wounded healer', and I suppose that's similar to what I've been doing, not healing, but using my own weaknesses and failings to help others move along in their personal journeys. Did I really just use the J-word? Something I promised myself I would never do, but sometimes it is unavoidable.

The fact of the matter is that the change I made suits me. It was not the choice I would have made if Liza hadn't been so negative about the alternatives, but it suits me. I can say what I think, explore ideas and share them with others without that constant pressure of expectation I had before. There are no wardens or PCC breathing down my neck. I find getting my thoughts down on paper very satisfying. It's not always literally paper of course, I have to have my laptop surgically removed to go on holiday.

Slowly, my relationships have started to recover. I didn't see Pete and Anne for nearly a year. The excuse was that I was writing in my cottage in Nidderdale, but we all knew that was not the real reason. I now see Pete occasionally, and it's starting to feel like old times. I've no idea what he knows, what he allows himself to know. With Liza things are a bit up and down. We're technically together, but in practice I'm spending most of my time in Nidderdale, and she has her studio – a new one – in Ferring now, close to Mum. Times together are special, but we haven't quite got back to where we were. Maybe that's not a bad thing. What I mean is, we haven't yet got to where we want to be. I think she suspects something about Anne and me. I'm not sure. I do know I don't want to go there.

This introspective stuff is tricky to get down, but the thing is that I feel I've changed. Liza's changed too in some ways. I'm just not sure if the two sets of changes are compatible. I mean, we've been through some challenging stuff; her affair, my slip with Anne. It would have been so easy to fall into a pattern there, for me anyway. I was very tempted. And what sort of man would that make me? Then there was all the Church stuff; rejection on the one hand, promotions offered on the other. And I think I ran away, hid. Not that leaving the Church was running away. I think Liza's instincts were right there. I've outgrown it, moved on, and finally started to undo the shackles of my upbringing. Now I need to build again; Liza, Anne, Pete, the children – Dad too. There's work to do.

Sisters

It is autumn in Ferring, and Liza's studio is bathed in mist as she experiments with borders for her latest painting. In the distance, a doorbell rings. She swears softly, drops what she's doing and heads for the main house. Her studio is a converted stable in the grounds of a Victorian terrace which she and Tom bought when he switched jobs five years earlier. It's not as grand as the vicarage but with plenty of character and space for the two of them, especially considering they also owned (outright in this case) the cottage in Yorkshire.

The visitor is Anne, standing slightly awkwardly on the doorstep. They embrace. Liza leads the way into the lounge, a comfortable room with cushions and candles identifying it as more Liza's than Tom's. There is a slight chill in the atmosphere which Anne is keen to dispel, but Liza is all politeness.

'Come in, sit down. How are you?'

'Okay, I think. You?'

'In the pink.'

Anne wells up a little, and looks at her sister.

'God, it's good to see you.'

Liza smiles a tight-lipped smile.

'I'm not far away, you know.'

'I know. It's just…'

'I know. Want some tea?'

Anne declines, declaring that she is 'all tea'd out', having drunk multiple cups of tea already that morning, largely because she had not wanted to appear ungracious. So, Liza wonders, does Anne accept everything that's offered to her? Only tea, is the response, to which Liza comes back with a tart 'Not what I've heard'. Anne looks pained but lets this one go. Liza hasn't finished with the tea conversation though. Perhaps it's safer ground for the moment. Perhaps she senses Anne's discomfort. She probes a little more. Why accept every cup that's offered to you? Obligation seems to be the answer. The vicar's wife comes round, you offer her a cup of tea, and it's rude of her to refuse. This fails to satisfy. Why? Because it's an important ritual, the giving and taking of tea establishes a mutual relationship; breaks down the barriers a little.

'But you know these people. Surely you can be yourself.'

'Not really. I'm the vicar's wife.'

This is an interesting concept to Liza. Is being a vicar's wife what defines Anne? To the parishioners, yes – some of them anyway. Most of them, perhaps. Liza is appalled.

'God, how dreadful.'

'Isn't it. Didn't you find that?'

'I was never that kind of vicar's wife.'

'Tom was never that kind of vicar.'

'We both know what kind of vicar Tom was.'

There's a moment's pause while Anne tries to work out what Liza is saying. What does she know? How much should she, Anne, reveal? There is a tassel on the cushion next to her. She fiddles with it. She settles for defending Tom. He was a good vicar, inspirational. Perhaps not the right word to choose as Liza makes a pointed remark about different kinds of inspiration, and who he chose to inspire, or be inspired by. Anne lets this one go too and enquires after the subject of their conversation. How is he? The answer, which amounts to a vague 'Okay I guess, last time I saw him', raises more questions.

'Not with you then?'

'Still unsettled.'

'Him or you?'

'Him, me, both of us. Lots of loose ends, Anne. He visits me for sex.'

'Liza!'

'What? Why not? The old spark's still there, we're just not sure we can live together. Too many compromises needed, too much trust.'

'He doesn't live here?'

'Not so you'd notice. He's in Yorkshire a lot, writing, and he travels a lot – lecturing and stuff for Jonny, you know.'

Anne is hesitant. 'I heard you'd got back together.'

Liza answers with an apparent non sequitur. 'What happened to us?'

Anne doesn't answer, looks ever more uncomfortable.

'How did we get to the point where you hear rumours and you don't know if they're true?'

Anne tries to evade the issue. 'You know what happened.'

Liza is not about to let her off the hook. 'What happened, Anne?'

'We… just drifted, I guess.'

'No, you can do better than that.'

Anne weakens. 'Tom happened, Liza. And then Pete happened.'

'We lived with that for long enough.'

'And then Tom happened.'

Liza feels she is getting to the nub of things. 'So, Tom happened twice?'

Anne looks chastened, seeks for an explanation.

'When you left him he went to pieces, started coming round. He chatted to Pete, argued mostly. Chatted to me, flirted mostly. I tried to help him.'

'Clearly.'

Anne is quick to respond.

'I tried to keep him at arm's length, Liza. God knows I tried. But it stirred up all the old stuff. And then, I thought you were back together, and I was relieved. I thought Pete and I could get back to normal.'

'And you failed?'

'In getting back to normal?'

'In keeping Tom at arm's length.'

Anne gives way a little. 'To some extent. Well, yes. Let's not go there.'

'No, let's. To what extent?'

'You're not going to like this.'

Liza is implacable. 'Try me.'

Anne tries to explain. She thought Tom and Liza were 'over'. She thought she and Pete were 'over'. Everything had changed.

'So you… you jumped into bed with my husband.'

'It was the couch, actually.'

'The couch?'

'In the lounge.'

'I don't care about the bloody furniture, Anne.'

Anne is nearly in tears now. She says she's sorry. Liza appears to think this is not enough – two marriages in jeopardy and the guilty parties are sorry? It's an inadequate response. Never one to mask her feelings, Liza is not about to start now. She is hurt, angry. Anne tries to bridge the divide, but Liza hasn't finished yet.

'My own sister. Of all the people I should have been able to trust. And you're sorry.'

'But I am. Truly.'

Liza would like to know if, after five years of silence, Anne thinks 'sorry' does it? Anne does not think so, but doesn't know what else to say. She has missed Liza. She didn't know why she wasn't speaking to her. She is really sorry.

Liza bridles some more.

'You didn't know why? Why did you think?'

'I don't know. I thought I should keep quiet. You didn't know about Tom and me.'

'Oh that's all right then. "I screwed her husband, but she'll never know." You screwed my husband and you lied to me. So much for sisterly support.'

Anne twists the tassel on the cushion round her finger, apologises again, is contrite, tries to get through to her sister, asks her to listen. This seems to fan the flames still more, Liza more or less jumps down her throat.

'No, you listen. My life was at a crossroads, my marriage in a mess. Tom and I were trying to work things out, or I was anyway. Maybe it could have worked. But no. My man pours out his troubles to my sister and does she listen and support? Does she buggery. She jumps his bones. She can't even wait to get to the bedroom. The two-faced, scheming bitch has her knickers off and Tom on the couch before he can pause for breath. Marriage over, friendship over, family kaput. Stupid cow.'

'I was stupid. I'm sorry.'

'No. I was the stupid one to ever trust either of you. Flirting, joking, laughing – and screwing.'

Anne answers in a small voice, almost a whisper, that it 'wasn't like that'. What was it like, Liza would like to know. Really. Anne tries. She was trying to help.

'We'd had this fun, innocent relationship for all those years.'

There's a snort of derision from Liza.

'No, really. Liza you have to believe me. Yes we were old flames but we'd made our choices. I was happy with Pete, and Tom was mad about you. I thought we were safe. But that day... He was so miserable; he thought he'd finally lost you. He opened his heart to me.'

'And you opened your legs.'

'You want to make it ugly, but it wasn't, Liza.'

'Oh, that helps.'

'I'm sorry, but you wanted to know. He was sobbing. I held him, stroked his hair. He responded. One thing led to another. That's it... I was sorry as soon as it was over. We were both in shock, I think.'

Liza wants to know if Anne enjoyed the experience. Anne does not want to share. Liza is insistent. She wants to know; deserves to know.

'Come on, Anne, out with it. Did you or did you not enjoy shagging my husband? Be honest. I think I deserve some honesty.'

Anne answers very softly. Yes, she did. Liza still wants her pound of flesh.

'I can't hear you, Anne.'

Anne capitulates.

'Yes, I enjoyed it. It was great, at the time. That do you?'

'If we're going to get over this we need a good dose of honesty, Anne. So it's my turn. I didn't know what had happened, but I'm not stupid. And Tom's a rotten liar. I hate you, Anne. I've spent the last five years hating you. But I can't carry on, it's eating me up. I need to lance the boil.'

Anne wants to know if she hates Tom too. It's Liza's turn to fill up. No, is the answer, she can't. She's wanted to, has tried, but no. So Anne is carrying the can? No, not entirely. Tom has been made to suffer. But Liza wants to draw a line under that as well.

The tears are flowing now. Anne is wretched. Can Liza ever forgive her? Liza has herself under control. She doesn't know the answer, but she is going try. She needs her sister back, she needs to move on. Being forgiving is Tom's territory, not hers, but she's going to give it a go. A little tentatively, Anne asks what she can do.

Liza is not sure. Her voice cracks a little as she admits this.

'I don't know. Sit there and take it? Be honest. Let me trust you again.'

There's a pause. Anne breaks the silence by suggesting that maybe that cup of tea might be a good idea after all. Liza starts for the kitchen but turns on the way to ask about Pete, how much he knows.

Anne manages a smile.

'Oh, Pete doesn't notice anything unless it's sobbing on his shoulder. Or he can read it.'

'And you've not been writing him notes.'

'Or sobbing. Perhaps I should try sobbing.'

'It's less disruptive than shagging.'

Anne is shocked. Liza tells her not to be.

'Sorry. You've just become so, I don't know, blunt, crude.'

'Whereas you very politely jumped into bed with my husband.'

Another go round the merry-go-round. Anne points out that Liza and Tom were not together at the time. Liza accuses Anne of making that assumption. Anne counters that that is what Tom told her.

'And you believed him?'

'He's a man of the cloth.'

'He's a man.'

'Fair point. I wanted to believe him, I guess.'

Liza looks shocked.

'You wanted our marriage to fail?'

'No, of course not. I thought it had. What I wanted was him. I wanted it to be okay to hold him, be held by him. I wanted to be wanted.'

Liza feels that that was Pete's job. Where was Pete while all this was going on? At a PCC meeting, Anne thinks. That's not what Liza meant. What she meant was why wasn't he holding you, wanting you?

'Pete? Not too good with intimacy, Pete. Has to be reminded about sex from time to time. It wasn't that he wasn't interested, isn't interested. God Liza, you know Pete. He's just not...'

'Not always on the same planet as everyone else.'

'Right. It's like, you've probably noticed, if we're eating, talking, he's not listening, his mind's on other things. Ask him to pass the mustard and he does, but he wouldn't know he was doing it.'

'And it's the same with sex?'

'That's right. You do it at the dinner table with friends and he doesn't notice.'

Anne giggles as she says this. They both do. The ice is breaking a little. She admits to feeling a little neglected, a little overlooked. So, Liza wonders aloud, was that part of the attraction, part of the reason she ended up in bed with Tom?

'It was on the settee, actually.'

Liza is still not interested in the detail of the furniture. Anne apologises. Liza feels they've covered that ground. Anne says apologising makes her feel better. Liza is not sure how much she actually wants Anne to feel better. Anne points out that if they are to move on they both need to feel better about it all. Liza is not convinced that it really does make Anne feel better as opposed to being simply a knee-jerk response. Anne is unsure what Liza wants from her. Liza moves to her, holds her hands and says, simply, that she wants a way out, a way out of the mess. And no, to Anne's question, she is not all sorted now she has decided to start over.

'Anne, you're my sister. We grew up together, remember. We're supposed to care. And you've been avoiding me for the last five years. Why?'

Anne thinks this a strange question. Quite clearly she has been racked with guilt, has felt unable to face Liza, and has had no idea what she would say when she did face her. The result, as Liza sees it, has been five years of Anne feeling guilty and of Liza seething with resentment – five wasted years. And now she has a husband she rarely sees, a sister she never sees, and a family with awkward questions about what's been going on. It's all a mess.

Anne does not feel that Liza has any claim to exclusivity on a messy life. There is a danger of this developing into another argument as Anne states her case.

'Look at me, Liza – I've a husband who can't focus on me for more than 30 seconds at a time, a sister I'm too ashamed to see, and a brother-in-law I'm now too embarrassed to see because I slept with him.'

'Not for the first time.'

'The first time in 30 years.'

'That makes it embarrassing?'

'Well, where do you go with a relationship after that?'

Liza suggests back to normal is worth a try. She is determined to put the last few years behind her, which she can clearly only do with support from Anne. So this is the way it has to be; sisters, friends, confidantes, a mutual support group. Anne is surprised.

'I thought you were mad at me.'

'I am. Was. I think a five-year sulk is enough, don't you?'

Anne thinks as long as you need is enough. For Liza it appears that the magic figure is five years. And she admits that she and Tom were not together at the time – although 'the bed was still warm'. That last remark highlights the struggle that is still going on, but it does represent progress. The discussion turns to Liza's relationship with Tom. Liza, it appears to Anne, is still keeping Tom at arm's length. Liza's view is more nuanced. She is unsure they can live together, not all the time anyway. There's too many compromises, too much unfinished business.

'So why not finish it?'

'I don't want to be without him.'

'No, not the relationship, the business.'

The time-honoured response is 'It gets more difficult as time goes on'. To which there is only one counter, which is 'All the more reason to do it now'. Liza, of course, is scared. Scared of losing Tom, scared of not losing him, scared of change. And no, she is not happy with the way things are right now, not entirely. But it works, after a fashion, and maybe that's all she can hope for. Anne thinks she is aiming low, but all Liza knows is that it feels risky. She and Tom seem okay in small doses, holding each other at bay. The upside is 'well it's a bit like dating again'. Anne does not see this as a positive.

'Sounds awful.'

'Awful? Didn't you like all that? The excitement, the special moments, the will he won't he, will I won't I stuff?'

'The nerves, the awkward moments, the "Oh God he's trying it on" stuff.'

'Oh come on, you loved it.'

'No, you loved it. I was very happy to leave it behind. And you're hardly a teenager now, Liza.'

Liza knows this but prefers not to be reminded.

'Don't you dare call me mature.'

'I'm not sure I'd call you that. Older perhaps, no longer in the first flush.'

That is enough honesty for Liza, who calls a halt. She has enough to cope with without the ageing process as well. Anne is, of course, a little older, but that is scant comfort when Anne is so relaxed about it. Especially when Anne thinks Liza is trying to recapture something which might have been okay at 20 but is unlikely to work now. Anne is both amused and exasperated, familiar emotions when dealing with Liza, so this is relatively safe territory for her. In her view, which she is perfectly happy to share, they are both middle-aged; middle-aged and attractive, not old, although they both will be one day, God willing. Liza finds this strangely unappealing. It is Anne's turn to lay down the law. Liza, in her view, needs to face reality. It might not be quite what she envisaged, but it's not a bad deal. She has her art, a husband who loves her, her children. She, Anne, has had to cope with being childless – 'And you'd have been a much better mother than me,' interposed Liza. 'I don't know, you were a loving mother,' was the response, but they both knew Anne would have focussed on the children more, for good or ill.

Whatever the truth of this, Anne argued, they had now reached a stage of life where they could choose – acceptance or more rebellion. Liza was not encouraged.

'Now you're really cheering me up.'

'Just speaking the truth.'

'Now you sound like Pete.'

'Speaking the truth to the heathen.'

'And I'm pretty heathen in his eyes.'

'He adores you, you know that.'

Pete does indeed adore Liza, but Liza knows that he also thinks of her as a flighty sister who might one day settle down and in the meantime can be indulged. She remembers many times when those aspects of their relationship had been in evidence. She is taken aback by the strength of a sudden feeling of nostalgia.

'It all seemed so good, so meant, you know. Tom and Pete so close, you and me. Where did we go wrong?'

'We're human. We made mistakes. We can get over it.'

Liza is unsure. Does Anne really think so?

'You said it yourself, we have to. What we had was good. It helped us all through a lot of things, a lot of years. But now, now we're in a different phase of life. We have to look forward, not back.'

'Say goodbye to the old stuff?'

'Adapt that's all.'

There's a pause. Liza needs a cup of tea. Is Anne sure she doesn't want one? Nothing? Anne thinks maybe an infusion. Liza has a good supply of infusions. What does Anne fancy? Camomile? Ginseng? Rose hip? Mint? Anne fancies blackberry. That may not be on the menu. Liza heads for the kitchen with Anne trailing in her wake.

'Or lemon? I like lemon.'

CHAPTER THREE

THE PLOUGH

The Plough is a typical Surrey country pub; horse brasses, tables made from converted Singer sewing machines, well-kept beer, a wine list, and a menu which Pete is absent-mindedly studying while Tom is at the bar. They are not eating, but Pete is choosing his hypothetical meal and is torn between the 'Plough burger' with all the trimmings (he has a weakness for gherkins) and a lamb shank with red wine jus. In the process he is mentally listing the many reasons he prefers gravy to jus. He is on reason number five (pretentiousness in pub food) when Tom reappears, bearing two pints.

'There you go. Get that down you.'

'Cheers.'

'Cheers.'

Pete licks his lips appreciatively.

'Good pint that.'

'Keeps his beer well does Mick.'

'Not like a lot of them these days.'

They agree that Mick does, indeed, know what he's doing and is a rare example of an old-time landlord, to be treasured. They then move on to pleasantries.

'So how's things, Tom?'

'Not bad. You?'

'Okay.'

'How are Fulham doing?'

Fulham, it seems, are struggling. 'Still as keen?' Tom wants to know. The answer seems to be that Pete is, but he's not sure how keen the team are. Pete is one of those football fans who would hate to admit his team had any merit, skill or application. It would ruin the whole experience. Tom comments that it makes good sermon material, and Pete responds that every vicar should have his team. Being a supporter of a run-of-the-mill team in the English football league is, in Tom's view, a salutary reminder that you might have assurance of the next life but things can still be rubbish in this one. A dose of realism, wonders Pete. Tom seizes on this. Is Pete recognising that all the stuff about the next life might not represent realism? What Pete means, though, is that we have high expectations as Christians. It's good to be reminded it's not a perfect world. It has been a while since they talked like this, but this is a conversation they could have had at any point in the last 30 years. Nothing has changed, except the greying, the thinning of the hair, and a slight thickening of the waistlines.

Tom asks after Anne. The switch in conversation throws Pete momentarily.

'Anne?' he says.

'Your wife,' prompts Tom.

Anne, it seems, is fine. So, on enquiry, is Liza. The conversation moves on to other things; writing, the Yorkshire cottage, Tom's current project, a book, entitled *The Ocean's Calm*. Pete wonders whether the ocean is really calm. That, it seems is not what Tom is suggesting. The title refers to the calm of the ocean, and is not a claim that the ocean is calm. This confuses Pete. Logically, he thinks, the ocean must be calm if Tom can write about its calm. No, counters Tom that, in a sense, is the point. The ocean can have calm in places while being anything but calm overall – and it is those calm places which are so special. And they are so special precisely because there is a seething, eddying, violent sea below and around – a good metaphor for life. Value the calm. Pete is not sure people will get it. They spend a good ten minutes arguing the point before Tom calls a halt and suggests they are getting nowhere. Pete reverts to enquiries about Tom's domestic arrangements.

'Still spending most of your time at the cottage?'

If this is intended to elucidate information about the state of Tom's marriage and domestic arrangements, it fails. Tom replies that he is spending a lot of time at his 'writing retreat', which leads them back to a circular discussion about the current writing project, whether the ocean really is calm. Tom is bemused. How is Pete not getting this? Maybe he should call it *The Calm of the Ocean*. Or *The Still Small Voice* suggests Pete. That, it seems, is too restricting. That's part of it, of course, but it's very Christian, Tom wants to be much more inclusive than that. So the ambiguity might be a good thing, suggests Pete.

The central thesis of the book is that in the midst of the storms and the power struggles and the emotional upheavals and so on that everyone gets in life, we all need a centre of calm. People naturally think of the eye of the storm, but the ocean is a good analogy because, when you've got storms and the power of the wind and the waves on the surface, there's still a calm and serenity on the ocean floor.

This catches Pete's interest. Is it really true?

'So I understand. And we all need that underlying calm to survive the storms of life.'

'And how do we get that calm?'

Tom smiles. 'I'm working on that.'

'Let me know when you find out.'

This gives Tom an opportunity to talk through the ideas he has been exploring. His thesis is that religion can be a source of that calm. And, to Pete's consternation (though not surprise), this means any religion. But, and this is a significant proviso, any religion can also destroy the calm. This seems counter-intuitive to Pete. How would a religion destroy calm? By the weight of expectations, guilt, 'all that kind of thing'. Pete finds this interesting. 'Is that your experience?' he asks. 'Isn't it yours?' is the response.

Pete reflects. In life as a whole, yes, expectations, guilt and so on are destructive of calm.

'But not in religion?' asks Tom.

'I'm not sure I can separate the two.'

'So we're not so different.'

Without intending any irony, Pete seeks to differ. He sees Tom's 'woolliness' as a significant difference.

'Woolliness?' queries Tom.

Pete takes a swig from his pint, thinks, and quotes Tom. 'All religions are valid, there are many paths, the Divine spark.'

'Oh you mean my inclusivity.'

'You're just scared to say we're right.'

Tom sees it differently. 'No, I'm just not arrogant enough to say everybody else is wrong.'

The Bible, it seems to Pete, is clear. Not the way it reads to Tom, who argues that while the Bible is many things, clear isn't one of them. And the Bible is not really the basis of claims to having all the answers. Pete is unsure where Tom is going with this. Tom points out that claiming exclusivity is not an exclusively Christian standpoint, it's a human one. It makes us feel superior; the chosen ones. We just rationalise it from the Bible. Pete struggles with this. After all, the Bible clearly states that anyone who accepts Jesus can be saved. Tom is unconvinced by the clarity argument but responds with a comment on human nature.

'So we get to be superior, and on top of that we can act like Lady Bountiful going round dishing out salvation.'

'That's a cynical view.'

'It's a realistic view. Look, it's difficult to separate faith from life, right?'

Pete accepts that, for him, yes, this is difficult; impossible even. Tom's position is that the same is true for everybody. The only thing special to Pete is that he has the vocabulary, the ability to articulate what he believes. Everybody has some underlying belief, some faith – 'Except atheists' puts in Pete. Even atheists have a belief system, in Tom's view. So, this underlying belief system, this faith, or lack of it, underlies everything we do or say. It doesn't matter if you're an evangelical Christian, a Muslim, Hindu, or if you just have a vague feeling there's something beyond us, it's there; it's part of who we are; you can't get away from it. You can't just say it doesn't count, it's arrogant.

'Still passionate about this stuff, aren't you?'

'Yes, because all this 'you've got to believe what I believe' stuff causes pain, war, suffering, splits families, and it's man-made. You heard the story about the vicar who got to heaven, did you? Well, he dies, gets to the Pearly Gates.'

'So there are Pearly Gates?'

'Symbolically. He gets to the Pearly Gates and St Peter greets him, and gives him the guided tour. He points out the different areas. Over there, he says, are the Methodists. The noisy lot over there are the charismatics. Over there, by the stream, are the Baptists.'

'And the Anglicans?'

'They were all holed up in a committee room discussing building repairs. And so on. Then the vicar notices a high wall and St Peter says "You need to be quiet if you go near there". "Oh, why?" says our vicar. "Behind that wall," says St Peter, "is the area reserved for the Exclusive Brethren. They don't believe there's anyone else here." '

Pete is not sure of the point. Tom's point is that these divisions are man-made. And not just within the Christian Church.

'Within marriage too,' comments Pete. 'So how is Liza?' Tom thinks Liza is fine. Only thinks? wonders Pete.

'Knowing how Liza is is not my strong point.'

'Meaning?'

Tom has been playing with a beer mat during this exchange. Now he puts it down before replying.

'Meaning, I thought we'd get back to normal when I gave up the Church. I suppose I had this notion that I'd do my writing, my talks and so on, she'd go off to work, and we'd settle down together in the evenings like a normal couple.'

'But she had different ideas?'

'I don't know really. I just know I end up spending most of my time at my retreat, and we get together every now and then. It's not what I had in mind.'

Pete suggests talking about it, which Tom opines is something he is 'not good at'. This seems odd.

'You're one of the most articulate men I know.'

'Not in this context.'

'So get out of your comfort zone. Try doing something you're not good at for a change.'

Tom accepts this but switches the conversation to Anne. How is she? Pete thinks she is fine. Fine? Fine as in happy, busy, settled.

'No problems?'

'No,' says Pete. 'All good on that front.'

'Good. Glad to hear it. Another beer?'

'My shout I think, but I should go.'

'Because it's your shout?'

'Because I said I'd pick Anne up.'

Tom wants to know where Anne is. Pete is a little surprised that he doesn't know. She's gone to see Liza. It's Tom's turn to be surprised.

'Really? Been a long time.'

'Yes, I can't work out what happened between those two.'

'Oh, woman stuff I expect.'

Whatever the problem was, in Pete's view, they seem to be burying the hatchet. Both men see this as a good thing. Pete has missed seeing Liza. Tom hopes, even prays, that the reconciliation is going well. He is reluctant to accept Pete's suggestion that they go back together; he has things to do. Pete is insistent. The four of them together would be like old times. Tom thinks it will just be awkward. Pete concedes a degree of awkwardness but not enough to kill the idea. What, he wonders, is Tom afraid of? Tom is unable to come up with anything – anything he can say to Pete anyway – so he is caught, gives way gracefully and finishes his pint.

'Go on then. Sup up.'

Pete does so and they leave the pub, heading off to join the sisters.

CHAPTER FOUR
LIKE OLD TIMES

Anne and Liza are in the middle of some serious reminiscing when they hear the door. They exchange glances. They were expecting Pete to pick Anne up, but it sounds like Tom is with him. And indeed he is, bursting into the room with no sign of the awkwardness he could, or should, be feeling. He kisses Liza, hugs Anne, and expresses delight. Pete follows him in.

'I gave Tom a lift.'

'So we see.'

Now Tom shows a little embarrassment. He drinks in the atmosphere in the room like a dog sniffing the night air. He shows little sign of the dawning realisation that the two women have talked. Liza invites Pete to take a seat. He declines; he is just picking Anne up. Liza's invitation was really more of a command. He sits down.

'Just for a few minutes.'

Anne breaks the silence.

'It's nice to see you, Tom. Been a long time.'

'Yes, hi. How are you?'

Anne thinks she is 'good'. Tom wonders whether there is any tea going. Liza points out that he knows where the kettle is.

'Sorry, yes.'

Liza's patience is wearing thin. 'Don't you start.'

'What?'

'Apologising without meaning it.'

Pete is nonplussed. Liza tells him not to worry, it's not his fault. Pete and Tom both react with relief, at which Liza pointedly reminds Tom that she was talking to Pete.

'You should worry,' she tells him, 'and it probably is your fault.'

'Situation normal' is Tom's response, which does not go down too well. Sensing the beginnings of a marital row, Pete and Anne start to make their excuses – Pete because he doesn't know what is going on; Anne because she does. Liza is not letting them off the hook that easily.

'No, stay,' she says. 'Have some more tea. Take a seat – not on the settee.'

Pete is out of his depth again. He is told to relax.

'Why?' he wants to know. 'Why do I have to relax?'

Tom volunteers to put the kettle on; make tea. Anne offers to help him. Liza plumps a cushion and suggests they should not take too long.

'Trust, Liza,' says Anne. 'Trust.'

They head off for the kitchen. Pete turns to Liza. He is a little uncomfortable. He is aware that this is odd given their long and close relationship.

'Is… everything all right, Liza?'

'It's heading in that direction, Pete.'

'I'm not sure I understand what's gone on.'

'Ask Anne.'

Pete digests this. He has missed Liza.

'It's been a long time since the four of us were together.'

Liza nods. 'Too long.'

This gives Pete the opportunity to ask questions he has been avoiding. He takes in Liza's art decorations, and the touches of chintz which seem a little out of place but somehow work, surprising himself by noticing this. Stress is maybe making him act out of character. He tackles the first subject.

'Are you and Anne…?'

'We're mending fences.'

'And you and Tom…?'

'You see Tom regularly, you know how it is.'

'Not really.'

'Not really?'

'Not that regularly, and he doesn't talk about it.'

Liza laughs, a hollow, unamused laugh.

'I bet he doesn't.'

'I feel like I'm missing something here.'

Liza suggests, again, that he talk to Anne. Pete assures her that he will. At that point Anne reappears with a query. Has Liza got any more infusions? Yes, she has. Tom knows where they are. Anne has tried that. Tom denies all knowledge of any infusions. Liza mutters something about men and heads off to the kitchen, from where she can be heard giving Tom instructions. Pete and Anne exchange looks. Anne asks how the pub was. It was fine. How are she and Liza, Pete wants to know. Anne grimaces.

'We've cleared the air. No, it's good. Really.'

'Good. What was the problem?'

'I'll tell you later – on our own.'

Pete would like a clue, a hint, some idea of what is going on. Anne isn't about to start the conversation until they are on their own, at home, away from Tom and Liza. This, in itself, gives the game away. Some things insist on being addressed, sooner or later, no matter how hard we try to avoid them. As they talk, Tom returns, talking to Liza as he does.

'Not now, Liza,' he is saying as he reappears. Liza can be heard disagreeing.

'Yes now, Tom. Today. We have to talk about this. It's eating us up.'

'Today. I promise. But not now.'

He re-enters the room, preceded by a tray of tea and biscuits.

'Anne, good chat with Liza then?'

'Oh yes.'

'What is going on?'

Liza enters at this point, looks at Pete with a mix of tenderness, pity and exasperation.

'He wakes.'

Pete has had enough. He stands.

'Okay. I think we should go.'

Liza looks a little hurt.

'Must you? We just made tea.'

'I'm sorry Liza, but Anne and I need to talk. Now.'

Liza nods, smiles and hugs him.

'You're right. You do.'

It is Tom's turn to be bemused. He has trouble recognising Pete's position, not for the first time. He thinks they can all have tea and biscuits. Pete disagrees. He makes his position clear.

'You all think I'm thick, don't you? In another world. Can't see what's under his nose. Well it's not true. I just try to make the best of things. I thought I could avoid this, but I can't. So we're going home. Now.'

They all look chastened, especially Anne. Pete turns to her.

'We need to, Anne. We have to talk. You and Liza have talked, and I'm glad you have, but now it's my turn. Sorry Liza.'

He embraces her; the bond between them is still strong. He turns to Tom, touches his arm.

'We can catch up later, Tom, be in touch. See you.'

And with that he is gone, with Anne in his wake. Anne pauses to kiss both Tom and Liza.

'Better go. Wish me luck. I'm glad we talked.'

'Me too. Go.'

And then they are alone; Tom and Liza – the golden couple – faced with rescuing their marriage, with speaking truth, listening, and retrieving. Tom is first to speak.

Indicating the door, he ventures, 'So, that was quick.'

'I think they're going to have a difficult conversation.'

'And so are we.'

Liza smiles, though without humour.

'We certainly are. And, before you ask, yes, we must. No more false starts. No more messing about. I want honesty, plain speaking. We need to face up to things.'

Tom is not sure he likes the sound of this. His hesitation, uncertainty, and fear are palpable. Liza softens a little.

'Face up and fess up. We've messed up; both of us. Hurt each other, right? And we've spent years making it worse by avoiding the issue. So now I'm going to the loo. I'm going to spend five minutes thinking about my conversation with Anne. You're going to pour the tea and then we're going to sit down and talk.'

Tom sees the sense in this. Maybe it's time.

'A serious talk, Tom, a long one – probably a painful one – but no ducking out. We sit and talk this out, okay?'

'As long as it takes.'

Liza heads off. Tom looks round the room; their lounge. It's Liza's really, since he has rarely been there. The fact was that she had furnished it, decorated it, and chosen the pictures, all without him. Technically it was his home too, but he had allowed himself to become a visitor. Why? Because it had seemed the easy option, because he could run away to Nidderdale whenever things got tough or, perhaps more to the point, whenever he and Liza were in danger of getting too close. Closeness might lead to difficult conversations. He had been frightened of the consequences of those conversations. No ducking it now though. He sends up a silent prayer, a single word prayer. 'Help'.

He stirs himself, picks up the debris of mugs and biscuits, heads off to the kitchen with the mugs that had been intended for Anne and Pete, turns and pours tea. Rude to refuse, he thinks. If we can get through this, relatively intact, he reflects, I should write our story. We have something special, the four of us. We very nearly threw it away – might still – but if we don't, I want to record it, in my own words as much as possible – it might be cathartic.

Liza comes back into the room. Looks at him. Sits opposite him.

'Right,' she says. 'I'll start.'

***

22246920R00192

Printed in Great Britain
by Amazon